Praise for the

WHISPERS OF THE FLESH
"Enticing and erotically intriguing... A fabulous read!"
—Fresh Fiction

"*Whispers of the Flesh* is a fast-paced, sexy, energetic, twisty romance.... It definitely gives a lot of fodder for our own fantasies."—Romance Reader at Heart

"As erotically charged as the previous books, *Whispers of the Flesh* weaves humor, romance, and a dark sensuality with an interesting plot that easily jumps back and forth in time.... For another charmingly erotic glimpse into the adventures behind the doors of Grotte Cachée, pick up your copy of *Whispers of the Flesh* today."—Romance Reviews Today

BOUND IN MOONLIGHT
"Within these pages are three tales that carry heat, sizzle, and passion.... Louisa Burton forms well-developed characters, strong conversation and enough sparks to keep the fires always lit. For those who enjoy erotic journeys that lure the audience, these tales will satisfy in every way."—Coffee Time Romance

"Louisa Burton is an absolute genius!... Refreshing and erotically sexy... The surprising last pages are keeping me breathless for the next installment."—Fresh Fiction

THE HOUSE OF DARK DELIGHTS
"Exquisite and riveting literary erotica... Readers willing to be seduced into a world of dark sensuality and sexual taboos will be spellbound."—*Romantic Times Book Reviews*

"A very sexy bit of Victorian erotica to entice the mind and senses... a captivating tale... Pick up
House of Dark Delights and indulge yourself."
—Romance Reviews Today

ALSO BY LOUISA BURTON

Whispers of the Flesh

Bound in Moonlight

House of Dark Delights

In the Garden
of Sin

Louisa Burton

🐓 BANTAM BOOKS

A Bantam Books Trade Paperback Original

Published in the United States by Bantam Books, an imprint of The Random
House Publishing Group, a division of Random House, Inc., New York.

BANTAM BOOKS and the rooster colophon are registered trademarks of
Random House, Inc.

Library of Congress Cataloging-in-Publication Data

Burton, Louisa.
  In the garden of sin / Louisa Burton.
    p. cm. — (The Hidden Grotto series ; bk. 4)
  ISBN 978-0-553-38531-1
  1. Incubi—Fiction. 2. Vampires—Fiction. 3. Castles—Fiction. I. Title.
  PS3602.U769815 2009
  813'.6—dc22   2009014245

Printed in the United States of America

www.bantamdell.com

2 4 6 8 9 7 5 3 1

Book design by Lynn Newmark

For my Evil Twin and her husband,
Pamela Burford Loeser and Jeffrey C. Loeser,
with love and gratitude for your support,
friendship, and kick-ass Thanksgivings

The English Courtesan

Being the True and Candid History of an
Innocent Maiden's Schooling in the Arts of Eros

Blessed Isidore, in the last chapter of his 8th book, says: Satyrs are they who are called Pans in Greek and Incubi in Latin. And they are called Incubi from their practice of overlaying, that is debauching. For they often lust lecherously after women, and copulate with them; and the Gauls name them Dusii, because they are diligent in this beastliness. But the devil which the common people call an Incubus, the Romans called a fig Faun; to which Horace said, "O Faunus, love of fleeing nymphs, go gently over my lands and smiling fields." ...

That which appears true to many cannot be altogether false, according to Aristotle (at the end of the *De somno et uigilia,* and in the 2nd *Ethics*). I say nothing of the many authentic histories, both Catholic and heathen, which openly affirm the existence of Incubi.

Malleus Maleficarum
by Heinrich Kramer and Jacob Sprenger, 1486

❧

Fair ladies, if man were to spend a thousand years in rendering thanks to his Creator for having made him in the form of a human and not of a brute beast, he could not speak gratitude enough.

The opening of "The Pig King," the inspiration for
"Beauty and the Beast," from *The Facetious Nights of Straparola*
by Giovanni Francesco, 1553

One

$\mathscr{I}$ AM IN MY AUTUMN YEARS now, sitting quill in
hand before a high, arched window in the library of
my marble palazzo overlooking the Grand Canal, preparing to
record the events that had driven me, as a virginal young
Englishwoman of gentle birth, to seek an education in whoredom.

Almost four decades have elapsed since my fateful decision, following much deliberation and prayer, to pursue such
a course, but that decision and its aftermath, which altered my
life in ways unimaginable at the time, are branded indelibly
into my memory.

The curtain opened on my tale on the eighteenth day of
July in the year of our Lord 1626, when I still lived in London,
where I had been born and reared. Through covert inquiries, I
had ascertained that there was a visitor to that city, a Venetian

nobleman and poet named Domenico Vitturi, who acted as a
Pygmalion of sorts to young women from every corner of
Europe who sought to improve their circumstances through
the exalted form of prostitution for which Venice had long
been notorious. Under his direction, the prospective courtesans were groomed in the social graces and such gentle pursuits as singing, dancing, gaming, and rhetoric, as well as in
the mysteries of the bedchamber, in preparation for their introduction by him to aristocratic gentlemen who would pay
handsomely for their company and their favors upon their arrival in Venice.

Signor Vitturi, who was said to be worth four million
ducats—the equivalent of one million pounds sterling!—
assumed all costs pursuant to this endeavor. He paid for his
apprentices' transportation to Venice, bought them lavish new
wardrobes, provided houses, servants, food, even their own
gondolas. Their every need was provided for until such time as
they could support themselves in a queenly enough manner to
suit him. It was not unusual, I learned, for his hand-picked,
carefully trained courtesans, renowned far and wide for their
beauty and accomplishments, to enjoy the company of
princes, cardinals, even kings, and to amass extraordinary
riches of their own. They bedecked themselves in the finest
jewels and silks, and it was said that some even owned fully
staffed palaces as grand and opulently furnished as those of
their wealthiest benefactors.

I was astounded. Whores living in palaces?

Such was the depth of my ignorance in matters of a
worldly nature. As the only child of learned parents, well tu-
tored but cosseted on account of my sex, I had found myself,
at one-and-twenty years of age, a bookish innocent. Although
I prided myself on my erudition and my enlightened attitude

toward affairs between the sexes, my knowledge of those affairs was largely theoretical.

So naive was I that it did not even occur to me to wonder what benefit Signor Vitturi might accrue from all this beneficence until it was explained to me that his chosen few were expected to keep themselves at his sexual disposal from the moment he took them under his wing. In this way, he maintained a virtual harem of some of the most extraordinary and cultivated beauties in Europe. Aside from occasional visits to his bed, however, no other recompense was expected of them. Their earnings were entirely theirs to keep.

That summer, Signor Vitturi had selected three candidates, two Italians and an Englishwoman, to travel with him to a secluded French castle called Château de la Grotte Cachée, where their education in courtisanerie was to take place. It was Vitturi's custom when visiting Grotte Cachée for this purpose, which he had done five times previously, to bring along a few companions. This time, one of them was to be the most influential, if controversial, man in England outside of the royal family: George Villiers, Duke of Buckingham, erstwhile favorite of the recently deceased King James, and now chief minister to James's son, the new King Charles.

Desperate for a solution to an agonizing dilemma, the nature of which I was loath to admit openly for reasons that will become clear, I resolved to contrive an audience with Signor Vitturi in the hope that he would deem me worthy to partake in this venture. And so it was that I found myself, that damp and unseasonably chilly morning, being ushered by a liveried footman into the high-ceilinged, darkly paneled great chamber of York House on the Strand, where Vitturi was a guest of Buckingham.

The Venetian rose from his writing desk as I was presented,

bowing with his hand upon his breast, but not before I caught sight of his face—the face I had been warned to expect, lest my countenance betray any hint of distaste. His forehead, cheek, and jaw on the right side were badly scarred, the flesh there gouged and puckered but well healed. These ghastly wounds appeared to extend to his chin and neck, but were mostly concealed in those regions by a narrow, trim beard of the type that was in fashion at that time, as well as by the ruff at his throat.

"Don Domenico." I executed as graceful a curtsy as I could manage, given my state of nervous excitation. "I thank you for agreeing to see me."

Vitturi was a tall man, and younger than I had expected, the unravaged side of his face being smooth-skinned and fine-boned; he wore a small gold hoop in the ear on that side. His eyes, which were the same deep brown as his shoulder-length hair, bespoke a perceptiveness that I found both appealing and unnerving.

"Are you chilled, Mistress Leeds?" he asked, nodding toward my tightly clasped, trembling hands. His Italian-accented voice was roughly soft, like the fur of a wolf, his manner courtly but distant.

"I . . . suppose I am."

If he knew that I was, in fact, trembling from nerves, and I suspect that he did, he gave no indication of it. Instead, he led me to a trio of stately, tall-backed chairs before a fireplace in which low flames sputtered and popped. Pulling one chair a bit closer to the fire, he gestured for me to sit.

From the corner of my eye as I arranged my skirts, I noticed his gaze shift from my face to my modest linen coif to my dress, which he surveyed from neck to hem. Although fashioned with a modishly short-waisted basque and full sleeves, it was made entirely of black crepe save for the white muslin cuffs and a plain, turned-down collar that fell from the throat in two long points over the bodice. The somber costume was a far cry from that of most Englishwomen, who were notorious throughout Europe for their uncovered heads and low-cut bodices.

In fact, Vitturi himself was attired entirely in black, including an overgown of lustrous matte satin worn open over his close-fitting doublet and breeches. The latter were less puffy and somewhat longer than those being worn in England at the time; as I recall, they extended over the knees. The overgown, with its togalike flap over the left shoulder that was, like the rest of his costume, peculiar to the patrician gentlemen of Venice, imparted an aura of archaic dignity; few Englishmen wore gowns as a matter of course anymore.

"Claret?" he asked, lifting a silver ewer from the elegant little black and gold lacquered table around which the three chairs were clustered.

I accepted with thanks, hoping the wine would soothe my nerves. No sooner had he filled two silver bowls than the footman reentered the room, bowed, and announced the arrival of a "Mademoiselle Elle." With a glance in my direction, he asked his master, "Shall I see if Mademoiselle would be amenable to returning at a more convenient time, signore?"

"Nay, show her in," Vitturi replied, explaining to me that he had requested the lady's presence at this meeting so that she might help in determining my suitability for "the undertaking in question."

"Elle makes her home at Château de la Grotte Cachée," he told me. "She assists me in the selection of promising young ladies and imparts a distaff perspective to their tutelage that I have found to be indispensable."

He rose again as a golden, statuesque beauty swept into the

room with a whisper of rose-hued taffeta and a merry "*Bonjour*. Pray pardon my lateness, Domenico. So this be your supplicant, eh? Upon my faith, but she is a pretty little thing."

"Mistress Hannah Leeds," Vitturi said, "may I present Mademoiselle Elle, who serves as abbess to my novices."

He fixed me with that dark, trenchant gaze, as if gauging my reaction to his likening of courtesans-in-training to Brides of Christ. Schooling my expression, for in truth I did find the comparison a bit unseemly, I rose and greeted the luxuriously attired "abbess" with a smile and a curtsy. " 'Tis a pleasure to make your acquaintance, mademoiselle—or should I address you as Mother Elle?"

As quips went, it wasn't much—I was far too wrought up for genuine cleverness—but Elle laughed appreciatively as she returned my curtsy. " 'Elle' is fine all by itself—*Sister* Hannah," she said. "And the pleasure is mine, I assure you."

Elle was the most resplendent woman I had ever seen, with radiant blue eyes and a beguiling smile. Her hair, like pale amber spun into the finest silk, was smartly styled in a chignon flanked by twin masses of side curls. Her gown was cut in the French fashion, with a face-framing winged collar of starched point lace trimming a neckline so wide and deep as to reveal a breathtaking display of bosom, compressed by her stays into high, creamy-soft mounds. Pearls encircled her throat and dangled from her ears; her fingers and thumbs glittered with rings. An ivory fan hung from a golden girdle around her waist in the Continental style.

Vitturi motioned Elle into the third chair, poured her a bowl of claret, and fell into a contemplative silence as she chatted amiably about this and that without seeming to expect much input from either Vitturi or myself. I sensed, with much appreciation, that she was attempting to put me at ease. It worked—until I glanced toward the Venetian and found him studying me over the rim of his claret bowl. I quickly looked away, not because of his scars, for I had already learned to focus on the unblemished aspect of his face, but because of the intensity of his gaze. It felt as if he were peering right through my skin—or trying to.

When he did finally speak, he got right to the point. "I cannot help but wonder, Mistress Leeds, why a highborn Englishwoman such as yourself should wish to move to Venice and become a *cortigiana*."

The honest answer was that I had no desire at all to become a courtesan, nor any intent to pursue such an occupation. What I did wish—what I urgently needed—was to get close to the Duke of Buckingham as soon as possible, but my attempt to maneuver an introduction had failed miserably. As soon as he'd learned whose niece I was, he had adamantly refused to see me. Ah, but at Grotte Cachée, I would be just another of Domenico Vitturi's "novices." Buckingham's guard would be down. He wouldn't recognize me, having never met me in the flesh. Nor would he recognize the name "Leeds," which was not my true surname, but my grandmother's maiden name.

It was an imperfect plan, in that it required me to present myself as a candidate for whoredom, with all the degradation that was likely to entail, but the situation was dire, and it was the only viable plan at my disposal.

Of course, I could reveal none of this in response to Vitturi's query as to my motives. Instead, I delivered the little speech I had rehearsed over and over in my mind the night before, while I tossed and turned and fretted about what to say and how to say it during this crucial interview. "I find myself in a bit of a dilemma, signore. My mother met her maker in March, and—"

"Ah," Elle said, nodding toward my funereal gown, "I

suspected you might be in mourning. Either that, or a Calvinist. Or both, perchance?"

"Nay, I am—" *Careful.* "—most definitely not a Calvinist. When my mother passed on, I was left with very little to my name, save a dowry so that I might contract an advantageous marriage. I've a cousin who has assumed the role of my guardian and protector, and he has negotiated my betrothal to a widowed gentleman who is . . . well, somewhat older than I, and whereas I am certain he is a fine man, and would provide well for me—he is a baron with an excellent holding—I doubt very much that he would find me a suitable bride."

"Your father is no longer with us?" Elle asked.

"Nay, he succumbed to a tertian ague when I was an infant."

"And why is it," Vitturi said, "that you feel your betrothed would find you unsuitable? Is it because you are not a virgin?"

"He . . . he is not my betrothed. The union has yet to be formally contracted. And as for . . . the other, you appear to suffer under a misapprehension, signore. I am, in fact . . . That is, I have never . . ." I gestured vaguely, appalled to feel my face stinging. They must have thought me an utter ninny.

"Are you saying you *are* a virgin?" he asked.

"That is a virginal blush if ever I've seen one," Elle observed as she snapped open her fan. "What an intriguing state of affairs. 'Tisn't often that an untouched maiden petitions to be one of Signor Vitturi's novices. In fact, I cannot recall a single instance."

"If your maidenhood be intact," Vitturi said, "why do you feel that your not quite betrothed will find you an unsuitable bride?"

"The gentleman in question has seven children, all of them still quite young and rather unruly from a lack of governance in the year since their mother's death, and he seems to think that I would make an ideal stepmother for them. When I speak to him of my interest in the Greek and Roman poets, and ancient history and such, he is apt to chuckle and wave his hand and tell me that I shall have no more time for such idle pursuits once I am 'chasing after his brood of little devils.' He has even told me that I shall have to put away my lute, because by the time I tuck the children into their beds, I will almost certainly be too fatigued to—"

"You play the lute?" Vitturi asked.

"Aye, signore," I said, "and the harpsichord."

"Do you sing?"

"I do."

"How well do you sing?"

"That would be for others to judge, I suppose."

With a weary little sigh, he said, "But these others are not here, are they? So I am asking you. How well do you sing?"

Leaning over to rest a hand on my arm, Elle said, "A beautiful singing voice is considered a great asset in a courtesan. Your modesty is charming and bespeaks a virtuous nature, but on an occasion such as this, frankness might serve you better. Given your lovely speaking voice, I would suspect that you sing like a bird. Am I not right?" She smiled and gave my arm a surreptitious little squeeze.

"I have ofttimes been complimented on the quality of my singing," I said.

"Have you any other talents?" he asked. "Favorite pastimes?"

"I compose madrigals to perform with friends, the words and music both."

"Indeed," he said, his eyes sparking with interest—perhaps because he was a poet, and what was a madrigal but a form of poesy? "How many have you written?"

"Seventy or eighty, perhaps more. I would have to count

them. I transcribe my favorites in a notebook bound in red leather that my unc—that was given to me as a gift."

"Are they any good?"

Having learned my lesson as regarded false modesty, I said, "I believe so, signore."

"A scholarly young lady such as yourself must speak one or two languages," he said.

"French, Latin, Greek, a little Spanish, and . . . *parlo Italiano fluentemente.*"

Vitturi's look of surprise was immensely gratifying. He ducked his head toward me, granting me a real smile, one that warmed those large brown eyes for the first time since we'd met. "*Ciò è inattesa,*" he said. "A delightful discovery, Mistress Leeds."

I returned his smile. For the briefest of moments, the space of two heartbeats, he held my gaze, and we shared—or so I fancied—a wordless communion of startling intimacy. But as quickly as one might snuff out a candle, his eyes grew opaque and his studied reserve returned.

He leaned over to lift his cup, took a long swallow, and said, without looking at me, "So you have concluded that the life of a Venetian *cortigiana onesta,* with the freedom, riches, and intellectual amusements that such a life provides, would be preferable to that of the wife of an English baron."

"And stepmother to seven little hellions? I have, Don Domenico." It wasn't a lie per se. Everything I'd told him was the truth. I had indeed found myself without property or prospects save for the singularly unappealing marriage that I had described. It was a grim predicament.

But it was not what had driven me to Domenico Vitturi's doorstep.

"In my part of the world," Vitturi said, "a female in a situation such as yours might very well take the veil. Of course, there are no nuns in your English Church—which is a pity, really. The convent has been the deliverance of many a young lady whose only alternative was a marriage they found abhorrent."

Vitturi's assumption about my religion was understandable, considering Parliament's decades-long campaign to purge the British Isles of "Romanists." Catholics who failed to attend worship services of the Established Church risked fines, ostracism, and imprisonment. The punishment for attending Mass was hanging. Although the persecution of Catholics had eased up a bit since King Charles's coronation, especially after he dissolved Parliament in June, official British policy was still fervently anti-Rome. Vitturi may have been Catholic himself, but he was also on intimate terms with many high-ranking men in Parliament. As such, he was the last person in whom I would confide such potentially damning information.

"Have you any close relations," Vitturi asked, "other than this cousin who has been endeavoring to marry you off?"

"There is no one," I lied.

Elle said, "You are fleeing a marriage—a life—that you foresee as repugnant, but are you aware, *really* aware, of what is entailed in the life of a courtesan? 'Tis true that you will enjoy a level of independence and intellectual liberty quite foreign to most women, especially to the matrons of Venice, who are kept, by and large, secluded in their homes with their children and their Bibles. The courtesan pays a price for her precious freedom, though. She has benefactors, half a dozen perhaps, whom she is obliged to entertain according to a schedule of her own devising, not grudgingly, but with true passion and a sense of adventure. The gentlemen who pay for her favors—most generously, mind you—expect to be pleasured in ways their sheltered and pious wives could never imagine. Given your lack of experience in carnal matters, I want to make sure that you understand what will be involved."

"I understand," I said, and at the time I thought I did. I knew the essential facts of sexual intercourse, and I had surmised that the act could be performed in various positions, but aside from that, what else was there? The finer points of kissing, perhaps, or of conducting oneself flirtatiously? Despite my scholarly open-mindedness, I really was woefully uninformed about the myriad ways in which men and women enjoyed each other's bodies.

Looking back upon that morning, I believe Elle sensed my ignorance despite my reassurances. "At Grotte Cachée," she said, "you will be taught certain practices that may shock you at first, and you will be expected to perform these acts with men who are virtual strangers to you."

Before I could truly digest that, Vitturi said, "You should be aware, Mistress Leeds, that you may be observed either with or without your knowledge during the course of your training by myself, Elle, or your fellow novices, in order to benefit your own education and that of the other young ladies."

God have mercy, I thought, but I merely said, "As you will, Don Domenico." I was in no position to take umbrage with this or any other condition he might choose to set forth. It was imperative that I be included among the prospective courtesans traveling with Vitturi and Buckingham to Grotte Cachée. It was a mission at which I could not, would not, fail; the life of my beloved uncle depended upon my success.

"For your own sake, Hannah . . ." Elle began. "I say, do you mind if I call you Hannah?"

"Please do."

"For your own sake, there is one thing that ought to be clarified ere we proceed further. You do understand the manner in which you are expected to repay your indebtedness to Signor Vitturi, do you not?"

I stole a glance in the Venetian's direction, expecting him to be discreetly sipping from his cup or otherwise averting his gaze while the indelicate subject was broached. But no, he met my eyes directly, albeit with an inscrutably blank expression.

Looking away quickly, I said, "I believe I do."

"And this arrangement is acceptable to you?" Elle asked.

Were I to reply that it was not, I would no doubt be escorted forthwith from Signor Vitturi's presence, and that would be that.

" 'Tis acceptable. However…" I paused a moment to recall the wording of the caveat I had composed during my long, sleepless night, which I prayed would safeguard my virtue during my "novitiate" at Grotte Cachée. "There is a matter which I believe warrants some consideration. 'Tis my understanding that gentlemen of a sporting stripe take great pleasure in being the first man to lie with a maiden."

"Many do," Elle said. "Methinks it has oft to do with the male urge to capture the most precious and elusive game, but there are men with less predatory motives, those who pride themselves on the skill and tenderness with which they introduce young virgins to the pleasures of the flesh. My brother Elic, whom you will meet at Grotte Cachée, is one such gentleman." Leaning toward me, her impish smile hidden from Vitturi behind her fan, Elle said in a deliberately loud whisper, "From all accounts, Signor Vitturi is another. Do not be misled by his stern manner. They say he has the gentlest hands in Christendom."

Slanting Elle a look, Vitturi said to me, "You are suggesting, I take it, that a young lady who debuts as a courtesan with her maidenhood intact, but well schooled in divers erotic pleasures, might command an unusually high price of the gentleman to whom she grants the privilege of deflowering her."

His summation was actually quite close to what I had planned to say—but for the phrase about being "well schooled in divers erotic pleasures." I felt the same little tremor of foreboding as when Elle had made that comment about my tutelage involving the performance of shocking acts with virtual strangers.

Ah, but there would be no such acts required of me if I could convince Domenico Vitturi to allow me to remain a virgin, would there? I assumed that I would be taught various types of kisses and caresses, and made to practice them, possibly with Vitturi himself, in lieu of lying with him. Of course, given that his novices were sometimes "observed with or without their knowledge," I might be compelled to witness others engaged in actual acts of lovemaking, but surely that would be the worst of it.

"It makes a great deal of sense, Domenico," Elle told him. "Hannah can learn what she needs to learn—and compensate thee quite adequately for thy largesse, if she be inventive—without sacrificing that valuable little maidenhead. It only remains to determine whether she meets thy lofty standards."

"Does she meet thine?" he asked her.

Their use of the quaintly familiar *thee* and *thine* suggested an intimacy that surprised me, especially given Vitturi's air of reserve; I wondered if they were lovers.

"She already speaks Italian," Elle said. "She has a scholarly bent, which is a charming novelty in such a beauteous little thing. She sings, plays music, composes madrigals . . ." Smiling at me, she said, "I think the gentlemen of Venice will throw themselves at the feet of this quick-brained little English maiden with the dazzling red hair."

He scowled at my too-thick, too-wavy hair. " 'Tis yellow, not red."

" 'Tis somewhere in between," Elle said, "but it *does* dazzle, and she has the loveliest skin, translucent but full of color, like glazed China porcelain. Exquisite, no?"

"What little we can see of it." Vitturi sat back in his chair, using his hands to lift his right leg and cross it over the left. His left calf appeared well muscled through his black nether hose, the right somewhat less so. He regarded me in silence for a moment before saying, quite soberly, "Mistress Leeds, have you given this matter the clear-headed deliberation it warrants?"

"I have, Don Domenico."

"And you are absolutely convinced that this is the course you wish to follow."

"Aye, quite convinced."

He nodded. "Elle seems to think you a likely candidate, and I would tend to agree. However, given the nature of the vocation to which you aspire, and my reputation as a patron of the most desirable and sought-after *cortigianas* in Venice, our assessment of your person must needs be quite thorough. You understand?"

I said, "Of course, signore," although I didn't really understand at all, as I discovered a moment later, when he asked me if I would "be so kind as to disrobe completely."

Two

I STARED AT VITTURI, my hands clasped so tightly in my lap that I felt as if the little bones might snap from the pressure.

" 'Tis just as I thought," he said. "You fancy yourself a *cortigiana*, Mistress Leeds, but in truth, 'tis a vocation for which an innocent such as yourself is entirely unfit. You must trust me when I say that any efforts which you or I were to put forth on such account would come to naught. I pray you, leave here and put the matter from your mind."

"I . . . I am not unfit," I said, hating the quaver in my voice. "I know that I would make an excellent courtesan. I just didn't expect to be asked to take my clothes off in front of two perfect—"

"Hannah," Elle said softly, closing a hand around mine.

She's coming to my rescue, I thought, but then she said,

"Don Domenico is not only within his rights to ask this of you, he is wise to do so. His courtesans are expected to be not only learned, witty, and clever, they are expected to be—*must* be, above all else—exceptionally beautiful. A courtesan's beauty must extend beyond her face and hands. Her form must rival that of Aphrodite herself. Surely you understand why he cannot pass judgment on you until he sees you in your natural state. And after all, there is no shame in nudity. Your body is a wondrous machine, a thing of great beauty."

How could I argue with such straightforward logic? And had I not resolved most earnestly to use every means at my disposal, no matter how distasteful, to save my uncle?

"If you cannot bring yourself to undress in front of Don Domenico," Elle said, "then perhaps he's right. Perhaps you are simply not meant to be a—"

"I *am* meant to be a courtesan." I stripped off my gloves and started fumbling with the knot securing my coif at the nape of my neck. " 'Tis just that this is all so new to me. I need to . . . I just need to . . . *Blast!*" I yanked at the coif until it pulled free, mussing the neatly braided bun in which I had styled my hair, and then I set about untying my collar, which proved equally aggravating.

"Allow me," Elle said, leaning over to help.

I kicked off my shoes, reaching under my skirts to roll down my stockings. *Just do it. Do it and get it over with.* Domenico Vitturi had seen scores of unclothed women. He was used to it even if I wasn't.

Quietly, with an uncharacteristic note of earnestness, perhaps even compassion, in his voice, Vitturi said, "You need not do this, Mistress Leeds."

Both feet now bared, I sat up and looked him in the eye. "Will you allow me to accompany you to Grotte Cachée if I do not?"

He gave a sigh. "I think you know the answer to that question."

"Well, then." I stood, my face now scalding, and started prying open the row of tiny buttons that fastened my basque down the front.

My fingers felt huge, numb, hopelessly clumsy. I don't know how I would have managed without Elle's help.

Don't think about it and it won't matter, I told myself as she removed my basque. I had come to believe that one's mind and one's body were distinct and separate entities, with intellectual concerns existing on the higher plane, corporeal on the lower. No matter what indignities my body was subjected to, if I divorced my mind from them, in essence pretending they weren't happening, they would have no power to affect me. All that was required was a bit of mental discipline.

"You are Catholic?" he asked.

He was looking at the little gold crucifix around my neck, a symbol of the Roman Church that I wore beneath my clothes so as not to advertise my religion.

I winced.

He didn't smile, exactly, but there was a hint of reassurance in his eyes as he said, "Your secret is safe with me, Mistress Leeds."

Elle draped the basque carefully over the back of her chair, then did the same with my overskirt. She untied my bum roll, helped me to step out of my petticoats, unlaced and peeled away my stays...

As she pulled my shift up over my head, I wrestled with the urge to clutch at it, to squeeze my eyes shut and bow my head in shame. Instead, I lifted my chin and stared at the portrait of Buckingham over the mantel, reeling with the sensation of being utterly naked in a man's presence. Vitturi made not a sound as his gaze moved over my bare flesh, upon which no male had ever before laid eyes.

I hitched in a breath when Elle stroked a hand lightly down my arm, inciting a trail of goose bumps.

"She is exquisite, is she not, Domenico?" Elle asked. "Slender, without being skinny. Like a marble statue of a goddess, a true Galatea."

"Her breasts are rather small," he said.

"They are perfectly in proportion with the rest of her. Besides, a certain boyishness can be an asset in a courtesan, as you well know. 'Twas you yourself who told me about courtesans who dress in male clothing and even cut off their hair to entertain those benefactors who prefer the charms of their own sex, but do not wish to pay for their sport by losing their heads to the executioner. Hannah would be ideal for such purposes, would she not?"

"Pray turn around, Mistress Leeds," Vitturi said in a bemaddeningly calm, even voice.

I did so, fancying that I could feel Vitturi's gaze searing my very flesh—my shoulders and back, my buttocks, my legs— but of course, it was only the warmth of the fire.

His dispassionate appraisal made me feel all the more naked and exposed. Were he my lover, it would be a very different matter to feel his eyes upon me. It would feel natural, perhaps even exciting, the heat of his gaze serving as a prelude to his touch.

They say he has the gentlest hands in Christendom.

My skin felt peculiarly sensitized all over, as if it were suddenly just a bit too snug, pulling so taut around my breasts as to make their tips draw up tight and hard. This hot, prickly awareness shivered through me, settling in that secret, untouched place between my legs.

I imagined fingers there, warm, masculine fingers, stroking, exploring, ever so gently. As if it were really happening, the flesh there pulsed with heat.

I dug my nails into my palms so as to stifle arousal with pain. The drumming of my heart seemed to reverberate in my skull.

"What thinkest thou, Domenico?" Elle asked.

"Be prepared to leave for France in two days' time, Mistress Leeds. And bring the red notebook." There came a rustle of fabric followed by footsteps that sounded slightly halting.

I stiffened, my eyes flying open as I awaited, through a maelstrom of clashing emotions, his touch upon me.

A door opened and closed.

I turned around. He was gone.

Elle smiled as she handed me back my shift. "Welcome to the novitiate, sister."

After heaping me with advice and information while helping me to dress, Elle saw me to the door, kissed me three times near each cheek—another Continental convention—and bid me adieu. I started walking home, and was all the way to Fleet Bridge before I realized that I'd left my gloves behind on the little lacquered table.

I retraced my steps to York House, waiting just inside the front door while the footman who'd answered my knock went to fetch the gloves. Glancing around idly, I noticed, through a doorway off the entry hall, a harpsichord standing in the corner of an opulently furnished chamber. It was unlike any such instrument I had ever seen, more imposing by far than the plain little Flemish harpsichord in my withdrawing room at home.

I stepped through the doorway and approached the grandiose instrument, which was fancily carved and painted all over with peacocks, pheasants, and cupids amid an intricate network of scrolling tendrils and leaves. Even the inside of its raised lid was decorated with a lush pastoral landscape executed in vivid colors.

Curious as to its tone, I was debating whether to play a stanza of the madrigal I'd been working on, when I heard the muted groan of wood and what sounded like grunts of effort from beyond a slightly ajar door leading into another room. I cocked my head to listen, thinking perhaps it was a servant straining at some laborsome chore, until I heard a woman with a French accent—Elle, her breathing strident—say, "Thou art thinking of her."

"Who?" It was Vitturi's voice, as winded as Elle's.

"Hannah."

There came a moment's silence, or perhaps he muttered something I couldn't hear. "Nay," he said.

I crept closer to the door, which stood open perhaps an inch, peering cautiously into the chamber on the other side. By angling my head, I could make out in succession the edge of a marble mantelpiece, an ornately paneled cupboard, and a row of chairs covered in dark hide lined up against the wall.

Hanging on the wall over the chairs was a massive beveled mirror in a gilt frame, reflecting the upper body of Domenico Vitturi, in his black doublet but without his overgown. He was standing with a pair of upraised legs in embroidered stockings and red-heeled pink slippers propped on his shoulders, from which I surmised that Elle must have been lying before him on a table. All I could see of her aside from her legs was a great white lather of rucked-up petticoats.

Vitturi was leaning over her, his face obscured by hair that swayed with his movements, which were abrupt, as if he were trying to push some immovable object using his entire body.

But of course I realized what he was really doing—what *they* were doing. I was innocent, but I was not dimwitted.

I stopped breathing.

"If not Hannah, then whom?" Elle asked.

"*Merda*," he rasped. "No one."

"No one?" Elle said through a chuckle. "Thou lieth with me, Domenico, but methinks thy mind lieth otherwhere."

"Cease thy prating, woman, lest my cockstand grow as limp as thy wit."

Elle laughed.

Vitturi paused and straightened up, pushing his hair, which looked to be damp with sweat, behind his ears. "Vixen," he said with a little shake of his head—but he was smiling in an amused and indulgent way that took me completely by surprise, given how relatively aloof he had been with me.

The side of his face that was visible in the reflection was the uninjured left side, sheened with sweat. Without the wounds to distract me, I was awed by how striking he was, with those huge, dark eyes and distinctively Italian aquiline nose. What a shame, I thought, for such beauty to have been compromised. It occurred to me that a man's wounds ofttimes came to define him, even to himself. I wondered what sort of man Domenico Vitturi saw when he looked in the mirror.

Elle let out a kittenish little mew of pleasure as he resumed his thrusting. I backed silently away from the door and returned to the entry hall. When the footman reappeared with my gloves, I was standing exactly where he had left me.

Three

HAVE YE SEEN HOW Master Knowles looks at me?" Lucy Swanton asked her fellow novice courtesans as our carriage jounced along a rutted track through the woods enveloping Grotte Cachée Valley.

Jonas Knowles, Esquire, courtier and companion to the Duke of Buckingham, was the youngest of the seven noblemen accompanying Domenico Vitturi on this trip to Grotte Cachée. The other three novices, with whom I had shared the canopied cart during the ten-day journey from the Channel, could not stop whispering about Master Knowles, who was the fair-haired, charming second son of a baron. Lucy seemed particularly enraptured.

Saucily plump, with ruddy cheeks and gleaming silver-blond hair, Lucy was the most vivacious and chatty of the four of us, what my mother would have called a trittle-trattle. She was married to a Cambridgeshire gentleman farmer who was no gentleman, and from whom she'd fled after he'd throttled her almost to death for having paid a call on the rector's wife without his leave. She'd taken refuge in the home of a female cousin in London, a mistress of one of the king's ministers. When the cousin told her about Domenico Vitturi, she'd leapt at the opportunity to move far away from England and re-make herself into a woman of independent means.

Sitting next to her on the leather seat facing mine was Bianca Gabrieli, a delicate beauty with a fair complexion and light brown hair. Bianca was the widow of a Venetian glass merchant who had been rich as Croesus when she'd wed him but who had gambled it all away in short order. The previous winter, he was knifed to death over a debt he couldn't repay, leaving her in desperate straits.

Sharing my seat was the darkly exotic Sibylla Fierro from Florence, whose worldliness, elegance, and rigorous convent education were the envy of the rest of us. The impoverished orphaned daughter of a patrician, Sibylla had chosen cour-tisanerie over the nunnery.

"Master Knowles looks at all of us that way," Sibylla told Lucy. Her English, the only language we all had in common, was remarkably polished. " 'Tis Elle he truly lusts after, and who can blame him?"

"Has he bed her yet?" asked Bianca, whose Italian accent was much stronger than Sibylla's.

"Nay, nor will he," I said. "She doesn't fancy him. She told me so."

"Then she be mad," Lucy said. "I'd lift my skirts for him in a heartbeat if Don Domenico would allow it."

Don Domenico's companions were free to avail themselves of the intimate company of the novices, myself excluded, pro-vided they first obtain his consent. The only man who had been denied this privilege was Jonas Knowles. According to Elle, the Duke of Buckingham considered it unseemly for his principal retainer, who had a wife and child back home, "to be seen skulking from bed to bed like some goatish runagate."

On the seventh morning of our travels, when Lucy had talked of being summoned to Don Domenico's bed the previous evening, I'd felt an absurd little twinge of envy despite my resolve to remain a virgin. The memory of him taking Elle in the dining parlor of York House, his driving thrusts, his grunts of effort, his sweat—*Thou art thinking of her*—had only grown more vivid with time. I couldn't help but wonder what it would be like to lie with such a man, to transform him with my powers of seduction from an urbane and self-possessed gentleman into a rutting beast, to feel his sex moving in and out of me, rubbing me from inside, my heart hammering faster, faster...

I had even dreamed about it at the inn we stayed in the night before, only to awaken with a start, hips squeezing as I lay facedown in my little bed, the flesh between my legs hot and swollen. The urge to press down hard, to grind my aching sex against the prickly straw mattress, was almost overwhelming.

The dream had likely been inspired by the squeaking bed ropes and rhythmic thumping coming from the bedchamber next to mine, which housed the gray-haired but brawny Marquess of Tarwick. A female voice, muffled but recognizable as Bianca's, cried *"Sì! Sì! Dio santo!"*

"Like it good and hard, do you?" Tarwick rasped as the squeaking speeded up.

"Aye, my lord, *come una lancia.* Stab it in. Sì...Sì..."

I lay there with my eyes wide and my ear trained, grudgingly fascinated by their raucous coupling.

"By the rood, you're good at this," the marquess said, "bloody good. Can I fetch in you?"

"Sì, I want you to. I want to feel the...how you say? Spitting? Spurting, that is the word."

The moans from the next room took on an urgent quality. Wedging a hand beneath me, I found my night rail soaked through at the juncture of my thighs, a phenomenon I had experienced occasionally, but never to such a degree. I stroked my sex through the saturated linen, inciting a sharp tremor of pleasure that seemed to emanate from a little knot of flesh at the apex of the cleft. It was the first time I had ever experienced such a sensation, having never touched myself there except when bathing. Drunk with arousal, I reflexively pressed my mons against my hand. There came a second tremor and an urge to thrust that was so powerful, I shook with the effort of resisting it. I felt as if I were on the threshold of a crisis of pleasure that might burst my heart were I to surrender to it.

"*Oh Dio!* Oh...oh..." Bianca let out a series of sharp cries that alarmed me for a moment until they devolved into breathless chuckles and I realized she was reacting to pleasure, not pain.

"Oh, God," the marquess groaned as the squeaks and thumps grew louder, faster. "I'm coming. Ohhh..." The squeaks slowed as he let out a long, low groan.

I knew I should pull my hand out from under me, put the pillow over my head, and try to get back to sleep. I was no voluptuary enslaved by base physical urges but a scholar, a thinker, a creature of the mind.

But not only did I leave the hand there, I pressed my finger into the slit through the drenched linen, brushing the little knot, which was hard as a pearl now. That light, fleeting touch triggered a contraction in my sex that sucked the very breath from my lungs. There followed a flurry of spasms so intense that I had to bite my lip—*hard*—to keep from crying out as I convulsed with a pleasure I had never known before.

As I lay there afterward, catching my breath and marveling at what had just transpired, I reflected that I might have a great deal more to learn about carnal matters than I had previously thought. That realization only magnified my unease as our procession of carts, carriages, and horsemen drew ever nearer to Château de la Grotte Cachée.

Lucy was complaining about Don Domenico's "interfering in our love lives like some meddlesome old auntie."

"Love lives?" Sibylla said. "These are all wedded men, Lucy, most with mistresses as well. 'Tisn't love they want from us."

"Is *he* a wedded man?" I asked. "Don Domenico?" The possibility had not occurred to me.

"Constanze say he have no wife and no mistress," Bianca told them. Constanze was her older sister, who had had been among Vitturi's first group of neophyte courtesans seven years ago and was now one of the most sought-after courtesans in Venice. "She say once he have many lovers, and a very beautiful mistress, but now he only bed his *cortigianas*. She say when he is young, the mothers of all the young ladies want him for marry the daughters, for he have much wealth, and fine family, and he write the *poesie di amore*. But then a bad thing happen…"

Besides already being a poet of some renown in his early twenties, Bianca told us, Vitturi had been an officer in Venice's vaunted Navy. Nine years ago, during a battle in the Adriatic against "the Uscocchi," whom I took to be pirates of some sort, he received such grievous injuries that he was no longer able to serve in the Navy.

Upon seeing him newly wounded, his mistress was so horror-struck that she vomited and cast him aside. He sought out Galiana Solsa, the wealthiest and most elegant courtesan in Venice, who had favored him in the past, but she hurled stinging insults at him and ordered him out of her palazzo.

When he lingered, thinking he might sway her with words, for he'd always been a silver-tongued charmer, Galiana had him dragged into the street and savagely beaten by three brawny footmen.

"She is a *demonio*, that one," Bianca said. "*Una striga.*"

"*Striga?*" That was a word my Italian tutor had never taught me.

"A thing of great evil, a devil of the night. Galiana Solsa hunt the peoples in the dark, like the owl hunt the mice, and she drink their blood. She stay young very many years. Her... how you say, *preda*, those she feed upon, they vanish in the night. Still, the men, they cannot turn from her, so great is her beauty. She have a strange power over them."

"Bianca, you superstitious little plebian," Sibylla said. "You don't really believe that."

"Do you defy the Church?" Bianca demanded. "The *Folleti*, the incubus and the succubus, they visit the peoples at night, when they sleep, and violate them. Some of these incubi, the ones called dusii, they can change from man to woman, and back again. Is how they steal the seed from the mens and—"

Sibylla snickered.

"The fathers of the Church tell us these thing," Bianca said heatedly. "'Tis not for us to question."

Like Sibylla, I was far too scholarly to credit such tales, but I kept my mouth shut so as not to vex Bianca.

Addressing Lucy and me, but not the smirking Sibylla, Bianca said in a low, mysterious tone, "Constanze, she tell me there is much strange things at Grotte Cachée. There is a cave which make you feel drunk inside, and things happen there that cannot happen. And by this cave, there is a pool of water that is bewitched. What others in this water feel, you will feel. Oh, and she tell me one day she hear the old lord of Grotte

Cachée, Seigneur des Ombres, speak an *incantesimo*. I do not know the *Inglese* word for this."

"An incantation?" I said. "A magic spell?"

"*Sì, sì, magico*. And she say she think is incubi at Grotte Cachée, but she say they don't hurt the peoples. There is a hermit who live in a cave who can take the shape of animals, or even make himself *invisibile*. And she say Inigo and Elic, the men who will teach us the arts of love, be no ordinary men. Inigo, the dark one with the beautiful smile, he have *il cacchio di uno stallion*. She say is like a pillar of stone. And Elic, this one is very tall and handsome, with golden hair, like Apollo, and he can take the womens again and again—ten, twenty times, with no rest between *orgasmi*."

"*È ridicolo*," Sibylla muttered as she gazed out at the passing trees.

Lucy cut off Bianca's rebuttal with a gasp. "He's coming!" she said, craning her neck to look behind them through the tied-back curtains draping their carriage. "He's riding toward us up the path."

"Don Domenico?" I asked.

"Nay. Well, aye," she whispered as she pinched her cheeks and patted her hair. "He's coming, too, and some of the others, but I meant Master Knowles."

"What ho, ladies," Jonas Knowles said as he walked his horse past the carriage, sweeping off his wide-brimmed, luxuriously plumed beaver hat with a low bow.

Lucy made sheep eyes at him as she returned his smile. "Master Knowles."

Next came Elle, riding astride in a billowing blue satin skirt that was split in front, revealing matching breeches and hose— a shameless style of dress unique to Venetian courtesans, which the Frenchwoman had adopted as a riding costume. She wore a mannish hat very much like that of the English courtiers, only perhaps with a few more plumes. The effect was actually quite fetching.

When Elle told us that we were but a few miles from Château de la Grotte Cachée, all four of us raised a cheer. Ten days in that jolting, rattling carriage had left us woozy and aching. Like the other noblemen, Buckingham usually rode, surrounded by his yeomen and retainers, although he did have a very elegant carriage in which he retired from time to time, often with Knowles for company. As Buckingham's gentleman of the bedchamber, it was Knowles's responsibility to keep the duke well dressed, well fed, and supplied with devoted and genial companionship.

Domenico Vitturi, who rode by next, not only greeted us warmly, but touched his heart as he bowed, a courtly gesture of which I had grown quite fond. His traveling costume consisted of a black doublet, breeches, and hose, with a buff leathern jerkin and tall boots folded over at the tops. In contrast to the Englishmen, he wore a flat, brimless, Venetian-style felt cap. To my mind, his attire—the cap in particular—bespoke a restraint and self-assurance that was more attractive by far than the peacock ostentation of his companions.

"We few shall be riding ahead to the château to ensure that all is in readiness," he said, meeting every pair of eyes in the carriage save for mine. He often appeared to be subtly dodging my gaze, just as I dodged his. I wasn't quite sure why this was. He didn't seem to harbor any mislike toward me, and I certainly felt no animosity toward him. In fact, the more I saw of him—of his gallantry toward the novices, his easy camaraderie with his fellows, and the evenhandedness and quiet authority he displayed with his staff—the more I admired him.

Bringing up the rear of the little group on horseback were

two stalwart yeomen of the Duke of Buckingham, followed by the duke himself, who was widely regarded as the handsomest man in England. Dressed in the dashing cavalier style favored by King Charles, he had wavy chestnut hair, a pointed beard, and deep blue eyes that were uncommonly striking. Yet for all his beauty, and his reputation for charm and wit—he was the courtier's courtier, after all—he rarely smiled, or engaged in good-natured banter with the other gentlemen. Indeed, there was an aura of melancholy about the man that evoked my pity despite his aloofness and his baffling accusation against my uncle.

"Your Grace," Lucy said to him with a little duck of her head.

The duke did not so much as glance in our direction as he rode past the carriage. Like Knowles, he was a married man with a child. This was the only reason I could fathom for his attitude of studied indifference toward the wanton beauties with whom he was traveling—that and perhaps his glum spirits. Buckingham's purpose in visiting Grotte Cachée was primarily to hunt wild boars in the woods and moorlands surrounding the castle, which were said to be teeming with them. French boars, Elle had told me, were known to be far superior to their English counterparts.

The duke was surrounded at all times by burly attendants charged with preventing anyone from getting close to him without his leave. Several times I had tried to speak to him, only to be rebuffed in no uncertain terms. Yeomen even stood guard over him while he slept. I prayed that he would be more approachable once we were at Grotte Cachée. If not, I would have to concoct some ruse to breach the fortification he had established around himself.

When he was just out of earshot, Lucy lowered her voice and leaned forward. "He thinks he's Lord God himself, being the favorite of two kings, first James and now Charles, but he very nearly got yanked down off that high horse of his after that wretched business with Spain." After half a year spent living with a mistress to a member of the king's inner circle, Lucy knew all there was to know about English court intrigue.

"What business with Spain?" Bianca asked.

"The duke headed up an absolutely disastrous naval expedition in October," Lucy said. "He tried to capture Cádiz and botched that up, so he mounted an assault on a fleet of Spanish galleons full of silver from the New World—only they took a different route than they were supposed to, and slipped the noose. It was a humiliating defeat for us. All fingers pointed to His Grace as a bungler, and there was a movement to impeach him as chief minister, but King Charles thinks he walks on water, so last month he disbanded Parliament."

"Disbanded...?" Bianca said with a little shake of her head. "My English..."

"Told them to pack up and go home, and that he'd call them together again when he felt like it—when he needs money again, most likely. Meanwhile, the duke has been saying he didn't bungle anything, that the mission only failed because Spain was warned about it in advance by a traitor, an English emissary to the Spanish court named Guy Goodbody."

"Goodchild," I said.

Lucy gave me a dubious little scowl. "Are you certain?"

"Quite. *I should know my own uncle's name.*

"Guy Goodchild, then," Lucy said. "He's been locked up in the tower for months, all the while proclaiming his innocence, although the duke says he has unassailable proof against him. It's probably true, because it's come to light that he's secretly..." She lowered her voice, as if to prepare us for something shocking. "...a papist."

Bianca and Sibylla, both openly Catholic—they were Italians, after all—exchanged a look of amused forbearance. I kept my expression carefully neutral.

"A Catholic would naturally harbor sympathies with Spain, would he not?" Lucy said. "And it doesn't help that it was the Duke of Buckingham himself who accused him. Everyone knows that Goodchild and the duke were close. After King James died, when His Grace was most in need of a friend, 'twas Master Goodchild he turned to. They fenced together, hunted together... Why on earth would the duke accuse his closest companion of being a traitor to the crown if it weren't so?"

That was the very question that I had come here to answer.

Lucy said, "Parliament was dissolved before they could hold an inquest to try Master Goodchild for high treason. They'll try him when they reconvene, whenever that may be. 'Tis all but certain he'll be found guilty, and then he'll be executed as all traitors are, by drawing and quartering."

Sibylla shuddered. "Barbari Inglesi," she said. *English barbarians.*

Just as I had feared, Bianca asked Lucy what she meant by drawing and quartering.

With cheerfully gruesome relish, Lucy described how the condemned man was to be drawn to the place of execution on a hurdle, then hanged by the neck, choking and writhing, until he was almost, but not quite, dead. After being taken down from the gibbet, his belly would be sliced open and his entrails pulled out, to be roasted before his eyes, often along with his privy members. The torment would finally end when he was beheaded, with the remainder of his body being cut into quarters.

"They take the four quarters and the head, shove them

onto stakes, and put them on display as a warning to others," Lucy said. "They're left to rot there till the flesh drops from the bones."

Bianca sat with a hand pressed to her mouth, ashen and wide-eyed. Sibylla yawned.

I stared out the window, eyes stinging.

Guy Goodchild, my mother's kind, funny, generous younger brother, had been like a father to me all my life. At forty years of age, he had never been married. He had no wife and no children to come to his aid. He only had me. I could not, *would* not let him end his days in such agony, especially for something he didn't do. Uncle Guy was fiercely loyal to his king, and to his friends, as well. He'd always spoken of the Duke of Buckingham with the greatest respect and affection. Once or twice, he'd even slipped and referred to him in my hearing as "George." Their friendship had meant everything to him.

What could this "unassailable proof" possibly be? Buckingham hadn't revealed it publicly, nor, apparently, did he mean to do so until the inquest, which would likely be brief and decisive, with the ghastly sentence carried out within days. The inquest would take place when Parliament reconvened, and since there was no way of telling when that would be, it was imperative that I establish my uncle's innocence as soon as possible. My plan was to do whatever it took to coax Buckingham into revealing his "proof" so that I could challenge it. If that required me to employ my womanly wiles, I would do so. All that mattered, all I cared about anymore, was saving my beloved uncle. I would gladly forfeit my modesty, my reputation, even my virginity if it came to it, in order to rescue him from such a hellish and undeserved death.

Four

"THERE IT IS!" exclaimed Bianca, pointing ahead of us as the carriage emerged from the shadowy woods, its wheels grumbling along a serpentine gravel path now instead of packed dirt. "I see it! *Il castello!*"

All four of us jumped up to lean out of the carriage, two on each side, shading our eyes as we peered at the distant castle nestled in the embrace of Grotte Cachée Valley. It was rectangular, with a tower rising from each of the four corners. The sinking sun, hovering just above the craggy, densely forested mountains looming over us, gilded the castle with a saffron luminescence. Having been told that it was constructed of dark volcanic stone, I had expected a bleak and forbidding edifice; on the contrary, from this particular vantage point, it might have been forged from pure gold.

"*È bello,*" Bianca murmured.

"*Sì*," I replied. "*Molto bello.*"

Even the jaded Sibylla appeared transfixed as she gazed at the building that was to be our home for the next few weeks.

"I can't wait to meet Elic and Inigo," Lucy said as we retreated into the carriage and set about tidying ourselves for our arrival at the château.

I said, "Will they be our only . . . the, er, only instructors teaching us how to . . ."

"Fuck?" Lucy said, erupting in laughter when I blushed.

"*Sì*," Bianca said. "Constanze, she tell me is just these two."

"Don Domenico doesn't . . . participate?" I asked.

Bianca shook her head. "He lie with us at night, but he don't teach."

He would lie with the rest of them, but not with me. I hadn't yet been summoned to his bed; nor, if he was as good as his word, would I be. Yet I couldn't help but recall Elle telling him that I could "compensate thee quite adequately for thy largesse, if she be inventive." I could only assume there were "inventive" ways to kiss and embrace and so forth, yet Vitturi had yet to solicit this sort of thing from me.

"He may not *mean* to teach us," Lucy said with a grin, "but every second spent in his arms is a revelation."

The other two emitted lustful little sighs that spoke volumes.

"Yet he never really seems to look at me," Sibylla said. "At my body, perhaps, but not at my eyes. He never lets me kiss him, nor does he let me sleep in his bed. When the lovemaking is done, I must depart."

Lucy and Bianca said he was the same with them, an accomplished and thoughtful lover, but one who never let his guard down all the way. When they spoke too familiarly to him, he seemed to shrink back into himself.

"I pity him," Bianca said, "because he keep his heart to

himself. I think he will never love one woman. But he love *women*, all women, more than any man I ever meet. And he know them. He know what they like, what make them ... *ec-statico*."

"He's that best of all lovers," Lucy said, "a gentleman, but also a bit of a savage. He's not afraid to let the beast out of its cage, you know?"

I nodded, although I didn't know, not really.

" 'Tis best he won't be the one to deflower Hannah," Sibylla said. "He would surely spoil her for other men."

"Aye, there's that," Lucy said. "The first time he bedded me, after agreeing to take me on as a novice, he did me in the French manner, and upon my honor, he didn't stop till I came seven times."

"The French manner?" I said.

"He pleasured me with his mouth," Lucy said.

"You don't mean ...?" My gaze strayed to her lap.

They all three burst out laughing as heat flooded my face.

"Oh, Hannah, your poor little lambkin," Sibylla said, clearly trying to stifle her laughter. "Surely you've heard of *Greek* lovemaking."

"Taking it in the bum?" Lucy added helpfully.

I gaped at them.

"Don't fret, sweeting," Lucy soothed as she leaned over to take my ice-cold hand. "At Grotte Cachée, you'll have the chance to master these things, and more. 'Tis why we've come here, so that we can practice all manner of novel bedsport with Elic and Inigo, so as to be prepared for any request of our benefactors."

So this, then, was what Vitturi had been referring to when he'd spoken of me debuting as a courtesan with my maiden-hood intact *but well schooled in divers erotic pleasures*.

And I'd assumed he'd been talking about kissing.

Imbecile! I thought, slumping back into my seat in a daze of horror. *Pathetical little dunderpate! What have you gotten yourself into?*

"Constanze say we will learn to take great pleasure in these thing," Bianca said, adding, with a suggestive smile. "She say Elic and Inigo are *ispirazione*. She say after Grotte Cachée, we never be the same."

"*Bonjour, mademoiselles!*" came a booming voice as the carriage rumbled over a drawbridge, shuddering to a halt before a gatehouse manned by red-coated Swiss Guards. "Good afternoon, ladies! *Buon pomeriggio, signore!*" The speaker, a bearded giant, swung open the carriage door and gave a deep bow. "I am Serge Pépin, *mon seigneur*'s *administrateur* and your servant, ladies. *Bienvenue au château*. Signor Vitturi tells me your lingua franca is English, *oui*?"

Before any of us could respond, he bellowed, "Excellent! We love English here!" Offering me his gigantic hand, he said, "Welcome to Grotte Cachée, mistress. May your stay with us be an adventure."

৵৫

Assembled in the castle's central courtyard to greet us were some two dozen men and women retained by Signor Vitturi for the purpose of transforming us into courtesans worthy of the most discriminating benefactors. There were Venetian dressmakers, seamstresses, milliners, and shoemakers; French and Venetian ladies' maids; strapping footmen; dancing, singing, and painting masters; instructors in rhetoric, deportment, harpsichord, and lute; French, Italian, and Latin tutors; even expert card players and sportsmen.

Vitturi and Elle were not in attendance, although the Marquess of Tarwick and Sir Humphrey Quade, Buckingham's master of the hunt, lingered about the central fountain drinking tobacco from long clay pipes as they observed this singular reception. I couldn't keep from stealing glances at the fountain, which was majestic in scale, with a fat column rising from the middle of a round stone pool. Atop this column was a sculpture of a couple united in coitus as a maidservant poured water onto them from a jug.

The last two people to whom the garrulous Monsieur Pépin introduced us were our *"professeurs d'amour,"* as the *administrateur* so tastefully put it: the by-now-legendary Elic and Inigo. I discreetly took their measure as we exchanged bows and curtsies, reflecting that Bianca's description of their physical allure had been no exaggeration.

Inigo, who struck me as a Greek or Italian type, had hair that grew in a mop of tight black curls, big dark eyes, and a disarmingly boyish grin. He was attired, for some reason, in the height of ostentatious English-style fashion, his doublet of ivory silk and full, midnight blue breeches both thick with embroidery. No opportunity for embellishment had been neglected; his whisk and garters were edged in lace, a lovelock trailed over one shoulder, his earring dripped tassles, and his shoes, which were embroidered to match his doublet, sported immense silken rosettes.

Elic was, as Bianca had said, very tall and handsome, with long, honey-blond hair and pale blue eyes. He resembled his sister Elle to an extraordinary degree; one would never confuse them for anything but siblings. His garb, which was far more austere than that of his friend, reminded me of Domenico Vitturi's in that it was entirely black but for a good deal of linen showing through the open front and armholes of the doublet; he wasn't even wearing a collar.

I could barely meet the eyes of either man. If my tutelage proceeded as planned, they would soon be doing unpardonably sinful things to me and with me, things I had never even imagined before that afternoon. I couldn't claim that I hadn't been warned. Elle had been most explicit. *You will be taught certain practices that may shock you at first, and you will be expected to perform these acts with men who are virtual strangers to you.*

Elic greeted me warmly, but his brow soon furrowed. "Hannah, are you—" He caught himself, making a sheepish face at having addressed me so familiarly. "Pray pardon me. Are you quite well, Mistress Leeds? You seem terribly pale."

"I thank you for your concern, monsieur," I replied, "but I am quite well. I tend toward paleness."

He gave me the oddest look of skepticism—half scowl, half smile—as if he were well aware that I wasn't normally pale, though of course he had no way of knowing that.

Monsieur Pépin assigned us each a footman to run our errands, as well as a ladies' maid, whose immediate duty was to show us to our bedchambers, unpack our baggage, acquaint us with the castle, and help us to wash and dress for supper.

"A feast of Auvergnet delicacies will be served in the great hall at eight of the clock," Pépin announced, "after which we shall enjoy libations and sweetmeats in the adjacent withdrawing room."

As we were filing into the castle, the *administrateur* took me aside and said, "I understand, Mistress Leeds, that you were asked to bring with you a book of madrigals of your own composition."

"*Oui,* monsieur."

"Signor Vitturi asks that you bring it to supper so that he may choose one for you to sing when the company retires to the withdrawing room."

I had been anticipating something like this—just one more assault on my already frayed nerves. "They are meant to be sung by more than one voice."

The *administrateur* responded to that with a smile and a Gallic shrug.

I sighed. "Very well, monsieur. Please tell Signor Vitturi that I shall be happy to oblige him."

"Afterward, you and the other novices are invited to accompany Elic and Inigo to the bathhouse for the first of your lessons in, er, *les arts de la chambre à coucher.*"

"Oh." *Oh, God, so soon?*

"If you would be so kind to extend this invitation to the other ladies ... ?"

"Of course," I replied, thinking this was no invitation, which one might have the option of declining, but rather a summons.

"Excellent! Until supper, then, mademoiselle," he said with a bow.

"*À bientôt,* monsieur."

Five

"OH, ISN'T IT LOVELY," Lucy cooed that evening as we novices and our two *professeurs d'amour* followed a pair of footmen with torches around a bend in the gravel footpath leading from the castle to the base of the tallest mountain overlooking the valley—an extinct volcano, we'd been told. Built onto its side was a colonnaded structure of white marble that glowed from within with a wavering luminescence.

Sibylla, her hand curled around Elic's right arm—I held his left in a rigid grip—said, "It looks like something the Romans might have built."

"It is, actually," replied Inigo, who had his arms around the waists of the other two novices. He'd told us he relished the opportunity to practice his favorite language, English, which he spoke, curiously enough, with a British rather than French accent. "There was a Roman villa here for about three hundred years following the Gallic Wars, a sort of pleasure retreat for an important family. They built this bathhouse to take advantage of a cave stream they felt had mystical qualities."

"Did it?" Lucy asked. "*Does* it?"

"Why don't we all have a dip," he suggested, "and ye can decide for yourselves."

Of course, I thought. "A dip" meant disrobing, and this was, after all, to be our first lesson in "the arts of the bedchamber."

The footmen stood to either side of the bathhouse's arched doorway as we filed inside, to murmurs of awe from the novices, for the golden radiance was the product of scores of candles, a hundred or more, their flames trembling all around us. Some sat on low wrought-iron tables, but most had melted in place on little natural shelves and depressions on the rear wall, which of course was part of the mountain to which the bathhouse was appended.

Colorful pillows were scattered all about, and there were trays of brandywine and sack near the square marble pool, from which a haze of steam rose into the cool night air. A large section of ceiling over the pool was open to the night sky, the roof's remaining perimeter being buttressed by four columns, one near each corner of the pool.

Adjoining each column was a life-size marble statue of a nude couple, which I took at first for a god and goddess— Venus and Adonis, perhaps, given the amorous poses. But upon closer inspection, I saw that the poses weren't so much amorous as lascivious, being representations of explicit sexual union, and not just of normal intercourse. Two depicted what I now knew to be lovemaking in the French manner as described to me by the other novices that afternoon, the male being the recipient in one instance and the female in the other.

And the couple—it was the same man and woman in each

sculpture—was clearly not meant to portray Venus and Adonis, nor any of the pantheon of Roman deities. The female was voluptuous but otherwise unremarkable; however, the male had stubby horns and slightly pointed ears showing through his head of short, coiled curls, and a slender tail with a little tuft of hair on the end. He also possessed a colossal male appendage that was depicted in the erect state, something I'd never before seen in a work of art—or anywhere else, of course. The organ in question reared up in the air, which I assumed at the time to be, along with its size, a comically absurd exaggeration meant to convey outsized erotic appetites. After all, this was no god but a satyr.

Looking away from the statues so as to collect myself, I noticed an irregular, doorlike opening in the wall of mossy rock, and ventured closer to peer into it.

" 'Tis our cave," Elic said when he saw what had drawn my attention, "the hidden grotto for which our little valley was named."

He advised me not to venture too far into this *grotte cachée*, should I choose to explore it during my stay, no farther than the cressets illuminating the first quarter mile or so. "Not only does it get deucedly dark in there," he said, "and labyrinthine as well, but some people experience a certain derangement of the senses within its walls, what we call *le magnétisme hallucinatoire*. I'm told it can oft be felt here in the bathhouse as well. Occasionally a visitor will feel it in the castle itself, because it was constructed of volcanic stone from this mountain, but most only feel it here and in the cave."

I had, in fact, been a bit light-headed since entering the bathhouse, as if I'd drunk too much wine at dinner, when I hadn't. I had attributed the sensation to nerves, but perhaps it was, in fact, *le magnétisme hallucinatoire*.

An agitated chirping drew my attention to a small, bluish bird perched on the edge of the opening in the roof.

"Calm thyself, Darius," Elic told it as he unbuttoned his doublet. "Thy territory is safe from encroachment. She's not going in there tonight, and perhaps not at all."

"Er . . . is that bird a pet of yours?" I asked.

The bird let out a furious squawk as it swooped down, darting into the cave.

"He doesn't care to be thought of as a pet," Elic said as he shrugged out of the doublet and tossed it onto a chair.

I turned to find everyone else nonchalantly disrobing, the novices chattering away as they helped each other with the hard-to-reach buttons, laces, and hooks of their jewel-toned evening frocks. The iron chairs lining the walls were soon heaped with clouds of petticoats; stockings, sashes, collars, and gloves dripped from their arms and backs. The footmen were retreating up the path to the castle, the light from their torches growing smaller and smaller.

Elic stripped down swiftly and jumped in the pool. He submerged himself completely, then rose to stand hip-deep in the water, which sluiced off him in sheets. His body was long and hard and packed with muscle, the organ hanging between his legs—I didn't stare, of course, but I could see it out of the corner of my eye—somewhat larger than I would have expected.

"How's the water?" Lucy asked him.

He shook his head as he skimmed his hair back from his face. "It's perfect. It's always perfect, warm when the air is cool and cool when it's hot."

I took my time tugging off my gloves as I contemplated the predicament I'd gotten myself into. The only way to gain access to the Duke of Buckingham had been to follow him to

Grotte Cachée, and now the only way to remain here was to play the whore in training, to do things that would require hours—nay, *days*—in confession when I returned to London.

I'm doing this for Uncle Guy, I reminded myself as I untied my collar. He was doomed unless I could convince Buckingham of his innocence. I had come this far. I would do what had to be done, and simply not think about it.

Remove yourself from it.

When Lucy, half undressed now, offered to help me off with my sedate black gown and underpinnings, I let her, but I drew the line at complete nudity. Although Bianca and Sibylla were now frolicking in the pool alongside Elic without a stitch on, I insisted on retaining my shift.

Lucy said, "Don't be a silly goose, Hannah. The rest of us are taking everything off."

"*He's* not." I nodded toward Inigo, sitting on the pool's marble lip with his feet on the submerged top step, drinking directly from a ewer of brandywine. He had stripped down to his breeches—of purple silk tonight, embroidered in gold—so he was still covered from waist to knees.

Having heard me, Inigo shrugged and said, "I only like getting my legs wet, and I hate the feel of cold marble on my bare arse. Lucy's right, there's no point in wearing that thing. This is hardly the place for modesty, and I'm sure you have a very beautiful—"

"Inigo." Elic caught his friend's eye. "She's an innocent maiden, remember? Leave her be. These things take time."

Inigo sighed grumpily. "Do as you will, Hannah," he said, the courtesans having invited the *professeurs* to address them informally, "but you really ought to have a proper bath. This water is extraordinary. It tends to relax one's inhibitions."

I stepped down into the pool. The moment my feet

touched the water I felt a surge of erotic excitement that sucked the breath from my lungs.

And by this cave, there is a pool of water that is magico. *What others in this water are feeling, you will feel.* The pool was fed by a stream from the adjacent cave; I could see it flowing in through one hole and out through another. If that cave was, indeed, imbued with a magnetic energy capable of producing delusions, perhaps that energy was absorbed by the water running through it. That might also explain the temperature of the water, which was as balmy as Elic had promised.

And then there was the cave-dwelling bird Elic had called "Darius," which an overzealous imagination could interpret as a hermit with the power to shape-shift. Rational minds didn't accept myths and legends wholesale, but rather searched for the grain of truth at their core, and I was nothing if not rational—especially back then.

The novices cavorted like schoolgirls, and much as I tried to dodge their splashing, my shift ended up getting soaked. To my consternation, the damp, filmy linen clung to every contour of my body, becoming all but transparent. I could tell from the way Elic and Inigo looked at me that my effort to preserve my modesty had had the opposite result, the sheer garment adding an aura of titillation I hadn't counted on. At that point, I realized I would have been better off getting casually naked, like the others—if nothing else, it would have garnered less attention—but my pride wouldn't allow me to admit this.

"Methinks you would benefit from this," Inigo said as he offered me a beaker filled to the brim from the ewer in his hand. I took it and retreated to a corner of the pool, trying to look as inconspicuous as possible. The brandywine was sweet and syrupy, and I gulped it gratefully.

Inigo was offering instruction to Lucy and Bianca as they reclined on the steps to either side of him, stroking their own sexes. "Slow down, ladies. Savor your pleasure. Let it show on your faces."

Elic molded Sibylla's hand to his member, murmuring "Softly at first, like this . . . Tease me a bit, make me ache for a firmer touch."

To my surprise, Elic's sex thickened and rose in response to Sibylla's touch, like that of the satyr in the statues. It didn't grow quite that large, but large enough to make me wonder how a woman's body could accommodate such an organ. The sight of it straining upward, with its taut, polished skin and bloodred tip, incited in me a hot shiver of arousal.

Disconcerted by these lewd sights—and my reaction to them—I turned my back, only to find myself facing a ribald statue, the one with the satyr being ministered to in the French manner by the buxom female kneeling before him. He leaned back against the column with his hips cocked forward, clutching fistfuls of her long, wavy hair as she glided her tongue up his shaft. Her eyes were closed, and she was gripping the satyr's buttocks with both hands. The muscles of his torso and flanks were rendered in exacting detail, right down to a vein snaking downward across his abdomen. His head was thrown back in a grimace of ecstasy, the cords in his neck standing out in sharp relief.

How would it feel, I wondered, to give a man that kind of pleasure, using just one's tongue and lips? I tried to imagine being licked and kissed on my own sex, and it throbbed in response.

I guzzled the brandywine.

"Take my stones in your hand," Elic told Sibylla, "and pull down a bit . . . *gently.* Nay, keep stroking my cock, as well. Aye, that's the way."

"Push a finger or two into those sweet little notches," Inigo told Lucy and Sibylla, "keeping your legs spread wide so your benefactor can see—or you might ask him to frig you with a dildo."

Frig? I thought. *Dildo?*

Inigo said, "Tell him you wish it was his cock instead, because it's so much bigger and harder. There's no man on earth who doesn't love hearing that sort of thing."

Keeping my back to the ribald antics on the other side of the pool, I drained my beaker, hoping that it would dampen my senses—only to realize I was still just as wildly aroused, and also quite tipsy. Whether because of the magnetic energy permeating the water, or what I was witnessing, or both, I was consumed by lust. My sex felt engorged, hungry . . . I couldn't seem to draw in a full breath.

"When your gentleman is ready to take you," Elic told Sibylla, "ask him how he wants you, unless you be well enough acquainted with him to know his mind."

"How do you want me, monsieur?" Sibylla asked in a softly provocative voice.

"Lying back, like this." There came a splash, as of Sibylla being lifted from the water, she responding with something between a gasp and a giggle. "Open your legs as wide as you're able, and lift up a bit. Use a pillow, like this, if you have one. 'Tis a sight no man can resist, that of a beautiful woman offering herself so boldly."

She let out a tremulous little moan.

He said, "You're very wet, Sibylla." I knew he didn't mean wet from the pool.

"You are an excellent *professeur,* monsieur."

"Open your sex with one hand and put me inside you with the other," he told her. She sucked in her breath, then let it out in a luxuriant sigh. He made a soft little sound of gratification.

"Hold still with your legs locked tightly around me," he told her, "and squeeze me from within."

"Within?"

"Using the muscles in here, as if you were trying to pull on me, but without moving your hips. Try it. Ah . . . And again."

Inigo praised Lucy and Bianca for the "charming abandon" with which they gave themselves over to self-gratification. "Next," he said, "we shall practice our French. Before long, ye shall swallow a cockstand deeper than ye would have thought possible."

Lucy, her breath coming fast, said, "Shall we spend first, monsieur?"

"Certes," he said, "and pray, do not hold yourselves in check. Remember that you do this to inflame the ardor of your benefactor. The greater your display of passion when you climax, the greater his excitement."

I could hear the girls' shuddering breaths, their airy little moans. Lucy fell silent for a moment, then let out a guttural cry that went on for some time. Bianca's pleasure reached its zenith soon thereafter, accompanied by a stream of breathless Italian.

"Why do you look away, Mistress Leeds?"

I turned to find Domenico Vitturi, in his black overgown, standing in the doorway, his half-ravaged face eerily pale against the darkness of the night, making him look like an apparition.

"You are here to learn, are you not?" he asked as he crossed to one of the few chairs not heaped with clothing, his long-legged gait somewhat stiff because of his bad leg.

"Aye, Don Domenico. I just . . . I . . ."

"She just needs a bit of time, Domenico," Elic said as he knelt on the top step of the pool, hunched over with his weight on his elbows. Sibylla lay with her legs wrapped around his back, her hips propped on a pillow. From where I stood, I could see their privy parts united in coitus, his distended organ almost fully sheathed within her.

"She's *wasting* time, I say," Inigo countered as he unbuttoned his bulging breeches. The cockstand that sprang forth was unbelievably massive, like that of the satyr in the statues. Even Lucy and Bianca, who had seen their share of male appendages, gaped in wonderment.

Placing herself between his legs, Lucy lapped eagerly at the rampant organ, which twitched in response. Bianca, on the steps next to him, leaned down and licked the tip, murmuring "Mm..."

"One at a time, ladies," Inigo said, "so that I may give each of you adequate attention. Bianca, you first. Take it in your mouth and lower your head slowly until you've taken in as much as you think you can. Be careful to shield your teeth with your lips. That's right..."

Realizing I was staring with rapt interest, I looked away quickly.

"Hannah," Inigo said, gentling his voice, "I do realize this is all new to you, but you should at least watch. Sucking cock is a skill even a virgin can acquire, and one that will greatly enhance your desirability as a courtesan, especially if you learn to do it well."

"He's right," Vitturi said. "You claim to have the spirit of a courtesan, Mistress Leeds, but I've yet to see evidence of it."

He wore the same coolly impassive expression that he always wore on those rare occasions when he addressed me directly. No, not always. He'd slipped that evening at supper, where he'd sat next to me at a long, damask-draped table in the castle's cavernous great hall. We enjoyed a sumptuous banquet with Serge Pépin, Elic, Inigo, my fellow novices, and the gentlemen who had accompanied us there—with the exception of the Duke of Buckingham, who had chosen to sup in his rooms with only Jonas Knowles for company.

I was dismayed by the absence of the duke, who seemed no more inclined toward conviviality now that we'd arrived at our destination than he had during the long journey there, during which time he'd never so much as glanced in my direction. He still seemed determined to keep himself secluded in the best of the available accommodations—he had an entire tower to himself—attended to by the dozen or so retainers he'd brought with him. How was I to pursue my objective if I couldn't get anywhere near the man?

Also missing at supper was Elle, much to my disappointment, for I felt more at ease when she was around. She had become a valued friend and chatmate—not that I could confide to her my true purpose in apprenticing myself to Signor Vitturi, of course, for which I felt some measure of guilt. My hope was that, when all of this was over and I had, God willing, saved my uncle from the executioner, I could reveal everything to Elle and she would understand and forgive me my subterfuge.

During supper, Vitturi ignored me almost completely until the lull between the small entrées and the roasts, when he turned to me and asked if I'd brought my book of madrigals. I retrieved the little red notebook from the hidden pocket of my gown and handed it to him. While everyone else feasted upon pork with lentils, stuffed partridges, and glazed leg of lamb, Don Domenico turned the pages of my book with seemingly utter absorption. He did not look up even when the roast course was removed and replaced with entremets of fragrant sour cherry clafouti, prune tarts, and an assortment of Auvergnat cheeses and fruit pastes.

"You wrote all of these? By yourself?"

I turned to find him looking at me, the book open to the last of the two dozen or so madrigals written there. "Of course, signore."

My voice must have betrayed a hint of umbrage, because he said, "I don't doubt you, I just…" He closed the book and ran his thumb over the tooled design on the cover. "Your word choices are at times unorthodox, but so apt, and I find your restrained lyricism remarkably powerful. 'Tis quite accomplished work for a person of so few years."

So unforeseen was this praise that it took me a moment to find my tongue, and when I did, all I could do was stammer something about how most of my work was a good deal less impressive than these handpicked examples.

With a look that was both baleful and amused, he said, "Your inclination toward false modesty is not as endearing as you seem to think it is, Mistress Leeds."

I groaned in mock exasperation. "I was brought up never to brag."

"If someone points out how exceptional you are, 'tisn't bragging to simply thank him."

With a startled little smile—*exceptional?*—I said, "*Grazie*, signore."

"*Prego.*" He smiled into my eyes, the first time he had looked at me—*really* looked at me—since that all too fleeting moment of rapport on the day we'd met.

The moment seemed to stretch time itself. Once again, I felt a connection with him—with something inside him, something raw and needful that he kept locked in a box within himself.

And once again, his smile faded and he abruptly turned away.

"Um, which one shall it be?" I asked.

He scowled in puzzlement.

"Which madrigal would you like me to sing after supper?" I asked, indicating the book in his hand.

He thrust it at me, saying "You choose. One's as good as the next."

I sang my current favorite, to an enthusiastic reception from everyone save Domenico Vitturi. He clapped politely, but he didn't smile, and when the others stood and cheered and demanded an encore, he turned and left the room.

His frosty demeanor hadn't thawed between then and now. " 'Tis a skill you need to learn," he said, pointing across the steamy pool.

Inigo sat with Bianca's head in his hands, guiding her movements. Her sheaf of dark, wavy hair hid the sight of her mouth on his sex, but his directives left no doubt as to what she was doing. "Open your throat, Bianca. That's right, just relax it. I know you can't take it all, and I don't want you to gag, but perhaps another inch . . ."

"Inigo," Vitturi said as he lifted his bad leg over the good, "perhaps 'tis time for Mistress Leeds to try her hand at the French arts."

I closed my eyes, summoning the backbone to get through this.

My reluctance wasn't lost on the Venetian. "Pleasuring a man with one's mouth is a fundamental erotic skill, Mistress Leeds. If you want to be one of my courtesans, you must learn to do it—and not just tolerate the act, but relish it."

I looked toward Elic, who seemed to share his sister's inclination to protect and defend me, but he was clearly unaware of anything at the moment save his tutelage of Sibylla. He and the darkly beautiful Florentine were moving together slowly, sensually, his buttocks clenching and releasing, the muscles of his back and shoulders flexing with every languid thrust. His head was lowered toward hers, his hair draping both their faces in damp tendrils.

I turned to look at Inigo, his gaze on me as Bianca's head bobbed up and down, up and down. He said, "You needn't take it in your mouth, Hannah, not this first time. I just want you to taste it, to know the feel of it on your tongue."

"It taste *delizioso*," Bianca said as she lifted her head from the organ in question and moved aside to make room for me between his legs. "Come, Hannah, you must try. Is not so bad—you see."

I waded across the pool, thinking *Remove yourself from it. Just do what has to be done.*

Six

"COME," INIGO SAID, gesturing me closer. "Get comfortable."

I knelt on one of the steps with my face at the level of his glistening cockstand, which he held in his fist. It looked more than a little forbidding, with its twisting network of veins. There was a tiny slit on the purplish tip, from which oozed a bead of clear fluid.

Inigo took my hand and stroked my fingers up the shaft, which felt very warm and hard and surprisingly silken. "Touch your tongue to it," he said.

Remove yourself...

I closed my eyes and leaned forward, feeling a woozy sense of disbelief that I was actually doing this, and extended my tongue until the tip of it met hot, smooth skin. *I've done it,* I thought, but before I could pull away, Inigo closed a hand around my head and gently restrained me.

"Pretend you're a cat licking something delectable," he said. "Start down here at the bottom."

I drew in a steadying breath and licked the erect organ upward from the base, surprised to find its warm, fleshy taste not at all unpleasant.

"Don't let your hands be idle," Inigo said, guiding my right hand to the slippery head and tucking my left under his bulging "stones," as Elic had called them, to a stretch of firm flesh which he told me was actually the root of the shaft. "Rub it gently, in rhythm with your tongue...That's right..."

I wondered what Domenico Vitturi was thinking as he sat there watching me from across the pool. How did it make him feel, seeing me with my mouth on Inigo's sex? Did it please him? Trouble him? Did it arouse him as much as it aroused me?

I had expected to be disgusted by this act, but in fact, I found it strangely exciting. My nipples grew stiff and prickly beneath my sodden shift; my sex felt hotly inflamed.

"You're doing very well," Inigo murmured in a voice that sounded slightly winded. He had a length of my hair wrapped around his fist as he leaned back on a braced arm, hips rocking.

I licked and caressed him, gratified on a primal level by his quickening thrusts and harsh breathing. *I did this to him,* I thought. *He is consumed by pleasure because of me.*

Sibylla's moans drew my gaze to the couple at the other end of the pool. Elic's thrusts had grown sharp and hectic. "Hold still. Aye..." He reared over her, growling low in his throat.

"I'm about to come, too," Inigo rasped. I glanced up to see his head thrown back, the muscles of his neck and torso straining.

"Not with Hannah," Vitturi said sharply. "Bianca, you finish him."

I stepped aside for the other woman, who grasped his shaft and kissed the tip. "Shall I swallow it?" she asked Inigo.

Vitturi answered for him, saying "Nay. I want Mistress Leeds to see."

Inigo nodded to Bianca, who pumped him with her fist as she suckled him. "Now," he gasped. Stepping back, she gave him a few swift strokes, whereupon a burst of milky fluid shot from the tip of his sex. More spurts followed, all of them spattering Bianca's breasts, at which she was aiming his member.

I watched in astonishment as she leaned down to lick the last few drops that dribbled out. Inigo stroked her hair, then he took a handkerchief out of his pocket and used it to clean his spendings off her.

So ended our first lesson in the arts of the bedchamber, whereupon we climbed out of the pool and prepared to return to the castle. The air felt terribly chilly after the warmth of the water, and I shivered as I wrung out the skirt of my sodden shift.

As my fellow novices searched for their underpinnings among the piles of discarded finery, Inigo told them they needn't put everything back on, that the staff of Grotte Cachée were accustomed to their guests going about in a state of dishabille. Lucy, Sibylla, and Bianca merely donned their nice, dry shifts and gathered up the rest of their clothes, while I stood with my arms wrapped around myself, shaking from head to foot and dreading the long, chilly walk back to my chamber.

I started as I felt something heavy being lain upon my shoulders—Domenico Vitturi's black satin overgown. I turned to find him standing behind me, his expression impenetrable as he wrapped me in the capelike garment.

"Nay, signore, 'twill get wet," I said. "I would hate to ruin such a beautiful—"

"The next time you are instructed to undress, I suggest you do so," he said without looking at me. "My patience has its limits."

Before I could summon a response to that, he turned and walked away.

Inigo and Elic gathered up our clothing to carry back to the castle, an unexpectedly gallant gesture. As we left the bathhouse, Vitturi closed a hand over Sibylla's shoulder and spoke quietly into her ear.

"*Sì,* signore." She told the rest of us she was going to linger there for a bit, and would see us in the morning.

"*Buona notte,*" Bianca said with a sly little smile.

As I followed Elic, Inigo, and the two novices down the footpath to the castle, Bianca said, with amusement in her voice, "Don Domenico, it make him, how you say, *eccitato* to watch us take our lesson, *sì?*"

Tossing me a grin over her shoulder, Lucy said, "Methinks 'twas watching Hannah that excited him so. Gave him quite the cockstand, seeing her lick that splendid lob—I saw him shift his breeches to hide it—but at the same time, he looked none too pleased, never mind he'd ordered her to do it. I don't think I'll ever understand that man."

"He have too much of the black bile," Bianca said. "It make him *malinconico.*"

I paused to look behind me. The bathhouse still glowed from the light of all those candles. Through its wide, arched doorway, I saw Vitturi leaning against one of the statues, guiding the rhythmic movements of Sibylla's head as she knelt before him.

He lifted his own head to rest it against the column. His eyes closed, then quickly opened.

He'd seen me. Our gazes locked for a breathless moment. I turned and hurried back up the path.

As I was brushing out my hair that night, there came a knock at my bedchamber door. I draped a shawl over my night rail and opened the door to find Domenico Vitturi standing there.

"Signore," I said, reflexively pulling the shawl around me.

"Mistress," he said with a bow, taking in my nightclothes and unbound hair as he straightened up. His doublet was unbuttoned over his shirt, as if he'd thrown it on hastily on his way out of his own chamber. With a glance at the room behind me, he said, "May I?"

I stepped aside, clutching the shawl over my chest. He entered the room and perused it with an expression of idle curiosity, his gaze lingering on the ornate tapestries lining the walls. "Beautiful."

"Aye, they—" My throat clutched. "They are exquisite."

He looked at me. "What would you do if I were to offer you an income of ten thousand pounds a year for the rest of your life, with no conditions at all save that you leave here tomorrow and return to England?"

I hesitated only a moment before saying "I would turn it down, signore."

He came toward me until he was standing so close that I could feel the warmth emanating from him. There was only one candle lit in the room, and it was behind him, casting his face into shadow.

He said, "Then what if I were to tell you to get undressed and lie upon that bed?"

I held his gaze unblinkingly, the blood roaring in my ears. He didn't look away.

The shawl slipped down to puddle on the floor. My night rail closed down the front with half a dozen little ribbon bows, which I began clumsily untying. When the third bow came loose, the gown slid off one shoulder.

As I was plucking at the fourth, Vitturi took my hands and lowered them to my sides. Gathering my great rippling mane of hair behind me, he reached for the half-undone fourth bow, rubbed the satin ribbon between his fingers.

His throat moved.

I waited, my heart pounding.

He retied the bow, then pulled up the side of the gown that had slipped down and set about retying the rest.

Without looking up, he said, "What I had you do tonight in the bathhouse, with Inigo . . . There was a reason for that."

Was there a hint of contrition in his tone, or was it just a fancy of my imagination?

"I realize I must learn to pleasure a man in the French manner," I said.

With a fractional shake of the head, he said, "I told you to do it to see if you would." He tied the top ribbon, retrieved my shawl from the floor, shook it out, and wrapped it around me.

Turning away with a sigh, he said, "Why are you here, Mistress Leeds?"

"To become a courtesan," I said, as if it were obvious.

He glanced at me over his shoulder, looked away with a scowl. "Possibly."

I held my breath.

Rubbing the back of his neck, he said, "I don't know what to think. You bewilder me. The pieces of you . . . they don't add up to a whole that makes any sense to me."

As I was struggling to summon a response to that, he crossed to the door, saying "You'd better get to sleep if you're to be ready in time for your morning lesson. The dancing master is a temperamental sort. He doesn't like to be kept waiting."

"I won't be late. *Buona notte,* signore."

He paused in the doorway to look back at me, almost smiling. "*Buona notte,* Mistress Leeds. Sleep well."

Seven

"LUCY!" I CALLED, tapping on her bedchamber door the following morning. "Are you in there? We're all waiting for you downstairs. The dancing master's screeching mad."

I waited a moment, then knocked again. Upon hearing only silence, I opened the door and stepped into the room, which was cool and dark, the shutters and curtains being closed against the morning sun. By the light from the sconces in the hallway, I saw that Lucy's bedchamber was as lavishly appointed as my own, with a beautifully carved tester bed, its curtains pulled closed all around.

"Lucy?" I said.

There came a somnolent grunt from beyond the curtains.

With a groan of exasperation, I stalked to the bed and

whipped the curtains aside. "Lucy, you've got to get up and get dressed and come downstairs right now."

Rubbing her eyes, she said groggily, "In the middle of the night?"

"The middle of the . . . Lucy, 'tis a quarter past . . . Oh," I said upon seeing the man lying facedown next to her under betumbled sheets. No doubt she'd gotten very little sleep the night before.

Her bedmate hauled his head off the pillow to blink at me, and that was when I noticed his sleep-mussed sandy hair and the devilishly handsome face that Lucy had been mooning over ever since we'd set out from London.

"Mistress Leeds," Jonas Knowles said with a drowsily lecherous smile. "Take off that dreary frock and join us."

"Master Knowles?" I said. "Lucy, what on earth is he doing here? Don Domenico will be furious if he finds out you've been—"

"You won't tell him, will you?" Lucy, naked but for a snarled mantle of flaxen hair, sat up and pressed her palms together in an attitude of supplication. "I pray you, Hannah, we'll both be in such a pickle if—"

"Of course I won't tell, but you were mad to have . . ." I squinted in the semidarkness at her wrists, which were braceleted with knotted ropes. A strip of black fabric was looped around her neck. A gag? A blindfold? "What the devil . . . Were you tied up? Did he force himself on you?"

Knowles snorted in bemusement. "Cuds me, is she serious?"

"Hannah, you really are too much," Lucy said through a yawn. "I asked him to do it. 'Tis lovely, being tied up and ravished."

"Climb in and I'll show you," Knowles told me, patting the bed in invitation. "Better yet, you and Lucy can tie *me* up and use me any way you like, no matter how vile or degrading. I've always dreamed of being bound and gagged and mastered, and to have not one but two lusty little lightskirts forcing me to submit to their every nasty whim. Oh, I know, Luce!" He sat up excitedly. "You can ask Elle to join in, and the three of you could—"

"Aye, you'd like that, wouldn't you? He's mad for Elle," Lucy told me with a forbearing little chuckle. "I do believe he'd give his right arm to bed her."

Far from denying it, as I'd expected, seeing as he'd just awakened in the bed of another woman, he said, "I'd give every appendage I've got, save the one that matters most." He grabbed his crotch, just in case I hadn't grasped his meaning. "Go fetch her, would you, poppet?"

"Not till I've eaten," Lucy said. "I'm famished. I suppose I shall have to find the larder and help myself. 'Twill be hours till they serve breakfast."

"Breakfast is over," I said. " 'Tis a quarter past eight. Our dancing lesson was supposed to have started—"

"*A quarter past eight?*" Knowles bolted out of bed, utterly naked, tore the curtains aside, and grabbed a shirt off the floor. "Fuck! *Fuck!* Fuck fuck fuck fuck fuck." He yanked the shirt over his head and struggled into his breeches, tumbling to the floor in the process. "I was supposed to be in the court-yard at dawn."

"Jonas is hunting boars with the duke and his men this morning," Lucy explained as she tugged at the rope around her left wrist.

"I know which direction they're headed, so perhaps I can catch up with them," Knowles said as he snatched up the re-mainder of his cast-off garments. "Buckingham will be livid if he finds out why I was late." Hurrying to the door with his trailing wad of clothing, he said, "Prithee, Mistress Leeds, you cannot breathe a word of this to a soul, I beg you. The duke will cut me loose and send me home in disgrace if it gets back to him that I spent the night with Lucy."

"Is he that opposed to adultery?" I asked.

Knowles blinked at me. "Ah. Adultery. Aye, he, er ... he takes a very dim view of it, very dim indeed."

"I shall keep your secret," I assured him. "But may I suggest that in the future—"

"Thank you!" he called out as he raced down the hall. "Thank you, thank you, thank you! I am forever in your debt!"

Shaking my head, I asked Lucy, "Are all of the duke's retainers in such thrall to him?"

"Jonas is His Grace's favorite," she said through her teeth as she tried to bite through the knotted rope. " 'Zounds! Can you help me with these bloody things?" she asked, extending her arms in my direction.

"His favorite?" I said as I worked on the knot, which Knowles had tied more thoroughly than I felt was truly necessary. "He took my—Guy Goodchild's place in the duke's affections, then?"

"Aye, and after the way Goodchild betrayed him, His Grace is determined to keep those closest to him on a short leash."

I nodded pensively as I freed her left wrist and started on the right.

Misinterpreting my brooding expression, Lucy said, "You mustn't judge Jonas, Hannah. He's a landless younger son with no prospects save preferment at court, for which he's entirely dependent upon the Duke of Buckingham's patronage. You and I are in much the same position, you know. Jonas is no more beholden to His Grace than you and I are to Don Domenico."

It was a concept I needed no help in comprehending, for had not my uncle's advancement to the rank of emissary to the

Spanish court been due in large part to his friendship with Buckingham? Would that he had never become the favorite of such a powerful man. Then he would not be chained up in the Tower of London, awaiting his execution.

Most of our tutelage focused on those skills in which a first-rate courtesan was expected to be proficient when mingling in public with the gentlemen of Venice. During our dancing class that morning in the great hall, Lucy, Bianca, and I were taught the branle, courante, and galliard. Sibylla already being an accomplished dancer, Vitturi directed her instead, via a message delivered by a footman, to meet Elic and Inigo in *la Chambre des Voiles et des Miroirs.*

The Chamber of Veils and Mirrors, more commonly referred to as the Training Room, was where much, but not all, of our sexual instruction was to take place. Located in the southeast tower, it featured, I had been told, an "observation area" from which Vitturi and others could view the novices' erotic tutelage without being seen. It was a prospect that appalled me but didn't seem to bother my three fellow novices in the least.

"Just Sibylla?" I asked Lucy as we aped the movements of Monsieur Fluet, our fussy, temperamental little dancing master. "What can two men do with just one woman?"

"Could be a bit of fore and aft, but I hope not—not if they plan to do it to all of us."

"What is that—fore and aft?"

"One in the quim and one in the bum."

"*Nay.* Is that even possible?"

"Aye. Some women claim to love it. As for me, I can't stand the feel of a cock in my arse, so I've never even done it Greek style—not for more than a second or two—let alone Greek and regular at the same time. I *have* been with two men, though, two footmen in my cousin's house."

"Verily?" I couldn't resist the urge to question her about it. "What was it like? What did you do with them?"

"The first time," she said, "I took one in the mouth whilst the other fucked me from behind. The one I was sucking, Jack—bright red hair, lovely eyes—he shot off real quick, filled my mouth with spunk. But the other one, Harry—tall, black-haired brute—he didn't come at all, not in me, anyway. After Jack fetches in my mouth, Harry pulls out of me, throws Jack facedown over a sack of flour—we were in the pantry—and buggers him senseless."

"Buggers?"

"Fucks him in the arse," Lucy said. "Surely you know about sodomites. Men who fancy other men?"

"Well, aye. I just didn't know what they . . . did with each other."

" 'Tisn't just arse-fucking," she said. "They use their mouths, their hands . . . After that first time in the pantry, Jack and Harry would let me watch them when I had the itch. Nothing gets me wet like two big, strapping bucks fucking and sucking and working each other off. Jack fancied quim as well as cock, and there were times he'd fuck me after Harry gave it to him in the arse—or I'd lick his spigot while Harry was doing him."

"My word."

"Once," Lucy said, "they got into a tiff over something, and they didn't touch or even talk to each other for days, each of them waiting for the other one to admit he was in the wrong. Well, I was having none of that. I was bored, living in hiding, and constantly fearful that my beastly husband would find me and drag me back home. Playing with Jack and Harry was my only real diversion, and I wanted it back. I told them only a duel could settle it—dueling cocks. I had them meet me in the stable that night and made them strip down but for their boots and gloves. I told them to fight it out right there, and the first one to spend would have to tell the other he'd been wrong and he was sorry. The only rule was they had to keep their hands off each other's privy parts."

"Did they actually agree to that?"

"They loved the idea. Their cocks were rock hard before they even started fighting. They went after each other like animals, punching, kicking, spitting, biting... They ended up wrestling in the dirt, each of them thrusting against the other and gritting his teeth, trying to force the other one to come without coming himself. Finally, Harry slams Jack onto his back with his arms pinned down and their legs locked together. He starts rubbing against Jack real hard and fast, their cocks all slick. Jack's thrashing and grunting, trying to throw him off, but it's no use. He starts moaning, 'Oh fuck, oh fuck...' And then his eyes roll up, and this roar fills the stable. His whole body bucks, and come starts spraying out from between them."

I was rendered speechless.

"So then," Lucy continued, "while Jack's lying there covered with sweat and dirt and blood and his own milt, Harry kneels over him and says, 'Open your mouth.' He gives his cock a couple of hard pulls and fetches onto Jack's face, but mostly in his mouth, and Jack swallows it and says he's sorry and he was wrong. And Harry says, nay, *he* was wrong, and the two of them lie there crying in each other's arms till they both get hard again. And then I stripped down and Jack fucked me in a pile of straw while Harry fucked *him*. 'Twas the best tumble of my life."

"I... had no idea there were men who did this sort of thing," I said. "I never imagined anything like this."

"That's why you're here, sweeting," Lucy said as she patted my arm. "To learn."

After the dancing lesson, Elle reappeared for the first time since the previous afternoon and escorted us into the courtyard for a lesson in graceful deportment—specifically, how to walk in the absurdly tall shoes called chopines that were part of the uniform of a Venetian lady of fashion. Sibylla, flushed and slightly unkempt after her training with our *professeurs d'amour*, rejoined us for this lesson, but Bianca, who hailed from Venice and had been walking in such shoes for years, was exempted. Instead, Sibylla relayed a message from Don Domenico summoning her to the Training Room. She walked away smiling.

Following our midday dinner, we were measured for extravagant new wardrobes by our personal dressmakers and their teams of seamstresses, and then Don Domenico himself delivered a discourse on poetry, literature, and drama in the castle's library. The library was enormous, with carved oak wainscoting, Persian carpets, and five comfortably furnished, book-lined bays. Elle was present for this lesson, during which we practiced reading aloud from classical Greek and Latin verse. At one point, she took a book of Vitturi's poetry off a shelf and suggested we read from it, but this he curtly refused. I was disappointed—and suddenly intrigued as to what type of verse might flow from the pen of this enigmatic man.

That night after supper, everyone gathered in the withdrawing room for an evening of cards and table games. Don Domenico wanted his novices to be able to play and wager on primero, taroccho, chess, and tables. These were the games most popular in the *ridotti*, private clubs frequented by Venice's patricians, poets, and scholars—as well as by the *cortigianas* who provided them with female companionship in social settings while their wives remained secluded in their homes.

Most of the gentlemen participated with enthusiasm in our evening instruction, with the unfortunate exception of the Duke of Buckingham. Having come back empty-handed from his early-morning hunting foray along a nearby river gorge, the duke had launched a second outing to a marsh where the boars reputedly liked to feed at dusk. He and his party, which included Jonas Knowles and Sir Humphrey Quade, had yet to return when we sat down for our gaming lesson, although night had already fallen. About half an hour later, there came triumphant whoops from outside. Looking out the windows into the torchlit courtyard, we saw Buckingham's men hauling a reeking, cloudy-eyed boar on a pole toward the kitchen behind the great hall. Knowles and Sir Humphrey were with them, basking in the congratulations of the other gentlemen.

" 'Twas His Grace who made the kill," said the steely-haired, sinewy Sir Humphrey. The duke, however, was nowhere to be seen.

As the decks of tarot cards were replaced with chessboards at the conclusion of our lesson in tarrocho that evening, I excused myself to nurse a fictitious headache, explaining that I was already adept at both chess and tables.

Instead of returning to my chamber, however, I went directly to the library, where I located the book Elle had pulled off the shelf that afternoon. Handsomely bound in black, gilt-adorned calfskin, *La Poesie di Domenico Vitturi* was a recent compilation of poems written by the Venetian over a twelve-year period. I lit an oil lamp, set it on a little writing desk next to a Roman couch in the middle bay, and settled in to read.

The earliest of the poems, which were set forth in chronological order, had to do with military heroics and love affairs in roughly equal proportions. I skipped over most of the former, but found the latter unexpectedly passionate and stirring, considering who the author was. Of course, these pieces were written before the sea battle that changed his outlook on relations with the fairer sex. Those composed afterward were still beautifully written, but there was a darkness to them that hadn't been there before, and most of the emotion that had infused the earlier poems was replaced with a detached, academic tone. Of these later works, the only ones I found truly moving were three epic poems that retold in evocative language the myths of Europa and the Bull, Andromeda and the Sea Monster, and Leda and the Swan.

I heard a hiss of silken skirts, and then Elle appeared in the entrance to my little alcove, ethereally beautiful in silvery satin with a pearl-adorned stomacher—a striking contrast to my own demure black gown. She had a silver bowl cupped in each hand; I smelled cloves, ginger, and cinnamon.

Pinning me with a look of mock severity, she said, "A headache, eh?"

"Wherefore should I subject myself to lessons in games I already play perfectly well?"

"When you could be striving instead to decipher the puzzle that is Domenico Vitturi?" Elle's voice was ever so slightly thick, and there was a hint of bleariness in her gaze. It was the first time I'd ever seen her in her cups.

She handed me one of the bowls as she seated herself next to me on the couch. The spiced wine was warmly fragrant. I took a sip and set it on the writing desk.

"These later poems," I said, thumbing through them, "the three long ones, all seem to explore the same theme."

Elle nodded as she drank her wine. "The beauty and the monster."

"Aye, but the monster . . . he's not a monster, not really. 'Tis the same in each of the three poems. He has a monstrous visage, the outward form of an uglisome beast, but inside, he...he..."

"He has the soul of a man," Elle said. "He has a man's desires, a man's needs, a man's loneliness. When he ravishes or abducts the unattainable beauty, 'tisn't so much an act of brutality as one of desperation. He knows she'd never willingly give herself to the likes of him."

I closed the book and studied it in silence for a moment. "Loneliness," I murmured. " 'Tis odd to think of a beast being lonely."

"Every being in existence gets lonely," Elle said quietly. "We all crave affection, love, a companion of the soul. If we can't have that, we at least want to be touched, to...to feel the warmth of another body next to ours, to make love with our bodies, if not with our hearts. Lust is a sort of refuge for those of us who will always be alone." She lifted her bowl and took a long swallow.

She'd been speaking not only of Domenico Vitturi, I realized, but of herself. "I don't understand," I said. "Why must you be alone? You're beautiful, witty, exciting. Surely there have been men who've wanted to marry you, or at least take you as a mistress."

Studying the bowl with an unfocused, somewhat forlorn gaze, she said, "I can never marry, nor take a lover, not a real lover. I...I'm not like you, Hannah. My kind needs—"

"Your kind?" I said.

She sighed, closed her eyes for a moment. Setting her near-empty bowl aside with a groggy chuckle, she said, "Too much wine and too little supper. I really should be more careful."

"What did you mean by 'your kind'?" I asked.

"I suppose I meant..." Elle looked away, frowning. "Elic and I. Inigo, too. We're different from people...other people.

Our blood is more readily stirred, our passions more easily roused. The lust that drives us is more profound than you can imagine, Hannah, and much more relentless. It surpasses all other needs."

"Are you saying you're incapable of love?" I asked.

"If only I were," Elle said bitterly. "I *can* love, but I mustn't allow myself to form that kind of attachment with a—with anyone. 'Twould only bring pain, both to me and to the person I'd fallen in love with. My need for carnal sustenance is too overwhelming. No one woman could ever satisfy—"

"Woman?"

She looked at me for a second, then, realizing her mistake, said, "I meant 'man.' 'Tis the wine muddling my mind. Pray, forgive my maudlin blathering."

"So, then, you and Don Domenico aren't lovers—*real* lovers."

"We enjoy each other, we like each other, but we aren't in love, not remotely. He is as wary of that sort of thing as I am— for different reasons, of course. Nay, we aren't lovers in the sense you mean. I fear he shall be alone forever. My heart aches for him, but when I try to talk to him about these things, he tells me he has no desire to be 'shackled in holy matrimony,' as he puts it, and that he's perfectly content with his courtesans."

"Do you believe him?"

Elle took her time answering. "I believe that *he* believes it. I believe that he has made the best of an ill-fated situation."

"The wounds to his face? They're . . . well, they're unsightly, of course, but not monstrously so."

"Ah, but when he was freshly wounded, and cruelly scorned by the selfsame women who had found him irresistible before, he began to think of himself as monstrous."

"Perception became reality," I said.

"I understand he approached a famous courtesan who had him beaten almost to death."

I nodded, remembering Bianca's description of the notorious Galiana Solsa. "She's reputed to be something called a striga, which is a—"

"A striga?" Elle sat forward. "Really?"

"Surely you don't believe in such things—bloodsuckers, demons, incubi who can change their sex..."

"Dusii?" Elle smiled slowly. "There are many mysteries in the world, Hannah. Humans like to think they know all there is to know about the world and the beings who populate it, but they don't, nor do they really want to, most of them."

Before I could ask her to elaborate on that, she said, "Domenico came to the conclusion that he would always be repulsive to women. He knew there might be some who would sleep with him out of pity, but he found that prospect appalling. He was still a man, though, and he had the needs and desires of any man. He was willing to pay to have those needs appeased, but not by poxy street whores. He had always enjoyed the company of witty, beautiful, accomplished women, which in Venice means the *cortigiana onesta.*"

"And so he became a Pygmalion to high-level courtesans who would owe him their sexual favors in return for his patronage."

"Aye, although I understand he frequently sends them gifts after he beds them, even though 'tis they who are in his debt, and not the other way round."

"Why does he do it, then?" I asked.

Elle smiled as she pondered that question. "To make them happy, I suppose. Domenico adores women, but he never allows himself to forget that his protégées are servicing him out of obligation, not affection. He keeps his feelings reined in tight."

"Does he kiss you?" I asked, recalling what Sibylla had told me. "When . . . when you and he are intimate?"

Elle shook her head. "That would be *too* intimate. It would imply a connection of the heart rather than merely of the body."

"No one should feel that he can never love, or be loved," I said. "I feel sorry for him."

"Well, don't," Elle said with uncharacteristic sternness. "Domenico detests pity. He is no victim in some Greek tragedy, Hannah. He has a full life, the respect of everyone who knows him, and his lovers are the most beautiful and desirable women in Venice."

"Aye, but they're not true lovers, are they? They're just women who owe him the use of their bodies."

"Do you think they don't enjoy it as much as he does?" Elle asked.

He's that best of all lovers, a gentleman, but also a bit of a savage. "I think they enjoy it on base level," I said.

"You really do think of sexual desire as sordid, don't you?"

"In the absence of love, lust is naught but an animal instinct—and in the final analysis, the most exalted *cortigiana onesta* is naught but an expensive whore."

"Aye, but there is, after all, much of the animal in man, and it must find release somehow. Even St. Augustine knew that. He said, 'Suppress prostitution and capricious lusts will overthrow society.'"

"Thank God I'm a woman," I said, "and not at the mercy of such base drives."

"You never feel erotic desires?" Elle asked dubiously.

"Well, I suppose I do," I admitted, "but I'm hardly in their thrall."

I realized even as the words left my mouth that this claim

was no longer entirely true. In fact, my blood had been so stirred after our "lesson" in the bathhouse and Vitturi's visit to my room that I hadn't been able to get to sleep. I stroked my sex as I had at the inn, this time lying on my back with my night rail pulled up, my fingertips playing lightly on the hot, slippery petals while I imagined a man—Domenico Vitturi— pleasuring me with his mouth as I had pleasured Inigo. Resisting the urge to stroke myself faster and more firmly, or to directly touch the sensitive little pearl, as I had come to think of it, I kept my touch soft as a breath of air, slick as a wet tongue. I came with jolting force, then lay there gasping and shaking until my heart stopped thudding and sleep drifted over me like a veil.

"You should accept your desires, as I do," Elle said. "Stoke them. Revel in them. Embrace the animal beneath your skin. You're being groomed to be a courtesan, for heaven's sake. Sooner or later, you're going to have to get comfortable with all of this. Ideally, you should learn to love it."

"I know, I just . . ." I shook my head helplessly. "This is all so new to me. I've never even imagined most of the things the other novices have told me about. No man has ever touched me. I've never even been kissed."

A male voice said, "That won't do."

I turned in my chair to find Domenico Vitturi stepping out from behind the wall of bookshelves behind me.

"Domenico! Shame on you," Elle scolded. "How long have you been lurking there?"

Ignoring the question, he told me, "Kissing is as much of an art as making love, and one that even a virgin courtesan should be expected to master."

Elle said, "Perhaps Elic or Inigo could be prevailed upon to teach her the finer points."

"You can do it right now," he told her as he folded his arms and leaned his shoulder against the bookcase. "A female perspective might be useful."

"You have a point." Turning toward me on the couch, Elle put her hands on my shoulders, and said, "Face me and close your eyes, Hannah. You want your mouth to be—"

"Nay," I said, shrinking away from her. "I can't kiss *you*."

Raising his gaze to the ceiling, Vitturi said, "Mistress Leeds, your aversion to even the tamest aspects of your instruction is becoming—"

"He's right, Hannah," Elle said quietly. "Just close your eyes and pretend I'm a man. Pretend I'm Elic."

I considered this for a moment—no doubt I appeared to be sulking—and then, reminding myself what was at stake, I faced Elle squarely and shut my eyes tight.

"Soften your mouth," she said.

I felt her hand on my chin, tilting it up, and tensed.

"Relax, Hannah. Give yourself up to it." Elle's breath was warm and redolent of mulling spices.

Her lips touched mine.

A giggle erupted from me, and I broke the contact, my hand over my mouth. "I'm sorry, I . . . I just feel so silly kissing another woman."

Elle said, "Hannah, you do realize you may be called upon at some point to do more with another woman than just kiss her. There are many men who find it exciting to watch two females pleasuring each other. If one of your benefactors is of that ilk, he may bring another woman to your bed and ask you to use your mouth, or a dildo, to—"

"Nay!" I said. "You cannot be serious."

Vitturi pushed off the bookcase, growling something in Italian under his breath. "This is pointless. Come, let us rejoin the others. Give that to me." He took his book of poetry from my hand as I rose to my feet, but instead of returning it to its shelf, he tucked it into a pocket in his breeches.

The library was in the south section of the castle, the great hall's withdrawing room in the north. As we came to the tower door at the junction of the west and north ranges, Elle, pleading fatigue, excused herself to retire to her suite of rooms in the tower's top two floors.

Worried now that I'd just given Domenico Vitturi one more reason to send me packing, I started babbling, as we walked down the corridor toward the withdrawing room, about how I didn't really need instruction in kissing, how people kissed all the time without having received lessons in it, that it was natural and not something one could really do *wrong*.

Looking straight ahead, he said, "One certainly can do it wrong, especially if one is as inexperienced and apprehensive as yourself. You are very much mistaken, Mistress Leeds, if you suppose that I'm going to introduce you to Venetian society as one of my courtesans without some assurance that you know how to properly kiss a man. Given your reaction to Elle's attempt to demonstrate for you—"

"Had she been a man, I would not have reacted that way," I said.

"Is that so." He stopped walking and turned to face me in the darkened corridor. Through the closed door to the withdrawing room, I heard Sibylla exclaim "Checkmate!" followed by laughter and applause.

He said, "A kiss between a man and a woman is not something an unblemished maiden's instincts will have prepared her for. Such a kiss, if it be done well, should be filled with heat and mystery and the promise of erotic intimacies to come. 'Tis nothing like the dry, chaste kiss one bestows upon the cheek of a dear old uncle."

"I think I know that, signore. And I am confident that when the time comes, my instincts will guide me well enough."

"Let us see, shall we?"

I stopped breathing when he tilted my chin up, as Elle had done. His fingers felt rougher than hers, and stronger.

"Did you learn nothing from Elle?" he asked.

"Signore?"

"Close your eyes," he said as he cupped my upturned head in his hands. "Part your lips."

Eight

$\mathcal{A}$FTER WHAT SEEMED an interminable interval, but was probably only three or four seconds, I felt the soft hot shock of Domenico Vitturi's mouth upon mine.

I drew in a breath.

"Easy," he murmured against my lips. "Don't fight me. Yield to me."

His lips moved over mine with terrifying tenderness, making my heart hammer wildly even as I returned the kiss.

"Put your arms around me," he whispered.

I did, tentatively at first, then more firmly as the kiss continued. My lips felt as sensitive as my sex. When he glided the tip of his tongue between them, I actually moaned.

With one arm encircling me, he stroked my face, my throat, and my breast, which he gently squeezed through my stays. I held him tighter, pressing my body to his as he kissed and caressed me. His breath came faster when I touched my tongue to his. He deepened the kiss, one hand gripping the back of my head, the other banded possessively around my waist. His whiskers tickled my lower face, only accentuating the voluptuous warmth of his mouth.

At long last, he broke the kiss, meeting my eyes with a look of dazed wonderment. I think I may have looked very much the same to him.

He dipped his head again, his gaze on my mouth. I closed my eyes.

A door creaked open, accompanied by footsteps on the corridor's stone-paved floor.

He drew back, thrusting me from him. Reeling, I braced an arm on the wall. I turned and saw Inigo standing just outside the open door to the withdrawing room, his hand on the doorknob. He was smiling, his too-insightful gaze shifting between Vitturi and me.

"I was sent to fetch you," Inigo told Vitturi. "We, er, could use one more player. But if you are occupied with something more important…" He glanced in my direction.

" 'Tisn't important," Vitturi said, "merely a … an instructional demonstration. Mistress Leeds." Bowing briefly in my direction, but without meeting my eyes, he ducked into the withdrawing room.

I let out a pent-up breath.

"Hannah?" Inigo stepped toward me with a frown of concern. "Are you all right?"

I took my hand off the wall and smoothed down my hair. "I'm fine."

"Are you sure? Your hands are shaking. Come, rejoin us," he said, reaching for my hand as he gestured toward the withdrawing room. "I'll pour you something to settle your nerves."

"I would really rather not," I said, backing away. The notion of being in the same room as Domenico Vitturi right then, pretending nothing had transpired between us—nothing *important*—was too excruciating to contemplate.

Nodding thoughtfully, Inigo said, "I understand."

I was quite certain he did. For all his devil-may-care demeanor, he struck me as highly perceptive, even empathetic.

With a conspiratorial smile, he said, "Shall I tell them your head is still paining you, then?"

"Please do," I said, although it was my heart, not my head, that had begun to ache.

※

By the time I awoke the next morning, Buckingham had already left for a dawn boar hunt with Jonas Knowles, Sir Humphrey Quade, and a few yeomen and lacqueys. The duke was, if anything, even more inaccessible than he'd been in London and during the journey to Grotte Cachée. How could I convince him of my uncle's innocence if he spent every day far from the castle?

We novices began the day with a lesson on enhancing our natural beauty with antimony, lead, and a purplish dye for lips and cheeks that came from snails, of all things. We were taught, as well, how to perfume ourselves with a mixture of frankincense, musk, and oils extracted from orange flowers and lavender.

As that lesson ended, Sibylla was summoned not to the Training Room but to the "Punishment Chamber" in the cellar beneath the southwest tower, for a session with Elic.

I was filled with alarm on her behalf. "Punishment Chamber? Have . . . have you done something you might be disciplined for?"

"One can only hope so," she said with an impish little smile as she sauntered away.

While the Florentine beauty was being subjected to mysterious indignities in the castle dungeon, the rest of us had strands of our hair pulled through straw hats and coated with a noxious lightening paste. Since the paste required exposure to the sun in order to work, we spent the remainder of the cloudless morning on the castle's sprawling west lawn, learning the fundamentals of tennis, shuttlecock, archery, pall mall, and bowls.

Sibylla returned, looking none the worse for wear, as our hair was being rinsed. To hasten its drying, we were served dinner outdoors in a lovely rose garden adjacent to the castle, just the four of us around a small, linen-draped table. Sibylla described her interlude in the Punishment Chamber with Elic, who was charged with teaching her to find pleasure in submitting to benefactors with "certain medieval tastes." He took her twice while she was bent over a whipping stool getting "a red-hot spanking," twice more as she stood with her hands chained to the ceiling, three times as she lay tautly stretched on the rack, and for the eighth and final time while she was confined in a hanging cage, gagged and blindfolded. "That one took a bit of contorting," she told us, "but 'twas worth it."

She and Bianca told us about their sessions in the Training Room with our two *professeurs,* during which they were, indeed, penetrated by both men simultaneously. Lucy was aghast when they revealed that it was Inigo, not Elic, who had entered them from behind. "That thing's bloody huge!" They swore it wasn't at all painful, that in fact they'd both enjoyed it immensely, but Lucy was convinced they were lying to reassure her.

After dinner and a lesson in Venetian hairstyling, we convened in the library, where Signor Vitturi explained the more pragmatic aspects of courtisanerie: the taxes we would owe to the Venetian Senate; how to discreetly collect our monthly fees from our benefactors; our tradition of relaying political messages "from pillow to pillow"; the staffs we would require, including a *ruffiano* for dealing with troublesome men; how to avoid pregnancy and the French pox; and how to best equip our chamber of recreation, which might be a different room altogether from our private bedchamber. The entire time he was addressing us, Vitturi never once spoke to me, nor even looked in my direction.

Later that afternoon, we novices were escorted to the upper hall, now a temporary sewing room, to be fitted for luxurious garments especially suited to our particular figures—save for Lucy. She had just begun to disrobe for the fitting when a footman came and told her that her presence was required in the Training Room. She left with an expression of dread, knowing what was in store for her.

My seductive new apparel included gossamer shifts trimmed with lace, embroidered satin stays, gold-fringed red petticoats, and veils of shot silk adorned with tassels. I was shown drawings of my new gowns, a few of which were remarkably modest, for church and other occasions when it was best not to trumpet our profession, but most had a look of elegant dishabille. Two featured an open skirt over snug breeches, like those that Elle had worn during our journey. Unlike men's breeches, ours buttoned up not just in front but along an opening that extended between our legs, "for the convenience of your benefactors," as my dressmaker, Signora Tozzi, put it. Most of the bodices were shamelessly low-cut to display as much of my corset-plumped bosom as possible. One, a costume for the winter Carnival season, had even been constructed to display my bare breasts within triangles of lace.

The gown that was closest to completion was of apple-green damask. Its most notable feature was sheer sleeves meant to be worn partially detached from the arm-eyes, so that the tops hung nonchalantly open with ribbons dangling, upper arms and shoulders fully exposed. Eight petticoats gave shape to the skirts, which were to be hemmed about ten inches longer than the floor, because of the chopines I would presumably be wearing.

As Signora Tozzi and her gaggle of seamstresses hovered about me, one adjusting the drape of the drooping sleeve, another tying a girdle about my waist, the others pinning and basting, a footman entered the hall. He bowed and came toward the three novices standing on platforms in the center of the room, scanning our faces.

His gaze settled on me.

"Your turn," Sibylla whispered.

Oh, God.

The footman approached me and bowed again. "Mademoiselle. Monsieur Vitturi requests your immediate presence in *la Chambre des Voiles et des Miroirs.*"

"Are . . . are you quite sure that is where I'm wanted?" I asked, since Lucy had been summoned there not fifteen minutes ago.

"I am, mademoiselle."

"Er, I shall need to take this off," I said, indicating the green gown. "Please tell signore that I shall be along anon."

"Forgive me, mademoiselle," the footman said as he extended his hand to help me down from the platform, "but he requires that I escort you there forthwith."

I was led to the top floor of the southeast tower, where Vitturi waited on the landing, arms folded. He dismissed the footman and bowed to me, taking in my calculatingly disheveled green gown as he rose.

He met my eyes, then quickly looked away. Quietly he said, "The color suits you."

I opened my mouth to agree that Signora Tozzi had chosen well, but he put a finger to his lips, saying, "Speak softly, if at all, lest our presence be a distraction."

Before I could quite grasp that, he stood aside and gestured for me to precede him into an unlit passageway that curved around the perimeter of the tower.

La Chambre des Voiles et des Miroirs did not occupy the entire top floor of the tower, as I had supposed, but just the central part. It was a room within a room, a round chamber inside the round outer walls of the tower, separated by the carpeted passage into which Vitturi had led me. The tower walls were of dark volcanic stone, of course, but the Training Room was delimited by a ring of wooden panels lined on the inside with quicksilvered glass; even the ceiling was mirrored. Between each of these wall panels was a space of about a foot, every such gap being swathed with black draperies so sheer that I could see right through them to the candlelit interior.

A peculiar piece of furniture occupied the center of the room. At first glance it appeared to be a tall bed with a carved wooden canopy, its underside mirrored. Where the mattress should have been, however, was a flat surface like a tabletop, lightly padded and covered in black leather studded all around the sides with nailheads. The headboard, also covered in nail-studded leather, was divided horizontally, with one large hole and two smaller ones, like a set of stocks. There were no bed-clothes, no pillow. At its foot stood a hat stand from which a collection of leather straps and chains dangled menacingly. The other furniture consisted of a cabinet, a couple of tables, and several chairs and strangely shaped benches, the latter covered, like the bed, in black leather.

So dazzled were my eyes by the myriad reflections in this Chamber of Veils and Mirrors that it took me a moment to notice that there were people in the room.

I ducked behind a wall panel.

"They can't see you," Vitturi whispered. " 'Tis too dark on this side of the veiling. You'll notice the arrow slits have been covered against the sun."

So they had, each one draped with a narrow black curtain.

"Come." He led me halfway around the circular passage, our footsteps silent on the thick carpeting, to a couch—black leather, of course—facing a veiled gap that was somewhat wider than the others. He gestured for me to sit, then sat himself, lifting his bad leg over the good.

The view through the filmy black drapery was only slightly blurred, like looking through a glass window that needed cleaning. The mirrors produced multiple angles of the same images, giving the initial impression that the Training Room was *filled* with people, when there were actually only three occupants: Lucy, Elic, and Inigo. The two men lounged in chairs sipping from beakers, their gazes riveted on Lucy, who stood before them in naught but her thin silken shift.

As she started to lift the diaphanous garment, Elic said, "Lucy, Lucy, why must you rush so? There is much to be gained from teasing your benefactor, making him wait— especially if this be the first time he's seen you undress."

"Caress your breasts through the shift as you slowly lift it," Inigo said. "Pinch your nipples, too. Men love that. Aye, that's better. That's lovely."

"Watch yourself in the mirror," Elic told her. "See yourself as your lover would see you."

"Signore," I whispered, "must we spy on them like this?"

Leaning closer, so close that I could breathe in the warmth of his skin, he said, "Lucy agreed to be observed from time to time without her knowledge, as did you and the rest of the novices, and Elic and Inigo, for that matter."

Lucy. He called the other novices by their Christian names, I realized, whether addressing them directly or speaking to others about them. Yet with me, it was always "Mistress Leeds."

"I still don't feel comfortable watching this," I said as Lucy gradually drew the shift over her head.

"Yet watch it you will, so as to learn from it. Your training will unfortunately be lacking in practical experience, if you are to retain your maidenhead, but a courtesan must know what to expect if her benefactor wishes to share her with another gentleman."

God's pity. "Is . . . this sort of thing a common practice, signore?"

" 'Tis more usual for one man to bed two women, but there are men who enjoy seeing their courtesans or mistresses giving themselves to other men."

"Why?" I asked, since this flew in the face of what I knew about men, which was admittedly very little.

He sighed. "Just watch, Mistress Leeds."

Nine

$\mathcal{L}$UCY'S NAKEDNESS in the presence of two fully clothed men struck me as rawly prurient. It did make me uncomfortable; it also aroused me.

She was taking down her hair.

Inigo stood and started unbuttoning his crimson brocade doublet. "Have the other novices told you what to expect of this afternoon's session, Lucy?"

She nodded; even through the veiling, I could see her cheeks pinken. Women with coloring like Lucy's—and mine, for that matter—can hide nothing.

"Have you ever made love in the Greek manner?" Elic asked her as he raised his beaker to his mouth.

"Nay, not . . . not really," she said in an unsteady voice. "I tried it once, but it hurt, so I made the fellow stop."

Elic said, "Your patron has very exacting standards for his

courtesans. He insists they should not just endure this form of coupling but take pleasure in it. There are measures we can take to make it both comfortable and stimulating for you."

"Wh-what measures?" she asked.

Inigo, now in his shirtsleeves, patted the odd, leather-upholstered bed-cum-table, which stood at an angle to me. "If you will but lie upon the training bed, facedown, you shall find out soon enough. Come. I'll help you up."

She hesitated, regarding the bed uneasily.

In a grave tone, Elic said, "Lucy, if you don't cooperate, Don Domenico will send you back to London. He's done it before."

"Nay! Nay, I cannot go back. I cannot live in hiding again, and if my husband finds me, he'll beat me to death, I know it. I'll cooperate, I will. I . . . I don't mind it, not really, not the idea of it. But the pain . . ."

"We won't hurt you, I promise," Elic said as he rose and ushered her with a hand on her back to the training bed. "And you really will learn to enjoy it, you'll see."

She allowed him to lift her onto the bed, lying facedown when he instructed her to do so, her body starkly white against the lustrous black leather.

Inigo placed a small table next to the bed. From the cabinet, he retrieved a silver tray, which he set on the table. Opening a drawer in the cabinet, he chose four shiny black cylindrical objects of varying lengths and diameters. The smallest was as slim as my little finger, the largest about eight or ten inches long and almost as thick around as my wrist. Most had raised designs on them, and they all had fat knobs on one end and tapering, slightly rounded tips on the other. These items he laid out on the tray by ascending size as Lucy stared, wide-eyed.

"What are those things?" I whispered to Vitturi.

"Lacquered dildos from China."

So dildos *were* phalluses; I was glad to have this confirmed.

"Don't forget the oil," Elic told Inigo as he rested a comforting hand on Lucy's back.

His friend shot him a look as he pulled a tiny white porcelain bottle from his pocket. "Am I ever without it?"

Sitting on the edge of the training bed, he picked up the smallest of the dildoes by the bulb at its base, drizzled a bit of the bottle's contents onto it, and rubbed it to thoroughly coat it.

Lucy squeezed her eyes shut and clenched her teeth as he used his free hand to spread the cheeks of her buttocks.

"Becalm yourself, Lucy," Inigo said as he positioned the slender little phallus. "The less tense you are, the less this will trouble you."

She took a deep breath and appeared to visibly relax, but no sooner did he penetrate her with the little device than she yelped and twisted around to swat him away.

Groaning in exasperation, Inigo told Elic, "Just use your *liggia spiall* on her."

Fixing his friend with a look, Elic said evenly, quietly, "You know I can't do that."

"Why not?"

With a meaningful glance around the perimeter of the round chamber, Elic whispered something I couldn't hear.

Inigo winced. "Sorry, brother. Wasn't thinking."

Liggia spiall? I looked toward Vitturi, but he was frowning in evident bewilderment.

"Why don't we just, uh . . ." Inigo nodded toward the hat stand festooned with straps and chains.

"Not yet." Turning to Lucy, sitting on the bed with her arms wrapped around her upraised knees, Elic said, "I thought you wanted to cooperate."

"I . . . I do, I swear it, but . . ."

"Did it hurt?" Elic asked her.

"*This?*" Inigo held the tiny phallus up.

"Nay, it didn't hurt, but it felt so . . ." She shuddered. "When I felt it go in, I just panicked."

" 'Tis this or London," Inigo said, brandishing the phallus.

With a sigh of capitulation, she lay back down, promising to lie still this time, but when Inigo attempted again to insert the dildo into her, she leapt up kicking and flailing.

Her fist slammed into his nose.

He howled.

"Lucy!" Elic gripped her arms and pushed her back down onto her stomach. "For pity's sake."

"Oh, God, I'm sorry!" she said. "I'm sorry, Inigo. I just . . . I can't help it. It feels so, so . . ."

"Sh, don't fret so," Elic murmured. Folding her arms behind her, he clamped a hand around both of her wrists, pressing them to the small of her back. He caught Inigo's eye and cocked his head toward the hat stand.

Inigo went to it, dabbing a handkerchief under his badly swollen nose, which was trickling blood. "*Now* you come round," he said nasally, "after she broke my bloody nose."

" 'Twill get better." Elic's disregard for his friend's injury—the nose did, indeed, look broken—struck me as curious, given the compassion he displayed with others.

Plucking two short leather straps off the stand, Inigo hooked them to a pair of small rings on the bottom corners of the training bed, just two of many that I now noticed at intervals among the nail heads.

"What are you doing?" Lucy asked,

"Making this easier for you." Inigo pulled her left foot toward him and buckled the strap around her ankle, then circled the bed to tether the other ankle as well.

"You don't need to do this," Lucy said, craning her neck to

look over her shoulder at her widespread, tightly bound legs. "I won't move, I promise."

"That's what you said before you smashed my nose." Inigo fetched two more straps, one short and one long. He handed the short one to Elic, who wrapped it around Lucy's crossed wrists, trussing her hands behind her. The other, Inigo buckled across her waist, securing her firmly to the bench.

"You curs!" She struggled against her restraints, her upper body straining off the bed, those lush breasts swaying. Her lower body could wriggle a bit, but that was all.

" 'Tis for your own good," Inigo said. "You don't want to be shipped back to London, do you?"

"N-nay, but—"

"Well, then." He parted her bottom cheeks and plunged the little phallus in all the way to the knob.

She thrashed, swearing like a sailor. Elic held her still, murmuring soothing things into her ear until she settled down, red-faced and glowering.

"How does it feel?" he asked her.

She squirmed a bit, her expression sullen. "I loathe you, both of you."

Inigo smiled and gave the dildo a little jiggle. She sucked in a breath, but didn't budge as he slid it almost completely out of her, then in again, and again, and again. He moved it in a circular motion for some time, then asked Elic to take over while he oiled the next one, which was about as thick as his thumb, with little bumps all over it.

As soon as he pulled the first one out of her, he replaced it with the second, pressing it into her slowly. He paused when she cried out, her body jerking. If she hadn't been strapped down, she probably would have bolted off the bench.

"Does it hurt?" Elic asked.

"Nay, but . . . Gadzooks, it feels so big, too big."

" 'Tis just the right size," he assured her, stroking her hair as Inigo pushed the studded phallus deeper, deeper. "Think about how wonderful it feels entering you, filling you."

"And look at it from the man's perspective," Inigo said. "Imagine how it feels to be buried in such a snug little aperture. 'Tis a gloriously tight fit around a full cockstand."

Standing across the bed from Inigo, Elic slid his hand between Lucy's legs and under her mons, cupping it as Inigo manipulated the phallus this way and that.

" 'Tis best if you're as aroused as possible before your benefactor takes you this way," Elic said, "and of course, you want to remain so while he's inside you. You can touch your clit very softly, like this, or ask him to do it."

She gasped; it turned into a moan. *He's stroking her pearl*, I thought. I didn't know how I felt about the word "clit."

I started when Vitturi leaned over to whisper in my ear, "Like Lucy, you will need to learn to connect the sensation of being penetrated this way with erotic pleasure. That way, when one of your benefactors takes you in this manner, you'll still find it sexually arousing even when you aren't being directly stimulated."

Given his matter-of-fact tone, he might have been discussing politics instead of sodomy. I wondered if he had ever had a woman the Greek way, and concluded that he must have. I envisioned him rearing over a prone female, pushing himself into her as he caressed her breasts and her sex, thrusting, sweating, groaning... My own sex pulsed with desire as I imagined how it would feel to be breached in such a manner—by a man who was, as Lucy had said of Domenico Vitturi, a gentleman but also a bit of a savage, a man who was not afraid to "let the beast out of its cage."

"If you can time your climax so that you come first," Inigo told Lucy, "he'll feel every spasm with astonishing intensity."

The third phallus was about as big around as a broom handle, with a raised spiral down its length. Inigo pushed it into her, twisting and turning it, as Elic caressed her sex, murmuring "Accept it . . . Let it in. Let it possess you."

She lay still as it penetrated her from the tip to the bulblike handle, her breath quickening, her color high.

"Is there any pain?" Elic asked, still caressing her sex.

"Nay," she breathed. "None at all."

With his free hand, Elic started unbuckling the strap around her wrists. "I don't think you need these anymore."

"I may," she said. "Perhaps you'd best leave them."

The two men shared a smile as Elic rebuckled the restraint. Inigo scooped a hand under her breast, kneading it gently as he maneuvered the phallus. Lucy's hips rose a bit every time he thrust it into her, lowered as he tugged it out.

She whimpered when he withdrew it completely, but smiled, lifting her bottom when she felt the tip of the final and largest one nudging her open.

"You can push it in harder," she said breathlessly as he worked it in inch by inch. "I don't mind."

"You see? The third one prepared you for the fourth, and the fourth will prepare you for this," Inigo said, stroking himself between his legs.

So fixated had I been on Lucy and what was happening to her that I hadn't noticed Inigo's condition until then—bizarre, considering how obvious it was beneath the shirt hanging down over his breeches. Elic's doublet had a long, pointed skirt that concealed his groin, but I assumed he was as aroused as his friend.

Without even meaning to, I looked at Don Domenico, at his lap. His doublet was skirted with square tabs that parted, revealing a sizable bulge.

Lucy's strident moaning drew my gaze back to the Training

Room, where Inigo was still frigging her—another coarse word I now knew the meaning of—with the big dildo. Her thrusting had taken on a strained, frantic quality as she rubbed her sex against Elic's hand.

"Nay!" she cried when he took his hand away. "I'm about to spend."

"I know," he said as he unbuttoned his doublet. " 'Tisn't time yet."

Much as I tried to concentrate on what was happening inside the Training Room, my mind kept returning to Vitturi, sitting right next to me, as aroused as I. I couldn't help but recall that first night, when we were walking away from the bathhouse and I turned to see Sibylla kneeling before him, relieving him of his lust.

Methinks 'twas watching Hannah that excited him so, Lucy had said.

I swallowed hard, licked my lips. *Do it. Say it.* "Don Domenico, I..." I glanced at him, then down at my nervously clenched hands. "If you wish it, I would be ... more than willing to ..."

I had run out of words.

He was staring at me.

Lifting my great mass of skirts, I knelt on the floor and rested a hand upon his knee. "You've asked very little of me, and—"

"You offer this as compensation, then, for my patronage."

I shook my head, gazing up at him in the dark, at his anguished beauty. "I offer it because ... I would like to. I want to."

Reaching slowly toward him, I pried loose a button of his breeches with trembling fingers. He seized my hand and pressed it against the rigid column. His eyes closed. A muscle flexed in his jaw.

Abruptly he flung my hand away and stood, looking down

at me as I knelt at his feet. "Did Elle not tell you I've no stomach for pity?"

So he *had* been listening to my conversation with Elle in the library the night before—or to enough of it to have heard me tell her that I felt sorry for him.

Bracing a hand on the couch to rise, I said, "Don Domen—"

"Stay here and learn something." He turned and strode stiffly away.

I sank onto the floor, my head in my hands. *You fool, Hannah, you absurd little ass.*

"Nay, don't unbind me, I pray you," Lucy said.

I looked up to see Inigo unbuckling the strap across her waist. A tiny speck of blood under one nostril was the only remaining evidence of his broken nose. The swelling had completely subsided; it wasn't even red.

It must not have really been broken, I thought. It had certainly looked that way, though.

"I'm just taking off this one," Inigo said as he hung the strap back on the hat stand. "The rest can remain as they are."

As Inigo held the dildo in place, Elic, shirtless now, helped Lucy to rise to her knees, still widespread because of her tethered ankles. The way her wrists were bound behind her forced her back to arch, thrusting out her breasts. Elic suckled her nipples as he opened his breeches, and then he lay on his back between her thighs. Guiding her with one hand and his cockstand with the other, he lowered her onto the tumescent organ.

"Oh, God, I'm so close," she moaned as she began to writhe atop him.

"Not yet," he said, holding her still as Inigo leapt up onto the training bed.

Elic spread his legs to make room for Inigo behind Lucy.

Crouching on his haunches, Inigo whipped off his shirt and popped open the buttons of his breeches. He retrieved the little white bottle from his pocket and dripped oil down the length of his cock, using his fist to coat it in three swift strokes.

Slowly he withdrew the lacquered dildo, which, despite its size, didn't approach the length and girth of the phallus rising between Inigo's legs. He parted her buttocks and touched the broad head of his cock to the tiny opening.

"Do you want it fast or slow?" he asked her.

"Fast."

Planting one foot on the bed to brace himself, he got a good grip on her and rammed himself in.

From her seemingly tortured groan, I was worried for a moment that he'd hurt her, but it was a groan of ecstasy, as I soon realized. Elic stroked her between her legs as she writhed like a wild thing, rasping "Deeper, both of you. Oh, God, deeper. Fuck me! Fuck me harder. Oh . . . oh . . ."

She came with an explosive scream, but she didn't even slow down, just kept thrashing and thrusting and moaning and begging them to fuck her harder, deeper.

Elic arched his hips and shuddered, his face darkening, a vein rising on his forehead. Inigo paused for a moment, stilling Lucy with one hand banded around her waist and the other gripping a breast. When Elic's climax ended and he started thrusting again, so did Inigo and Lucy. Elic came again, not long afterward; this time, I saw thick white fluid oozing out from where he was joined to Lucy.

Inigo's thrusts grew more frenzied. He shifted his position, lowering the bent leg. As he did so, his unbuttoned breeches slipped down. He yanked them up, but in the split second before he did, I saw something that made my jaw drop.

I can still see it, when I close my eyes and revisit that afternoon in my mind. The breeches fall, revealing something that doesn't belong there, a fleshy, whiplike something growing out of the base of his spine. *A tail,* I think as I sit on the floor in that dark, carpeted passage, staring. He's already covered himself back up again, but I know what I saw.

I think.

"What's wrong?" Elic asked, wondering why Inigo had gone still. Lucy, oblivious, was still thrusting away.

"You don't suppose someone's watching right now, do you?" Inigo looked around fretfully, pushing a hand through his wild mop of hair, in which I saw, or imagined, a pair of small, bony stumps. The tips of his ears, which I hadn't seen before, were ever so slightly pointed.

I stood up, staring and shaking my head. *Nay. I'm imagining things.* If so, however, it would be the first time in my life that my mind had ever conjured up something that wasn't there.

"Is anyone there?" Inigo asked loudly, glancing one by one at the veiled gaps between the mirrored panels.

I bit my lip, weighing the pros and cons of responding.

"What says that bloodhound's nose of yours, brother?" Inigo inquired.

Elic drew in a breath slowly. "There might be a female. I smell orange flowers, lavender, frankincense..."

"That's just Lucy."

Elic scowled in concentration. "Possibly, but—"

"*É!*" Inigo happened to be looking in my direction when he yelled this.

I lifted my skirts and ran.

"*Qui va là,*" he called out, but I was already sprinting down the stairs.

Ten

FOUR DAYS LATER, while Elle and I were strolling arm in arm across the west lawn toward the castle for dinner, I stopped walking, forcing her to stop, as well.

She looked at me expectantly, her face shadowed from the noon sun by the broad brim of her straw hat.

"I didn't come here to learn to be a courtesan," I said.

After a moment, she pointed to a swing bench beneath a vine-covered arbor in the rose garden adjacent to the castle's west wall. "Let us go sit in the shade, shall we?"

We sat on the swing, our skirts mounding into a crackling, colorful heap. My black mourning attire had been supplanted by the luxurious new wardrobe Signora Tozzi and her staff were busily sewing day and night. Two days ago, we novices were told that every morning we would be given a newly finished dress to wear that day, so that Signor Vitturi could pass judgment upon it, while the dress from the day before would be taken away for alterations.

That day's gown, which I found both exquisite and scandalous, had been designed to make the most of my slender frame and dainty breasts. It was fashioned of deep blue satin embroidered in gold, its heavily boned bodice featuring a wide gap in front that was laced together with gold cords. As it was intended to be worn with neither shift nor stomacher, the open bodice bared a wide expanse of my chest and stomach; any wider, and it would have exposed my nipples. The voluminous leg-o'-mutton sleeves, which were trussed to the bodice with ribbon rosettes, had been generously slashed, with undersleeves of fine white sarcenet puffing through the slits. The skirt was undivided, in the Venetian style, its deep hem lightly tacked so that it could be rehemmed longer and worn with chopines.

Signora Tozzi, who declared it to be the most beautiful and seductive dress she had ever created, called it *"il vestito dallo zaffiro"*—the sapphire gown. So enamored of it had Elle been when she saw it that morning that she'd asked the gifted dressmaker to create an exact replica for herself. Signora Tozzi had objected that Elle was too generously endowed on top for a bodice with such a wide opening, whereupon Elle had offered a thousand ducats for the gown, silencing Madame's objections.

Elle untied her bonnet and tossed it onto a nearby bench. "What you tell me will never pass my lips, Hannah. Not once in my life have I revealed a secret that I've been asked to keep. And I assure you," she added with an enigmatic little smile, "I am far older than I look."

Elle was my only confidante at Grotte Cachée, and a woman of singular insight. If there was anyone who might have some notion as to how to run the elusive Duke of

Buckingham to ground, it would be she. Not to mention that she was the only person there whom I could truly trust.

And not to mention that I was, at that point, pathetically desperate. My uncle's fate was in my hands, and I was failing him utterly.

I told her everything. Toward the conclusion of my account, I began weeping in frustration at Buckingham's continued inaccessibility, for so obsessed was he with his hunting that I'd scarcely laid eyes on him since we'd been there. I'd seen plenty of dead boars being lugged across the courtyard, and I'd eaten so much pork that I'd grown quite sick of it, but the duke had continued to keep himself well isolated from most of his fellow visitors to Grotte Cachée.

Elle dried my tears with a scented handkerchief and took me in her arms, murmuring pacifying things until my composure returned.

I told her I felt awful for having kept such a secret from her these past weeks, given what close friends we'd become.

She said, "We all have our secrets, Hannah. I've kept things from you, too, secrets about this place and those of us who live here."

As she said that, I was reminded of the many little enigmas I had encountered at Grotte Cachée—the bird named Darius who "didn't care to be thought of as a pet," the hallucinatory magnetism in the cave and bathhouse, Elic's unnatural sexual stamina, the erudite Elle's willingness to believe that a Venetian courtesan named Galiana Solsa was a bloodsucking demon...

Humans like to think they know all there is to know about the world and the beings who populate it, Elle had told me, *but they don't, nor do they really want to, most of them.*

Humans, she'd said, not *we humans. They* and *them,* not *we* and *us.*

And then, of course, there was what I'd seen in *la Chambre des Voiles et des Miroirs* when Inigo's breeches had slipped down. Since then, it had dawned on me how much he resembled the lusty satyr in the bathhouse statues, even as regarded his build, his facial features, and those tight corkscrew curls—although Inigo's hair was much longer than that on the statue, effectively hiding the horns and ears.

"Is Inigo a . . ." I felt foolish saying it, but I plowed ahead. ". . . a satyr?"

I'd asked it in order to gauge Elle's reaction. She should have burst out laughing. Instead, she stared at me for a second too long before looking off across the lawn with an uncharacteristically tight little smile. Pushing the swing back and forth with her foot, she said, "What an extraordinary question."

"I saw his tail with my own eyes," I said, with as much certitude as I could muster. "And I think I saw something that might have been horns, and pointed ears."

"Whom have you told of this?" Elle asked. Not *You can't be serious,* but *Whom have you told?*

"I asked the other novices if they'd noticed any unusual body parts on Inigo. Of course, they all laughed and pointed out the obvious. I told them what I'd seen, or . . . thought I'd seen. I asked if he'd ever removed his breeches in their presence. He hadn't. I asked if they'd ever felt anything unusual on his head. They all said he hated to be touched there, or even to have his hair stroked."

"Did they believe you about the tail and so forth?" Elle asked.

"Sibylla and Lucy thought I was imagining things. Bianca wasn't so sure. She truly believes in . . . what she calls *Folletti*—incubi and the like. She was talking in the carriage on the way here about the strange phenomena at Grotte Cachée that her sister told her about—and the strange beings. She said something about Elic and Inigo not being ordinary men, and how there's a hermit who lives in the cave and can take the shape of animals."

"Did she."

"What are you, Elle? Are you a dusii?" I asked, recalling her slip of the tongue in the library when she was talking about her need for carnal sustenance. *No one woman could ever satisfy me.*

"The singular is 'dusios.'" She looked away again with that forced smile. "How on earth did we end up talking about this?"

With quiet gravity, I said, "I've never betrayed a confidence either, Elle, upon my faith—never."

Taking my hand, she said, "I believe you, Hannah, but if I were what you suspect I am, can you not understand how dangerous it would be to confide in *any* human, even one in whom I have the utmost trust? There are still many places where Follets are being burned alive as witches, even those who've done no harm to anyone. Were such beings to find a safe haven, such as Grotte Cachée, they would be loath to jeopardize it by making their presence here known, would they not?"

I opened my mouth to pursue the subject, hesitating when I noticed her gaze shift to something over my right shoulder. Turning, I saw a figure in the distance walking with a slightly halting gait along the gravel drive leading from the gatehouse to the stable and carriage house tucked away in the woods. Domenico Vitturi was wearing his usual black doublet and breeches, and he had a book in his hand.

"Where does he go when he wanders off like that?" I asked, more to myself than to Elle.

Ever since the afternoon he'd summoned me to the Training Room, Vitturi had become virtually as reclusive as the Duke of Buckingham. He rarely ate with the rest of us, and when he did, he was uncommunicative. According to the other novices, the last time he was intimate with one of them was in the bathhouse that first night, and Elle told me he hadn't touched her since London. When in the castle, he often holed himself up in the library. Most of his time, however, was spent somewhere off in the woods with his books. He no longer observed our training sessions with *les professeurs de l'amour*—or rather, the other novices' training sessions. Over the course of the past four days, I had learned to hunt with hawks, paint landscapes, discuss political matters intelligently, and a host of other things, but although my fellow novices continued to receive erotic instruction, not once had I been required to observe or participate in it.

Nor, of course, had I been required to "compensate" Signor Vitturi for his patronage in any way. I realized at that point that he could have obliged me to perform any number of acts that would have gratified him sexually without compromising my virginity, but he had not done so.

"Perhaps you should tell him what you've told me," Elle said, still gazing at the spot where Vitturi had disappeared into the woods.

"Tell him why I'm really here? Nay!"

She looked at me. "He's Buckingham's friend, Hannah. He may know why the duke accused your uncle of treason. Is that not what you came here to find out?"

That, and if luck smiled on me, to convince the duke that it had been a mistaken accusation. The possibility that Buckingham might have confided to Vitturi the grounds for that accusation had never occurred to me. After all, Vitturi was Venetian; he would have little interest in political intrigues between England and Spain. Still, if there was a chance he might know something…

"You're right," I said. "I should question Don Domenico, but in an offhand manner, as if I were simply discussing current affairs. I absolutely cannot let him know I came here under false pretenses. He would almost certainly send me back to England, and if that happens, I shall have no hope at all of swaying Buckingham. Surely you can see the wisdom in that."

Elle acknowledged reluctantly that she did.

I said, "All that remains, then, is for me to contrive a private little tête-à-tête with Don Domenico. 'Twill be easier said than done, given what a recluse he's become."

Elle regarded me in silence for a moment with those radiant blue eyes that seemed to see everything. With a knowing little smile, she said, "Is this Buckingham business the only reason you want to be alone with Domenico?"

"Oh, honestly, Elle." I looked away so she wouldn't see me blushing. In truth, the notion of being with him in a secluded place filled me with a jittery excitement that had nothing to do with Buckingham and everything to do with the memory of Vitturi's warm mouth on mine.

Elle said, "You asked before where he goes when he wanders off like that."

I sighed. " 'Twas a rhetorical question."

"I know where he goes."

I turned to look at her.

"I asked him yesterday. He told me. If you'd like to know, I'll tell you."

"I thought you'd never betrayed a confidence in your life."

"He didn't ask me not to tell," she said. "He just assumed I wouldn't."

"Because it never occurred to him that you would," I said, beset with misgivings.

With a vexatious groan, Elle said, "Very well," and stood, puffing up her skirts. "If you don't care to know, then—"

"Where does he go?" I asked as I, too, rose from the swing.

"There's a path through the woods behind the carriage house—a network of paths, actually. One of them leads to a place called the Nemeton. 'Tis a clearing in the woods that was a place of worship for the Gaulish tribe that once lived here. They conducted rituals there, some of which amounted to sexual orgies."

"My word."

"They chose that spot because oak trees were sacred to them, and that area of the forest is mostly oaks. Only very special visitors are permitted to see it. I took Domenico there several years ago because I felt he would appreciate it, and he did."

"Is it very far?" I asked.

"Only eight or nine hundred yards from here as the crow flies, but over a mile by foot along the paths. 'Tis a rather tortuous route, the better to keep the Nemeton away from prying eyes. 'Tis rare that someone stumbles upon it. The directions are fairly complicated."

"You'll share them with me?" Was I "special" enough?

"But of course." Elle smiled. "I shall explain them on the way to the kitchen."

"The kitchen?"

Taking my arm, she said, "Come along."

I paused on the path, a blanket over one arm and a basket of food and wine over the other, when I spied an open, sunlit area up ahead. Looking down, I saw that my blue satin gown had gotten slightly dirty around the hem, but was otherwise unscathed after my mile-long trek along the web of narrow forest trails that led there. I wished, not for the first time since setting out, that my bodice didn't reveal an eight-inch swatch of bare skin, but there was no help for that; I had to wear what I was given.

Taking care to walk silently, I approached the clearing, stopping just short of it to have a look around. The oak trees surrounding the Nemeton looked to be very ancient, and many grew in strange, twisted shapes; birds chattered and sang within their branches. The grass was neatly shorn, indicating that someone took the trouble to come out there with a scythe on a regular basis. I saw the carved stone altar Elle had told me about, and a fire pit that looked to be long disused.

I did not, however, see Domenico Vitturi. Filled with disappointment, I stepped into the clearing, squinting against the sun . . . and stopped when I saw something black hanging from a branch of a massive oak about five yards to my left: a doublet.

I took another two steps, and there he was, sitting in his shirtsleeves—it was a warm day, after all—on a squarish boulder at the base of the tree, which he lounged against as he read his book. My view was of the injured side of his face. It wasn't quite a full profile, as he was facing slightly away from me, which would be why he hadn't noticed my presence; the silken rustle of my skirts might have been taken for a breeze drifting through the trees.

The early afternoon sun filtered through the leafy branches overhead, painting him with a lacework of light and shadow. He turned the page with an expression of fierce absorption that made him appear almost angry.

I licked my dry lips. "Don Domenico," I said.

He looked sharply in my direction. For several seconds, he just stared at me.

I curtsied.

As if suddenly remembering his manners, he leapt to his feet and bowed. As he pressed his right hand to his chest in the

Venetian manner, it appeared to dawn on him that he was greeting me in his shirt.

"Pray, pardon my state of undress," he said as he took the doublet off the branch and shook it out. "I wasn't expecting—"

"Nay, signore, please don't trouble yourself," I said, but he was already shrugging it on. As he did so, his gaze lit on my bosom, so brazenly exposed by the gold-laced opening in my bodice. For a moment, he seemed almost transfixed, which surprised me—he'd never been one to leer. A prickly warmth crawled up my chest and throat to my face.

Redirecting his attention to the buttons of his doublet, he pushed them one by one through their loops. "Elle sent you here?"

I shook my head. "She just told me where to find you."

He looked up, his gaze shifting from my eyes to the items I was carrying.

Eager for something to do to with the nervous energy trembling through me, I put down the basket and set about laying the blanket out on the grass.

"What is this?" he asked, taking a few steps in my direction to peer into the basket.

"Um, wine and food," I said as I knelt on the blanket, smoothing it out, making the corners lie flat. "Some cheese and bread, fruit pastes, tarts…"

"You came all the way here just to bring me dinner?"

I stopped my pointless fussing and sat staring at a rumpled corner of the blanket. Feeling starved for air, I said, "Nay," but it emerged as a barely audible whisper.

The ensuing silence was absolute. Even the birds seemed to have ceased their chirping.

Eleven

I KEPT MY GAZE TRAINED on the blanket as Vitturi came and knelt before me, a bit awkwardly because of his bad leg.

He said my name very softly—not "Mistress Leeds" this time, but "Hannah."

He reached toward my face, hesitating with his fingertips a hairsbreadth away.

I took his hand and pressed it to my cheek, closing my eyes. His palm was very warm as I leaned into it, savoring his touch.

He curled his other hand around the back of my head, tilted it up, and kissed me with a sweet, hot hunger that was more thrilling than anything I'd ever experienced. We crushed our bodies together, kissing at such length, and with such passion, that when our mouths parted for a moment, we both gasped, laughing in astonishment.

The sky reeled drunkenly as we fell upon the blanket. He kissed me again and again, his hands roving everywhere, squeezing, caressing, plucking the pins from my hair, untying the gold cord that laced up my bodice.

Sitting astride me, he yanked the cord through its eyelets and flung it aside. He opened my bodice and gazed upon me, his hair disheveled from my hands, a feral glint in his eye. Yet his touch, as he trailed his hands over my breasts, was gentle as a whisper. I gasped when his fingertips brushed my nipples, which instantly stiffened. He stroked them very softly—maddeningly so—as I writhed to his touch, my sex growing damp in response.

They say he has the gentlest hands in Christendom.

I unbuttoned his doublet. He tore it off and whipped his shirt over his head. His torso was lean, but muscular, the epitome of masculine beauty save for a long-healed gouge from his right shoulder to the bottom of his rib cage.

He lowered himself onto me and kissed me again, his bare chest pressed to mine, our hearts pounding in unison. We moved together in a primeval rhythm; even through my skirts and his breeches, I could feel his arousal. Without breaking the kiss, he pulled my skirts up and caressed me with those deft, probing fingers until I was moaning and clutching at the blanket.

"Make love to me," I whispered.

"God, how I wish I could. I can't. I can't, Hannah. We can touch each other, pleasure each other, but if you're to be a maiden when you arrive in Ven—"

"That doesn't matter. I'm not . . . I . . . I don't care about that. I just want to make love to you."

He searched my eyes as he pondered that. "This has naught to do with . . . repaying my patronage?"

"Nay! 'Tisn't that, I promise you. I want you to be the first, no one else, just you."

He gathered me in his arms and kissed me again, groaning into my mouth when I stroked him between his legs. I unbuttoned his breeches and closed a hand around his erection. It felt impossibly hard, like skin stretched over marble.

He caressed me intimately until I was delirious with lust, and then he pushed a finger into me, igniting a climax that shuddered through me so long and so hard that I thought my heart might burst.

He kissed me as the tremors waned, murmuring how beautiful I was, how exciting it was to watch me come apart. "Your maidenhead is already torn," he said, still stroking me from within.

"How is that possible if I've never been with a man?"

"It happens," he said, lying on his back to strip off his breeches, hose, and boots. " 'Tis a good thing. 'Twill be easier for you."

He undressed me more slowly than he had himself, kissing and stroking every inch of skin he uncovered, and then he lay atop me, cradled in the juncture of my thighs. When I reached between his legs, he pulled my hand away, saying "I'm too close as it is."

I tensed when I felt his fingertips part my sex and seat his own within it—just the tip, but it felt far larger than I had expected, like the hard round head of a club pushing into me.

"Shh, *cara*," he whispered against my lips as he stroked my hair. "Easy, easy. Let me in."

I felt a burning as he stretched me open, using shallow, measured thrusts. It was a slow and steady incursion, made more bearable by the fact that I was so wet—no doubt this had been his purpose in bringing me to orgasm beforehand.

So this is what it feels like to be possessed, I thought when he was finally buried deep inside me. Despite the discomfort, I wanted to stay that way forever.

I could feel the strain in his body as he made love to me, every muscle quivering. I realize now that he was trying to hold himself in check so as not to hurt me. His undoing came when I wrapped my legs around him and raised my hips to meet his, as I had seen Sibylla do with Elic in the bathhouse.

"Dio mio." He thrust harder, his hands tangled in my hair, then stilled. A grinding sound rose from his throat. I felt goose bumps rise up all along his spine, and then his sex jerked inside me over and over again, the pulses gradually diminishing until he sank upon me, heavy and spent.

❧

"Don't become a courtesan."

I had just nodded off in Domenico's arms, the two of us curled up naked in the afternoon sun, when his soft-spoken entreaty brought me fully awake.

I lifted my head to meet his eyes.

Stroking a tendril of hair off my face, he said, "I can't bear the thought of you entertaining a different benefactor every night of the week. I only want you to be with me."

I rolled onto my back, an arm across my eyes to shield them from the sun. *Dear God, please don't let this hurt him as much as it's going to hurt me.*

He braced himself on an arm to look down at me. "You shall never want for anything, Hannah, not a thing. You'll live in luxury, with everything you desire. We'll travel, we'll go to the opera. I'll build you the biggest library in Venice and fill it with thousands of books." Trailing a hand down my throat and over a breast, he said, "I want the most brilliant and beautiful woman in Europe to be mine and mine alone. On mild evenings, I want to float through the canals on a gondola with you in my arms, watching the buildings turn gold in the setting sun. 'Tis one of the most enchanting sights in the world."

"I'm sure it is," I said recalling how exquisite Château de la Grotte Cachée had looked when I'd first seen it, gilded by the sunset. But I wasn't going to Venice. My plan—my vital mission, at which I mustn't fail—was to return to England as soon as possible with the information I needed to clear my uncle's name and save his life.

Whereupon Domenico Vitturi would realize that I'd been deceiving him from the beginning. I dreaded to think how he would react to that.

He must have misinterpreted my pensiveness, because he looked away, saying " 'Tisn't quite what you had in mind, I know. I suppose *I'm* not quite what you had in mind. I have no illusions about . . . what women see when they look at me, but—"

"Nay, I think you do." Sitting up, I took his face in my hands and kissed him lingeringly, deeply. "You foolish man, you have no idea how women view you, how much they admire you . . . and desire you. The problem isn't what they see when they look at you, Domenico, 'tis what you see when you look at yourself."

"Accept my offer," he said with a cagey grin, "and you shall have all the time in the world to convince me of that."

At a loss for words, I turned away from him and dragged the basket closer. In addition to the linen-wrapped food within, there were not one but two leathern bottles of wine. *You want him in his cups when you question him about Buckingham,* Elle had told me as she was packing the basket. *The looser his tongue, the more you'll learn.*

As I was pouring two bowls, Domenico said from behind me, "I pray thee, Hannah, think about it. Consider it seriously.

Then, if you decide that you would prefer the life of a *cortigiana onesta,* I will still lend you my patronage. I'll provide you with a home, a staff, clothing, jewels, a gondola ... I'll introduce you to the wealthiest, most desirable benefactors in the city. I will do all this because I'm a man of my word and I want the best for you, but make no mistake," he said, his voice low and rough. " 'Twill break my heart."

I studied the two bowls of wine, tears shimmering in my eyes. "Make love to me again, Domenico."

"Not so soon," he said, wrapping his arms around me from behind. "You need time to heal."

"Tonight, then?"

"Aye, and the next night ..." He nuzzled my hair. "And the next ..." He touched his lips to my cheek. "And the next, and the next, and the next," he said, planting a trail of kisses down my throat and along my shoulder. "I shall have your things brought to my bedchamber so that you can stay there ... if ... that is, if you wish it."

He never lets me kiss him, nor does he let me sleep in his bed.

"I would like that, Domenico. I would love it."

I handed him his bowl, which he touched to mine. "To your health," he said.

"Alla tua salute."

❧

"Are you trying to get me drunk?" he asked as I refilled his glass for the third time. It was late afternoon, and the sun had already dipped below the surrounding mountains. Domenico had lent me his shirt, which fell almost to my knees; he wore his breeches and unbuttoned doublet.

I stared at him with the bottle in one hand and the cork in another. "I ... er ..."

"Because you can have your way with me even if I'm perfectly sober, as I think should be evident by now," he said with a woolly chuckle that indicated the wine was already going to his head. As if to confirm that, he said, "We'd better eat something, or I shall fall asleep right here and not wake up till morning."

I laid out our dinner, and we ate, our conversation centering mainly on poetry, literature, and theater until I steered it toward affairs of state. I refilled his cup twice more, mine only once—and I barely touched it.

"Do you know anything about the Goodchild case?" I asked as I emptied the first bottle into his bowl and uncorked the second. I hated the studied nonchalance of my tone. I hated the subterfuge I was engaging in. *Please let him know something useful.*

"Goodchild." Lying propped up on an elbow, he lifted the bowl to his mouth. "The fellow who's been arrested for treason? I only know he's in the Tower awaiting trial. Buckingham's never mentioned him to me."

Damn it all to Hades, I thought.

"Why do you ask?" he said.

"I don't know." I looked down and shrugged. "It interests me."

"Because you're Catholic and they're saying that's why he spied for Spain?"

"Perhaps. I just thought, since you and the duke are friends, he might have told you something the rest of us aren't privy to. I suppose I'm prying into matters that are none of my affair."

"Buckingham wouldn't have talked to me about this. They tell me he's been melancholic ever since he found out what the blackguard did. 'Tis a painful thing, realizing one's lover has been betraying—"

"*Lover.*" I sat up straight, wine dripping from my bowl onto the blanket.

He groaned disgustedly. "Forget I said that. 'Twas all this wine. I don't normally drink so much, especially in the after—"

"Are you saying my—that Guy Goodchild and the Duke of Buckingham...?"

" 'Tis no secret in certain circles, and most members of the king's court know about Buckingham's proclivities, even if they aren't quite certain who's been sharing his bed since King James passed away."

"*King James?* You mean he and Buckingham...?"

"Oh, everyone knew about that. It had been going on for years."

"I didn't know." But then, it was hardly the type of thing that would have been discussed in my presence.

Domenico said, "After the king's death, Buckingham went into genuine mourning, and then early last summer, he took up with Guy Goodchild. Shortly after that, he arranged for Goodchild's appointment as emissary to Spain. As I understand it, Goodchild is a man of considerable refinement who's never been married, so there had been rumors for some time that he preferred men."

"But King James had a wife," I said, "and so does Buckingham."

"And so does Jonas Knowles. 'Tis done to keep up appearances and perpetuate the line, but—"

"Jonas Knowles?" I said through an incredulous chuckle. Recalling the morning I had discovered him in Lucy's bed, I said, "Jonas Knowles does not prefer men, I can assure you of that."

Cocking his head, Domenico said, "Do you know something I ought to . . . Nay, don't tell me. I don't want to know. I can assure you, however, that Knowles has spent every night in Buckingham's bed since we left London. He's been the duke's gentleman of the bedchamber for almost a year, but he didn't become his favorite—and his lover—until after Goodchild was arrested. If he's still disporting himself with women . . ." Domenico shook his head as he took a sip of wine. "God help him if Buckingham finds out. He gets wildly jealous, demands fidelity. Not that he gives it in return. He does like his pretty young men, and he'll take them where he can get them, but his favorites had better stay true or suffer his wrath."

"That doesn't seem quite fair."

"He doesn't have to be fair. He's the Duke of Buckingham."

"And no one minds that he beds men?" I asked. " 'Tis a sin, is it not?"

"The English aren't quite as intolerant of it as they are otherwhere. In Venice, such men risk execution if they're found out. They're beheaded, and their bodies burned."

"Hence courtesans who cut their hair short and dress in men's clothing," I said, recalling what Elle had said about the advantages of my small breasts.

Domenico nodded. " 'Tis a good deal safer than seeking out a male for the same purpose."

"But how satisfying can it really be?" I asked. "There are women in London who dress in breeches and doublets—churchmen are forever railing against them—but there's never any doubt as to their true sex. A woman could never pass for a man, not really."

"You'd be surprised how convincing a slim young woman can be, with her hair shorn and her breasts bound. Several times I've been in the company of such courtesans and never suspected that they weren't young men."

"Verily?" I said, as an idea began to take shape in my mind.

"Unless a woman has exceptionally voluptuous hips and breasts," he said, "such a disguise can work well enough."

Yes, of course it could, I thought. Of course.

It could actually work.

Twelve

TWENTY-FOUR HOURS LATER, I was sprinting across a marshy plateau after a pack of frantically barking dogs and the boar they were chasing. My lungs burned; my legs felt leaden. Try as I might, I could not keep up with the men running ahead of me—the Duke of Buckingham, master of the hunt Sir Humphrey Quade, five of the duke's yeomen, and a sturdy young castle lacquey named Yves.

Or should I say, my fellow lacquey, for I was posing as exactly that, a young servant-of-all-work sent along to perform tasks that were too lowly even for the duke's yeomen. It was Elle who had offered "Henri's" services to Sir Humphrey, saying I was new and untrained and getting underfoot around the château, but perhaps I could be of some use to the duke's evening hunting party.

My transformation into a young man had been accomplished by Elle that afternoon. To excuse me from my afternoon lessons and supper, she had reported that I had a stomach ailment for which she was nursing me in her own quarters.

"Domenico wanted to bring you a mint tonic," she'd told me, "but I convinced him you wouldn't want him to see you in such a state."

I was swamped with guilt to be heaping yet another lie upon the mountain of deceit that represented, God help me, the foundation of my relationship with Domenico Vitturi. My contrition was all the sharper because of my realization, as he took me for the second time in his bed the night before, that I was in love with him. With my resolve weakening, I reminded myself what was at stake. I was my uncle's only hope. If I didn't stiffen my spine and do what had to be done, he would be doomed.

The first thing Elle did while I was thusly "indisposed" was to shear off my wavy hair above my shoulders—as I squeezed my eyes shut and called up memories of my Uncle Guy carrying me around as a child, reading to me, teaching me to play the lute and the harpsichord...

It would be most prudent, Elle and I agreed, to darken my distinctively reddish blond hair. Although Buckingham himself would be unlikely to recognize me with my natural color, given his disinterest in women and the distance he'd maintained from us, such would not be the case with the other men in his party. In fact, Sir Humphrey had bedded both Lucy and Bianca during our journey. The duke's yeomen were not, of course, at liberty to approach us, but they could, and did, look their fill at every opportunity. Elle mixed up a dark brown dye using oak gall, henna, walnut shells, and a few other things— an ancient Roman recipe, she told me. I didn't ask how she'd come by it. I hadn't brought up the subject of incubi and so forth since the day before, nor did I intend to, given her disinclination to discuss the matter.

Elle came up with a set of laborer's clothes—coarse tunic and pantaloons, shabby boots, and a red knitted cap—that belonged to an adolescent scullery boy. She had me practice walking and talking like a male and speaking with a provincial French accent.

"You're supposed to be a nineteen-year-old boy," she told me as she wrapped a length of linen around my chest to flatten my breasts, "so don't forget to act like one. Don't get careless. But at the same time, don't forget to flirt with the duke."

The idea was to make Buckingham think that I, too, fancied those of my own sex, and in particular, him. Then, when he'd taken the bait and we were alone together, I could broach the subject of Guy Goodchild.

"How does a male flirt with another male?" I asked.

"The same way a woman flirts with a man. Let him notice you staring at him, but be subtle about it. Meet his gaze, then look away. If he says something witty, laugh just a bit too hard. You're naught but a young French peasant, if a comely one. He's one of the most famous men in the world, and one of the handsomest. Be awed by him. Oh, and it wouldn't hurt if you could contrive to come in physical contact with him, skin to skin, however briefly."

So that I wouldn't be forced to compete with Jonas Knowles for the duke's attention, Elle had sent Master Knowles a note asking him to meet her for a tryst at four o'clock on the top floor of the southeast tower.

"When he walks into *la Chambre des Voiles et des Miroirs* and sees me standing there with a pair of leather cuffs in one hand and a cat-o'-nine-tails in the other," she said, "he'll probably spend in his breeches."

Her plan was to keep him immobilized until Buckingham and his party, including me, had returned from the evening hunt.

"Knowles will worry about missing another hunt," Elle had said, "so I'd best gag him, too, to keep him from yelling for help. Although if I fuck him senseless ten or twelve times, he might not fret so about the hunt, and 'twould certainly make the time pass more pleasantly for me."

I told her I didn't think ordinary men, meaning men who weren't Elic, could climax that many times.

With a wily little smile, she said, "They can if they're in the right hands."

And thus did I take Jonas Knowles's place in that evening's hunting party. After some initial apprehension, I grew more comfortable with my role. I'd been charged by Sir Humphrey with carrying a bucket and a coil of rope and "keeping out of the duke's way." This I did, but without missing a single opportunity to catch Buckingham's eye as Sir Humphrey tracked their prey's feeding trails through twilit woods and meadows. I should say "the duke's prey," because although he had six men with him, not including Yves and me, this was indisputably the Duke of Buckingham's hunt. The others, the dogs included, were simply there to bow and scrape, fetch and serve.

It felt most peculiar indeed to not only be in such close proximity to the reclusive duke, but to have him acknowledge my existence. He made no attempt to avoid me, as he had when I'd looked like a woman. He gave me instructions, sent me on errands, he even asked my name! And after he'd caught me gazing moonily in his direction once or twice, I began to see a heat and interest in his eyes that hadn't been there before.

Then came the frenzied barking of the dogs, along with panicked porcine grunts, and the chase was on. Being a slower runner than the men, I caught only a fleeting glimpse of the boar, which was big and bristly and crazed, as the hounds pursued it across the field into a bog.

"Who has the duke's spear?" Sir Humphrey yelled as I arrived at the bog, where the six dogs were holding the boar at bay, nipping and tormenting it as it screamed and screamed. "Give the duke his spear!"

One of the yeomen handed Buckingham a long boar spear, whereupon he waded into the bog, taking careful aim. He jabbed the captive animal in the shoulder, yanked out the spear, and backed away.

"Well done, Your Grace!" exclaimed Sir Humphrey as he pushed the dying, squealing beast onto its side in the water. The yeomen praised him, too, with an exuberance that struck me as bizarre, under the circumstances. After all, it was the dogs that had done all the work.

Remember why you're here, I thought. "*Félicitations,* Your Grace," I said with a smile I hoped wasn't too coy.

He returned the smile, saying "*Merci,* Henri." It didn't escape me that I was the only one he'd thanked for congratulating him.

After tying the dead pig by its hind legs, the yeomen dragged it to an oak tree next to a stream and hung it from a heavy branch. One of them took my bucket and set it on the ground, while another pulled a knife from the sheath on his belt and slit the animal's belly open. Slippery ropes of entrails poured forth—along with half a dozen fetal piglets.

"Oh!" Clamping a hand over my mouth, I spun around. *Don't be sick, don't be sick, don't be sick . . .*

The men roared with laughter at my squeamishness—until Buckingham ordered them to shut their mouths, producing instant silence. Patting my shoulder, the duke said, "Henri is young, he's never hunted boar ere today—have you, boy?"

"I . . . I have not, Your Grace."

Buckingham moved his hand along my shoulder until his fingers grazed my bare neck. Lowering his voice, he said, "Some things take a bit of getting used to, eh?"

I looked up and met his eyes. He held my gaze, his fingertips softly stroking my throat.

I swallowed. "*Oui.*"

" 'Twill be dark anon, Your Grace," Sir Humphrey told Buckingham. "Why don't we have a look around whilst the boar's being dressed, see if we can locate the herd's bedding place before we head back to the château—matted grass, that sort of thing. Then perhaps we can come out especially early tomorrow and surprise them, eh?"

Spurred by the realization that I had to act fast if I was to get Buckingham alone, I said, "I know where they sleep, Your Grace! I can show you."

"*You* know?" Sir Humphrey said. "I thought you'd never hunted boar."

"I haven't, but I've seen matted grass not far from here. I could take you there," I told the duke. "I could show you."

Sir Humphrey said, "Let us go, then, afore there's no light to—"

"No need for you to come along, old man," Buckingham told him. "The boy can show me where it is. Why don't you stay here and make sure they get that boar properly dressed."

Sir Humphrey's gaze shifted from the duke to me, and back again, his expression carefully neutral. "As you will, Your Grace. I'd be quick about it, though. Night falls fast here in the mountains."

I led Buckingham into the closest patch of woods, walked until I couldn't see the hunting party anymore, then stopped.

He looked around, then gave me a canny smile. "There's no matted grass here. There's no grass at all."

"Nay, Your Grace. I wanted a private place to talk to you."

Apparently oblivious to the absence of my French accent, he came toward me, his gaze on my mouth. "What very red lips you have, Henri. They're as red as your cap."

He seized me and closed his mouth over mine, plunging his tongue between my lips. Shoving a hand under my tunic, he hastily unbuttoned my pantaloons.

I squirmed; he gripped me tighter. My pantaloons slipped down; I yanked them up with both hands. Wrenching my face away, I said, "Your Grace, please! If we could just talk—"

"Aye, that would be lovely, if there were time." Spinning me around, he pushed me down onto my hands and knees with seemingly little effort; he was a very strong man. "Humphrey's right," he said as he unbuttoned his breeches. "We must be quick about it."

Thirteen

I TRIED TO CLAMBER to my feet, but Buckingham held me down, saying "Come now, I know it's not your first time. It can't be, not the way you've been looking at me."

Throwing my tunic up, he spat in his hand and rubbed it on his member. I felt it brushing up against my bare buttocks, and struggled harder, crying "Nay! You don't under—"

He clamped a hand over my mouth, hard. "For pity's sake, do you want the others to hear?"

I could feel his cockstand, slippery with spit, between the cheeks of my bottom. I tried to wrest his arm from around my waist, but it was like trying to budge the limb of an oak.

He was shifting around behind me, trying to penetrate me without using his hands. "Hold still, will you?" A sharp jab missed its mark. He swore and thrust again, coming perilously close to his intended target.

He's going to do this, I thought. *He's going to do this to me, and there's nothing I can . . .*

Yes there was.

I stopped resisting, went absolutely still.

"There's a good lad," he said. "I knew you'd settle down. If I take my hand off your mouth, do you promise to hold your tongue?"

I nodded.

He released me and straightened up, giving his cockstand a few firm strokes as he fondled my bottom. "That's a fine little arse you've got there, boy, as round and soft as a girl's."

"There's a reason for that," I said as I took his caressing hand and drew it down between my legs.

"Want me to pull you off, eh?" he asked as he groped around. "Greedy little . . ." He fell silent as he discovered there was nothing there to pull.

"Fuck!" He pushed me away and bolted to his feet. "Bloody hell!"

I refastened my pantaloons as I clambered up off the ground.

Buckingham was backing away from me with an expression of outrage as he fumbled with the buttons of his breeches. "Who the devil are you? What the hell do you think you're doing?"

"I'm Hannah Leeds, Your Grace."

"Who?" he demanded, not taking his irate gaze off of me as he pushed his hair off his face.

"I requested an audience with you in London, but you refused to see me."

A second passed. "God's blood, you're Goodchild's niece.

What the devil are you doing here in France? Dressed like that?"

"I . . . I passed myself off as one of Signor Vitturi's novices when I learned you were going to be coming here with him, and I dressed like this so I could come along on the hunt. I desperately need to talk to you about—"

"Does he know about this ploy? Vitturi?"

"N-nay. Nay, he—"

"He shall find out about it as soon as I return to the château. I shouldn't think he'll be very pleased to have been played for a fool after everything he's done for you."

"Your Grace—" I began, but he was already striding away through the darkening woods.

"He loved you!" I yelled desperately. "My uncle loved you, and look what you've done to him!"

Wheeling around, Buckingham stalked toward me, his face dark with fury. "Look what *I've* done to *him*? The lying dog betrayed me! He betrayed England! The bloody papist gave Spain advance warning of our Cádiz campaign."

"Why do you think it was my uncle who told them?"

"I *know* it was your uncle. I have a coded letter that was sent to him from Olivares, which—"

"From whom?"

"Gaspar de Guzmán y Pimentel, Count of Olivares. He's the favorite and chief minister of King Philip of Spain, and a powerful and impiteous man. The young king is but a puppet. 'Tis Olivares who pulls the strings. The letter leaves no doubt that Guy was spying for Spain, and had been for some time. 'Twas to that end that he manipulated my affections. He never loved me, but he tricked me into loving—" Buckingham's voice broke; I saw not just anger but pain in his eyes. "He played me for a fool."

"How do you know this letter was really from Olivares?" I asked.

"Aside from the fact that I know his handwriting, 'twas written on Spanish-style laid paper with a Spanish watermark, and it bore the royal seal of Spain. 'Twas most assuredly from Olivares."

"If this letter was sent to my uncle, how did you come by it?" I asked.

" 'Twas found amongst his belongings in a trunk he kept in my chamber."

"Your bedchamber?"

The duke answered that with a withering glare.

"Who found it?" I asked.

"I don't have to stand here and be interrogated by the likes of you."

"That's all right," I said. "I think I already know."

❧

"Thank God you're back," Elle greeted when I entered *la Chambre des Voiles et des Miroirs* about an hour later. She wore black satin breeches with matching stays, and had a birch switch in her hand. "I can't tell you how bored I've been. I hardly ever get bored with sex, but he's just such an insipid lit-tle nit."

On the training bed knelt a naked Jonas Knowles with his whip-striped bum in the air and his head and hands locked into the headboard stocks. His good looks did not extend to his body, which was terribly soft and pale compared to the vir-ile beauty of Elic, Inigo . . . and, of course, Domenico.

"Who's there?" asked Knowles, who was facing away from me.

With an expression of weary disdain, Elle raised the birch

and slapped it down onto Knowles's posterior. "Did I give you leave to speak?"

"Nay, mistress. Pray pardon my insolence."

I said, " 'Tis I, Jonas."

"Mistress Leeds?" he said excitedly. "Two of you! Splendid!"

"I'm afraid not, Jonas." Extracting a big brass key from her bosom, Elle unlocked the stocks and raised the top half, which slid up through grooves in the bedposts. "Methinks you've had enough for one night." Yawning, she added, "I know I have."

I thanked Elle for her help in detaining Knowles and bade her good night; she kissed me on the cheeks and left. Knowles, coming down off the bed, gaped at my short dark hair and workingman's costume. "My God, what have you done to yourself?"

"These must be yours," I said, lifting a bundle of clothes and a pair of shoes from a chair and handing them to him.

"You aren't one of those Moll Friths, are you?" he asked as he pulled his shirt down over his head. Moll Frith was a character in the play *The Roaring Girl* who dressed in men's clothing.

"I wear disguises when my assignments call for them," I said as I seated myself in the chair where the clothes had been.

"Assignments?"

I sat back and crossed my legs. "From our mutual master, the Count of Olivares."

He stilled in the act of tugging on his breeches. After a couple of seconds, he pulled them up and started buttoning them. "Master? Olivares serves the king of Spain, which makes him an enemy of England."

"And yet we both spy for him. I do it because of my Catholic sympathies. I suspect your motives are a bit less noble."

"A spy? Me?"

"You tipped Spain off about England's plan to attack Cádiz

and capture that fleet of galleons. Don't deny it," I said when he opened his mouth to do so. "Olivares himself told me 'twas you. And then, so that you could usurp Guy Goodchild's place in the ducal bed, Olivares wrote that incriminating letter for you to plant in his trunk. In return, you were to exploit your position as the favorite of England's chief minister to spy for Spain, but Olivares is displeased with your performance in that respect."

Knowles, pulling on a stocking as he sat on the edge of the bed, looked up sharply.

I said, "He suspects your purpose in foiling the Cádiz expedition and framing Goodchild was merely to advance yourself within King Charles's court and that you don't give a fig about Spain. He sent me here in part to coax information out of Buckingham as to England's intentions toward Spain and in part to find out why you can't seem to do the job yourself."

"But I *have*—" Knowles flushed. "I ... I have no idea what you're talking ab—"

"Jonas, ask yourself how I would know all this if Olivares hadn't told me." After all, how could a mere "lusty little lightskirt" have sorted out such intrigue on her own?

Knowles looked around nervously as he donned his doublet, trying to peer through the veiled gaps between the mirrors.

"There's no one out there," I assured him. "Would I be talking about this if there were? Believe me, I've no more desire to be arrested for treason than you do. You're a cautious man, though. That's *one* point in your favor."

Rising from my chair, I went over to button his doublet, standing a good deal closer to him than was strictly necessary. "Cautious and clever," I said, my voice pitched low. "Maneuvering your way into the duke's bed was brilliant. Did Olivares suggest that, or was it your idea?"

" 'Twas mine." Leaning back against the bed, he closed his hands over my bum and pulled me even closer. "You should have seen Buckingham when I showed him the letter from Olivares to Goodchild. He blubbered like a baby, said except for losing King James, it was the most sorrowful thing that had ever happened to him, that he would never smile again. 'Twas all I could do to keep from bursting out laughing."

Dear God. "You fancy men and women both then, eh?"

"Nay, of course not," he said, a note of disgust in his voice. "Buckingham's the only man I've ever shared a bed with. To tell you the truth, it sickens me, the things he makes me do with him."

"But 'tis the price you pay for your ambition, eh?"

Grinding slowly against me as he kneaded my bottom, he said, "What better way to gain preferment at court than to attach oneself to the most powerful courtier in England? He's promised to knight me, and if I can continue to stomach... what I must stomach, I expect to be made viscount within the year, or at least baron."

"And thus shall you serve your interests as you serve those of Spain, eh?"

"Spain—aye, of course! Of course." Gripping me by the shoulders, he said, "You must tell Olivares that I shall endeavor to be more vigilant in digging up information for him. I've no desire to make an enemy of such a ruthless bastard."

Raising my voice as I backed away from Knowles, I said, "Have you heard enough, Your Grace?"

Knowles stared, aghast, as the Duke of Buckingham stepped into the chamber flanked by two brawny Swiss Guards.

"I've heard more than enough," the duke replied.

The guards wrestled Jonas Knowles into manacles and leg irons. As they half dragged their frantically gibbering prisoner from the room, Buckingham turned to me and said, "My most sincere and humble thanks, Mistress Leeds. Your uncle will, of course, be released from the Tower and exonerated of all charges."

"Thank you, Your Grace."

"I don't suppose he'll want to see me, but if you would be so kind as to bring him a letter from me..."

"Of course."

"I should never have trusted that snake Knowles. 'Twas my gullibility that landed Guy in the Tower. I don't expect him to forgive me after what he's been through, but I must make some gesture of appeasement. A title, perhaps. I could give him a barony."

"I am certain he would be most appreciative."

"Er... about what happened earlier, when we were alone in the woods... 'Twas shamefully crass on my part. I haven't been myself since your uncle..."

"Don't give it another thought, Your Grace."

Monsieur Pépin, looking uncharacteristically glum, was waiting for me at the bottom of the tower stairs.

"Mademoiselle Leeds," he said with a bow.

"Monsieur."

"Signor Vitturi has asked me to have your belongings moved from his bedchamber back into yours."

"Oh." *Oh, God. So he'd heard. He knew everything.*

"And..." He sighed heavily. "I am to tell you that a carriage will be waiting outside the gatehouse at dawn tomorrow to transport you and two attendants to Calais. This," he said, handing me a heavy kidskin purse, "should provide for your accommodations and your passage across the Channel."

I looked inside the purse. "There's... too much here, monsieur, far too much."

" 'Tis what the signore gave me to give you."

I nodded as I looked down at the bulging purse, my heart like a brick in my chest.

"*Je suis désolé*, mademoiselle."

Me, too.

Fourteen

MUCH LATER, after the castle's occupants had retired for the night, I eased open the door to the library, which was dark save for a corona of lamplight in the rear bay. I knew it must be Domenico with his nose in a book. He wasn't in his bedchamber—I had just come from there—and the library was, after all, his favorite refuge.

After packing my belongings—just the clothes I'd come with, not the courtesan's wardrobe Domenico had commissioned for me—I had bathed and washed my hair. Just as Elle had promised, most of the dark hair dye rinsed right out. I went to bed, but sleep eluded me entirely. After an hour of tossing and turning, I got up, threw my new ivory silk wrapper on over my matching night rail, and went in search of Domenico.

I crossed to the corner bay, my feet so noiseless on the

velvety carpet that I managed to get within ten feet of him without his realizing I was there. He sat facing away from me in a leather armchair, and although I couldn't see much of him, I could see that he was in his shirtsleeves. In his right hand, resting on the arm of the chair, he held an open book. He wasn't looking at it, though. From his reflection in the window across from him, I could see that he was gazing bleakly at nothing.

I took a few tentative steps in his direction, stilling when he lifted his head to look at the window. He must have noticed the pale shimmer of my wrapper against the blackness of the night.

He met my reflected gaze for a moment, then shut his eyes and rubbed his forehead. "Don't do this, Hannah," he said in a quiet, raw voice. "Please go. Go back to England."

The urge to turn and leave was strong, but I stood my ground, my hands tightly clasped. "I don't want to. Or rather, I don't want to stay there. I must return long enough to make sure Buckingham keeps his word and acquits my uncle, but after that, I . . . I would like to go to Venice."

He looked up, scowling in puzzlement at my reflection. "You *do* want to be a courtesan? I thought that was all pretense."

" '*Twas* pretense. I don't want to go to Venice to be a courtesan, Domenico. I want . . . I want what you were talking about in the Nemeton yesterday. I want to be with you, just you."

"Hannah . . ." He looked away grimly. "When I talked about that . . . 'twas before I knew that you were just using me, deceiving me."

"I did deceive you," I conceded, my chin quivering as I struggled to maintain my composure. "I hated it, especially after I grew to know you and care for you, but I was desperate to save my uncle. He's all I have, he's like a father to me, and they were going to execute him for a treasonous act he didn't commit."

"I can forgive you for that," he said meeting my eyes in the window. "I *do* forgive you for that. In your place, I might have done the same. But . . ." He wrenched his gaze from mine, his jaw set. "To come to me as you did yesterday, in the Nemeton, and seduce me for information while letting me think 'twas something more, that you had the same feelings for me as I . . . *Merda.*" Hurling the book across the room, he propped his elbows on his knees and clawed his hands through his hair. "Hannah . . . Why must we do this? Why can't you just leave?"

"Not—" My throat closed up; my eyes stung. "Not until I make you understand what really happened yesterday, and then, if you still want me to leave, I will."

Still leaning on his elbows, he rubbed his eyes.

Striving to steady my voice, I said, "When I came to the Nemeton, I had no intention of . . . seducing you, or anything like that. None at all, I swear. I will admit that I meant to loosen your tongue with wine. But making love, that was . . . It just happened. It felt . . . as if it was bound to happen, as if you were always meant to be not just the first man I ever gave myself to, but the only one."

Without lifting his head, he opened his eyes and trained them on my reflection.

I said, "You're accustomed to women who regard their bodies as . . . well, much as a merchant regards his wares. 'Tisn't for me to judge what others do, but as for myself, I couldn't imagine lying with a man for any reason but love."

He sat very still, his gaze fixed on me.

"I don't expect you to feel the same way about me, not after . . ." Tears spilled hotly from my eyes. I scrubbed them away and drew in a shaky breath. "Not after everything that's happened, but I have to tell you . . . You need to know . . . I love you. I love you so much, Domenico. Yesterday, when you asked me to be your mistress, it filled me with such joy—but anguish as well. God, how I dreaded this moment."

He wasn't looking at my reflection anymore but staring pensively at the floor.

I waited for him to say something. He didn't.

Desolate but resigned, I turned to leave, saying "I shall be gone in the morning."

I crossed the huge, dark room as quickly as I could without running, because I was perilously close to bursting into tears, and that was something I didn't want him to see. Better to hasten back to my chamber, close the door, and bury my face in my pillow.

I was almost to the door when I heard him say, "Hannah."

Turning, I saw him walking toward me with those lengthy but slightly halting strides that imparted an almost stately aura.

He stopped about a yard from me. Quietly he said, "If you really want to come to Venice, Hannah, then come. But not as my mistress."

I looked down, swallowing the sob that rose in my throat.

" 'Twas never what I intended," he said, "but I can be clumsy with words when it comes to certain matters. When I told you I only wanted you to be with me, what I meant was . . . that I wanted you to be my wife."

I stared at him as he took a step toward me, his eyes huge and glistening in the dark.

" 'Tis still what I want," he said hoarsely, "more than anything, if you'll have me."

I did start crying then, my sobs mixing with laughter as he gathered me in his arms.

"You knew how I loved you," he murmured, rubbing his cheek against my hair. "You must have known."

I shook my head.

"Well, I did," he said. "I do, with all my heart, and I intend to spend the rest of my life proving it."

Postscript

D OMENICO AND I were married the following spring in Venice's magnificent Basilica di San Marco, with my Uncle Guy there to give me away. Elle was among the hundreds of guests at the lavish wedding. Also in attendance were some two dozen young women who had become, through Domenico's patronage, among the most elegant and esteemed *cortigianas onesta* in the city. These included Lucy, Sibylla, and Bianca, with whom I have remained friends over the years despite my lofty status as Signora Domenico Vitturi.

No ordinary Venetian matron would deign to make eye contact with a courtesan, much less befriend one. In truth, they wouldn't have much opportunity even if they were so inclined, cloistered as they are within the thick stone walls of their homes. Domenico had promised me, however, that I would never suffer this benign captivity, that I would be free to go about as I wished, to mingle with thinkers, artists, and politicians, and even to accompany him to a *ridotto* on occasion for an evening of cards and witty conversation. By way of justification to those men who would raise their eyebrows at my unfettered ways, he explains that ours is not the customary Venetian marriage, but a *"unione Inglese."*

"When I wed an Englishwoman," he tells them, "I agreed to an English marriage. 'Tis a small enough price to pay for a lifetime with the most brilliant and beautiful woman in Europe."

That visit to Grotte Cachée in the summer of 1626 was to be Domenico's last. He never sponsored another courtesan, but a few months ago, at the urging of friends, he set about writing a memoir of his experiences as Pygmalion to a harem of wanton beauties. He's using the title I suggested, *Una Durata di Piacere,* A Life of Pleasure, and he plans to have a handful of copies privately published—under a nom de plume, of course, lest it bring embarrassment to our children and grandchildren.

I must now lay down my quill, not only because my tale has come to an end, but because Domenico has stolen up behind me and kissed my neck and told me it's time to come downstairs. Our head gondolier is waiting to take us for our customary twilight cruise through the canals.

Already, my husband tells me, the setting sun is painting the city gold.

Hunger

The Song of the Beasts

By Rupert Brooke

(Sung, on one night, in the cities, in the darkness.)

Come away! Come away!
Ye are sober and dull through the common day,
But now it is night!
It is shameful night, and God is asleep!
(Have you not felt the quick fires that creep
Through the hungry flesh, and the lust of delight,
And hot secrets of dreams that day cannot say?).
     The house is dumb;
The night calls out to you.—Come, ah, come!
Down the dim stairs, through the creaking door,
Naked, crawling on hands and feet
—It is meet! it is meet!
Ye are men no longer, but less and more,
Beast and God.... Down the lampless street,
By little black ways, and secret places,
In the darkness and mire,
Faint laughter around, and evil faces
By the star-glint seen—ah! follow with us!
For the darkness whispers a blind desire,
And the fingers of night are amorous....
Keep close as we speed,
Though mad whispers woo you, and hot hands cling,
And the touch and the smell of bare flesh sting,
Soft flank by your flank, and side brushing side—
To-night never heed!
Unswerving and silent follow with me,
Till the city ends sheer,

And the crook'd lanes open wide,
Out of the voices of night,
Beyond lust and fear,
To the level waters of moonlight,
To the level waters, quiet and clear,
To the black unresting plains of the calling sea.

One

Midnight, Early September
Greenwich Village, New York City

"HOW ABOUT A BITE?"

Anton Turek heard Galiana Solsa's seductively husky voice, raised a few decibels for his benefit, as he stood in a moonlit alley off Bleecker Street, lighting a fourth Gitanes off the third.

Took you long enough. Turek ground the unsmoked cigarette underfoot and retreated deeper into the brick-walled passage, ducking behind an artfully arranged jumble of old wooden pallets. He crouched, rather than knelt, so as to keep the knees of his new black Dolce & Gabbana jeans from coming into contact with the grimy concrete.

The *crack-crack-crack* of Galiana's stilettos grew louder, underscored by thudding from the big, multibuckled boots worn by the guy she'd been rubbing up against at The Fallout Shelter around the corner on MacDougal. Fallout was a

154 • Louisa Burton

teeming, murky, screaming-loud little joint with cinder-block walls that drew a punk-goth clientele of which Galiana's take-out du jour, who'd introduced himself as Oxy, was drearily typical: swastika neck tattoo, studded motorcycle jacket, striped stovepipe pants, the clown boots, and chopped-up lampblack hair that had been waxed and sprayed into a calci-fied semblance of disarray.

Oxy and Galiana had been tossing them back for about an hour—Irish whisky for him and silver bullets for her, both on her tab—when she whispered something in his ear while molding his hand to the crotch of her low-rise spandex booty shorts.

The mind is subtle, she liked to say. *The cock is not.*

She'd caught Turek's eye, smiled, and gave him a little nod. He'd drained his Booker's Manhattan, bit the cherry off the stem, laid a fifty on the bar, and made his way to this, her favorite alley in the Village.

That had been forty minutes ago. She didn't give a damn how long she made him cool his heels, she never had.

"Well?" Galiana's footsteps ceased, followed by Oxy's.

Turek's gums tickled as he peered between the weathered wooden slats of his "hunting blind," as he thought of it—although it was Galiana who did most of the actual hunting, per se. He had a hard time getting humans to let down their defenses enough to go off alone with him. Something about him put them off. It didn't used to be that way. Before his forty Lost Years, as he thought of them, he'd been fairly adept at the kind of interpersonal bullshit that won people over. It had come naturally to him; in fact, he'd been known for his savoir faire.

Not anymore.

Galiana and Oxy stood facing each other on the sidewalk right outside the alley. He was quite the strapping specimen by

punk standards, but Galiana, propelled to six and a half feet in
those heels and draped in one of the "zip-capes" she liked to
wear when she was on the prowl—long and hooded, with
linebacker shoulder pads—could have been Darth Vader next
to his puny Luke Skywalker.

"Are you hungry?" she asked.

"You fucking bitch, you gotta be shitting me." Oxy's booze-
thickened snarl made Turek smile. His cock twitched. Galiana
didn't care to be spoken to that way. It made her cross.

It made her ravenous.

"You rub a guy's hand on your snatch and whisper that
dirty shit in his ear," Oxy said, "you don't just take him outside
and tell him it's time to eat."

In a cartoonishly suggestive purr, she said, "I didn't say
what it was time to eat."

It took him a second, and then he snorted in an "I get it"
way that prompted Galiana, as she turned and strode into the
alley, to roll her eyes in Turek's direction. Tonight, her blue-
black hair was sculpted into fat coils and severe bangs—a neo-
forties, *Blade Runner* look enhanced by those ink-stroke brows
and kohl-limned eyes.

The zip-cape was fashioned, like her thigh-high boots, of
licorice-black vinyl. It billowed with her leonine strides despite the fifty pounds of lead ingots sewn into its hidden pock-
ets, since their weight was located mostly in the upper back
and shoulder pads. Most women could barely lift such a garment, much less wear it. Brass zippers lined every edge, from
the floor-skimming hem to the deep hood, and there were two
oversize belt loops, or what looked like belt loops, one on each
side.

"Yes," Turek breathed when, instead of hanging the cape on
the old wrought-iron lamp hook halfway down the alley, as
she most often did, she swung it onto the ground, lining side

up. She walked right over it, chuckling when Oxy hesitated to do the same.

"Go ahead," she said as she turned to face him in front of the alley's only window, which was tall, narrow, and iron-barred. "I'm chucking it tonight. I've had it for ages." Since 2002, to be precise, which was when she had ordered yet another gross of them from the Hong Kong raincoat manufacturer that had been producing them to her specifications for some twenty years. The remaining three dozen or so of the current batch were hanging in the twenty-by-sixteen-foot dressing room she'd created out of a spare bedroom in their apartment.

Galiana leaned against the window, leveling her most pheromone-drenched gaze at Oxy as she caressed her breasts through her spandex top. It had an ultra-deep U-neck that showed off not just a luxuriant expanse of cleavage but three glittering strands that might have been taken for the bottom loops of a triple diamond necklace—except that she wasn't wearing a necklace.

Oxy leered as she pulled the elastic fabric open, stretching it around her breasts. Inserted in each nipple was a small platinum ring to which the ends of the three diamond strands were attached.

"On your knees," Oxy said as he unzipped his fly.

"Yeah, right," she snickered as she shimmied out of the shorts. Beneath them, she was bare except for a little black lightning bolt of pubic hair and the five-carat diamond adorning her clit. "You're the one who's going to be genuflecting tonight, my friend."

"The fuck I am. Get on your fucking knees, bitch." He grabbed her shoulders and tried to shove her down.

She swatted him away as casually as she would swat a mosquito.

He slapped her so hard, her head snapped around.

Galiana smiled slowly as she rubbed her cheek. "Ooh, a bad boy," she said. "You like it rough, bad boy? You like to show your bitches who's boss? I guess that's something we have in common."

She hauled back and punched him in the face.

"*Fuck!*" Oxy stumbled back, cupping his abraded cheek. "*Shit!*"

He balled a hand into a fist and whipped it toward Galiana's head.

She seized his wrist, hissing with bared teeth. With her other hand, she reached into his pants, the muscles of her forearm flexing as she squeezed.

He yowled and tried to wrench her arm away, to no avail.

"Shh." She whispered some words in the long-dead Etruscan tongue of her homeland.

It was like flipping a switch. Oxy's mouth still gaped as if in midscream, but all that emerged from it was a strangled whimper.

Still gripping his balls, she said in the low feline rumble that Turek thought of as her Hell Voice, "Who's the bitch now, bitch?"

His throat spasmed as he tried in vain to form words out of the helpless gurgle rising from it.

Reverting back to her usual Kathleen Turner purr, she said, "I'm not letting go until I get an answer, and I am a very patient woman. Who's the bitch?"

"I . . . I . . . I am." It was a barely audible rasp, but an impressive effort, considering the grip Galiana had on him, both psychic and physical.

"You're what?" she demanded. "Say it."

Fucking drama queen, Turek thought as his stomach grumbled. Galiana loved to toy with her pigeons, get them in a corner with their wings broken, and bat them around a bit before she pounced.

"Th-the bitch," he croaked.

"Whose bitch?" she demanded.

"Yours."

"On your knees, bitch."

She pushed him down, clutching his spiky hair as she thrust herself against his mouth. "Work that tongue. Flick the diamond. Faster." She slapped his head. "*Faster.* Oh, yeah. Oh, yeah... Now slow down. Back off a little. Make it last."

Make it last? "*Verdammt,*" Turek whispered as he crouched there, his knees aching like a motherfucker. "*Blöde Fotze.*" When a swear word leapt to his lips, it was more often than not in the language of his Bohemian youth, although he'd trained the last vestiges of a Germanic accent out of his English after World War I broke out; too much bullshit to have to deal with during one's world travels. Galiana had cultivated an American accent, but Turek went with refined British, the better to score the best tables and otherwise throw his weight around in English-speaking countries.

Between the First and Second World Wars, he was occasionally mistaken for Edward, Prince of Wales, which he didn't get at all. Granted, they were both champagne-blond and Teutonic, and they both knew how to properly tie an ascot, but Turek was a hell of a lot taller and better built, and facially, there was a world of difference. Turek's eyes were pale gray, not blue, and he had—back then, before 1982 and his "Post–Fuck-up Makeover," as Galiana insisted on calling it—a much stronger jaw, a broader brow, fuller lips...

His virile good looks and that oh-so-flaxen hair had made him a pussy magnet for six centuries, so it had killed him to have to get the plastic surgery and hazel contacts, not to mention having to dye his hair and eyebrows a darker shade of blond every few weeks. Galiana had wanted him to go with brown or even black, but it wouldn't have looked natural with his pale complexion. The physical transformation was jarring enough without ending up looking like Wayne Newton.

When Galiana first started talking surgery, he'd tried to argue his way out of it, but eventually he'd had to concede that she was right. They had his mug shot; they knew his name. He was bound to be rearrested eventually; even if he were to leave the country, he could be extradited back to New York. Two centuries had passed since his forty-year stint in a Parisian prison cell, but the memory was still pretty fucking fresh. It wasn't going to happen again if he could help it.

And it wasn't like he hadn't brought the whole shit storm down on himself. He'd been an asshole to let himself be seen dumping that disco bitch's drained corpse in that Staten Island landfill. If Galiana hadn't pulled off her "Mission Impossible Jailbreak," as the *New York Post* had trumpeted it, he might still be serving time.

"Can you save the dimples?" he'd asked the plastic surgeon as the anesthetic was being injected into his IV.

"You don't have dimples," replied the doc, a guy Galiana had found who had his own private little hospital in the Caribbean for well-heeled Bad Guys. "They're just creases."

"Chicks think they're dimples. Can you save them?"

"Sure. Whatever."

Sure. Whatever. Just the kind of precise, scientific response you like to hear from a guy who's standing over a tray of knives and bone saws while you're heading into la-la land.

The dimples—and they *were* dimples—were still there after the surgery, but otherwise you'd never have recognized him from before. His jaw, while still manly, was narrower, and the cleft chin was history; his eyes were a little smaller, but not unattractively so. Turek's nose had gotten badly broken when one of New York's finest grabbed his head and slammed it face-first into asphalt. Injuries to his kind healed swiftly, but not always tidily. The nose was a mess, but rather than surgically reshape it, Dr. Whatever had suggested leaving it unset and seeing how it healed. It healed looking like some five-year-old had made it out of Play-Doh.

"It looks like shit," Turek had said as he inspected his new face in the little hand mirror they gave him after the bandages came off.

"You look like a prizefighter," Galiana said. "Women will want to kiss it and make it feel better."

"I can make your cock look like that, too, if you want," offered Dr. Whatever, and he'd laughed like hell without missing a stroke as he fucked Galiana against the wall next to Turek's hospital bed.

The good doc had altered his physical features quite thoroughly, right down to grafting on new fingerprints from "a guy who never even got a speeding ticket, so we're talking squeaky clean." Turek didn't ask whether the guy in question was a cadaver or alive, not because it made him queasy, but because he simply didn't care. He did care that his fingertips had looked a little odd ever since the surgery, but that was a small price to pay for a nice, shiny new set of prints.

By the time Turek got out of the hospital, Galiana, in an effort to make their after-dinner cleanup a bit simpler and more discreet in the future, had already ordered her first batch of zip-capes. She had also arranged for new personal documentation—driver's license, passport, the works—identifying him as Anthony Prazak, a name he'd chosen because it meant "from Prague," the city of his birth. He'd taken Galiana's suggestion to change "Anton" to "Anthony," only to find himself dubbed "Tony" by just about everyone he met. When he complained to Galiana about being saddled against his will with a nickname that he regarded as juvenile and low-class, her advice was for him to lighten the fuck up.

"My name for the first couple hundred years of my life was Thanchvil Vestarcnies," she'd said, "and it was a butt-ugly name even back then. Most people have to take what they get when it comes to names. At least you got to choose your *last* name."

Small comfort, especially four years later, when a new antidepressant hit the market, and "Prazak" morphed overnight into "Prozac," always uttered with at least a hint of a snicker.

Because it was just so fucking funny.

"Yeah, Oxy, that's the way," Galiana said in a shuddery voice. "Get some fingers up there. More, bitch. Fill me up. Both holes. Good boy..."

When she finally came, it was with a low, voluptuous moan that drew giggly whispers from a pair of hipster chicks in sloppy sweaters passing by on the sidewalk with their cigarettes. They glanced into the alley, but it was too dark for them to see much.

"Stand up," Galiana commanded, as imperious as before, if a bit more breathless. "Get those pants down."

Oxy unbuckled his belt and shoved the pants down to the knees. His ass was small and muscular. Not bad, if you ignored the testosterone-poisoned dickhead it was attached to.

"Now make yourself nice and hard. Good boy," she praised as Oxy masturbated with brisk strokes, ass flexing.

Reaching overhead, Galiana grabbed a high crossbar of the iron window grille, pulled herself up, and wrapped her vinyl-booted legs around his hips. "You know what to do."

He fumbled between them.

"Come on, *push*," she said. "Haven't you ever done this before?"

He grabbed the bars and flexed his hips, groaning.

"Deeper," she said. "*Deeper.* Now stop. Don't move. That's right," she said, the diamond strands glinting as she undulated in a slow, serpentine rhythm. "You just stand there nice and still and let me pump that cock."

Still gripping the bars, Oxy closed his eyes and let out a quavering moan, his head falling back. Galiana's internal muscles were amazingly strong, the most powerful Turek had ever experienced, and she had complete control over them. Fucking her was like sticking your dick in a milking machine.

"Not so bad *now*, are you, bad boy?" With one hand still gripping the iron bar, Galiana slid out the partial denture that mimicked lateral incisors to either side of her front teeth, whereupon her fangs—curved, sharply pointed, and longer than Turek's, because of her age—sprang down from their grooves in the roof of her mouth.

Setting the denture carefully on the windowsill, she yanked Oxy's head forward by the hair and glided her tongue up the side of his neck from collarbone to jaw.

Two

IT'S ABOUT TIME.

Turek stepped out from behind his blind as he removed his own two-tooth denture, which he tucked into a pocket of his lambskin blazer. His hollow fangs snapped down, sparking electric tingles that buzzed along the conduits in the roof of his mouth all the way to his cock, which grew half erect in anticipation.

Galiana tightened her legs around Oxy, giving Turek a feral smile. She moistened her lips with her tongue before positioning the tips of her fangs on the chosen "sweet spot" along Oxy's carotid artery.

And then she pierced it.

There came a moment of utter stillness while Oxy processed what was happening. He began to flail then, as they almost always did, unless they were well and truly hammered.

Dislocating her lower jaw, Galiana bit hard to keep his head still. She renewed her two-handed grip on the window bar so as to keep him upright with his erection, or what remained of it, trapped inside her despite his efforts to pry her off. His guttural moans of distress, muffled by her muting spell, sounded like nothing a human throat could produce.

She opened her long legs as Turek came up behind their quarry, wrapping them tight around both men. Oxy let out a grunt of distress when he felt Turek pressed up against him. Galiana just kept on feeding, her hips moving in slow, shallow thrusts.

Turek ran his fingers along the other side of Oxy's neck, feeling for the thrumming beneath the flesh. Having located the spot where the carotid was closest to the surface, he dipped his head and sank his fangs deep, through skin and muscle and arterial sheathing to the sweet, hot river of blood.

Oxy began thrashing in earnest when he realized that he was being fed upon by not one but two beings of a type he'd always considered to be monstrous figments of the imagination. Turek used a firm massage of his tongue to start the blood drawing up through his fangs. After a few seconds, he felt the rhythmic pulses in his palate that indicated a successful tapping of the artery.

Oxy's frenzied efforts to dislodge himself through punching and pushing wouldn't last much longer, Turek knew, but in the meantime, it was pretty tiresome. Grabbing the other man's hands, Turek curled them around the window bars and held them there while he suckled. Oxy still struggled, but that was all right. Turek rather liked to feel the agitation of his prey at the front end of a feeding. It only amped up the primal gratification.

The influx of blood—one surge with every beat of this human's heart—sent prickles up into Turek's brain and down his spine. Then came the euphoria, a vertiginous flood of it. *Yes, oh, yes, yes, yes . . .* It was this transcendent intoxication, not unlike that heart-stopping moment right before orgasm, that Turek lived for, hunted for, killed for.

The sensation quickened every nerve in his body, making his balls swell, his cock stiffen. The lust that accompanied a feeding was excruciatingly intense. Not all vampires experienced it, but Turek and Galiana's subrace, the Upír, almost always did—as did their prey, who tended to absorb this carnal blood-haze, entering a state of hypnotic arousal as their blood trickled away.

Turek rubbed himself against Oxy's tight, squirming ass, not caring that it belonged to a man. In the normal course of events, he preferred women. Ah, but when he was feeding, when he was hard and hungry and quivering, all he needed was a body, any body.

Oxy's writhing became less erratic and more rhythmic, the muscles of his ass clenching hard and slow as he matched Galiana's unhurried thrusts. Galiana growled in pleasure, doubtless because the cock inside her was growing thick and hard once again, filling up that voracious pussy. Oxy continued to grip the iron bars when Turek removed his hands.

Turek unzipped his jeans and freed his own erection, which curved toward his belly, tapering at the tip like the tusk of a boar. With his fangs still seated firmly in Oxy's neck, he withdrew the little plastic packet he'd tucked into his jeans pocket next to the stag-handled Sheffield switchblade that had been his constant urban companion for over a century and a half. He opened the packet and rolled on the super-lubricated condom. Galiana ridiculed him for using them with their male prey. *You want your blood-fucking to be smooth and fastidious, just like you, when a bit of nastiness and pain can add so much to the experience.*

Easy for her to say. When it came to pain, "Mistress G," as she was known in BDSM circles the world over, preferred to be on the dispensing end rather than the receiving.

Oxy hitched in a breath, his sphincter tightening reflexively when he felt the sheathed tip of Turek's cock against it. Turek grabbed Oxy's hips and snapped his own, breeching the little aperture with a grunt. Oxy let out a shuddery moan. Turek pushed again, driving in deep. One more thrust, and he was buried to the root.

Still shaking from the abrupt impalement, but lost in the blood-haze, Oxy began to thrust again, faster than before. It felt to Turek like a strong, greased fist gripping and pulling, the sensation enhanced by the rapture of fresh blood pumping through his body. Blood-fucking was always blissful, but especially so when he knew that he wouldn't have to cut it short, that he would get to feel a human's lifeblood draining slowly away, pulse after gradually diminishing pulse, as his pleasure spiraled up, up, up . . .

The lure of a death feed was dark, beastly, seductive. It was a penchant that Galiana didn't share. She would rather take just enough to satisfy her appetites and leave the human alive, if a bit groggy. It was safer, she insisted, and certainly less troublesome. And, too, she felt that fixating on killing during a feeding was akin to fixating on coming during sex, rather than on the exhilarating journey. Yes, Turek would reply, but if there were no orgasm to look forward to, how exhilarating would the journey really be?

When Galiana did consent to bleed their prey dry, it was usually as a sort of reward to Turek for having pleased her somehow—a way of throwing him a bone. From time to time, however—tonight, for instance—the impulse to "thin the flock," as she liked to call it, came from her.

Galiana Solsa, as Turek knew all too well, was not a woman to be fucked with. Oxy should never have spoken to her as he did, and he certainly should not have raised his hand to her. This was to have been a harmless little midnight snack, with this "bad boy" coming to around dawn on a bench in Washington Square Park. When Turek hunted alone and planned to leave the pigeon alive, he targeted prey that was already drunk or stoned, and therefore forgetful, and he made sure to do enough physical damage to the neck to disguise the fang marks. Such measures were unnecessary with Galiana, whose physiology had had three millennia to adapt to her vampiric needs. Her saliva not only encouraged speedy healing of the fang wounds, it induced a mild amnesia. Had Oxy not acted like such a dick, he would have awakened on that bench tomorrow woozy from blood loss, but with no evidence that he'd been fed upon.

But there would be no more sunrises for this "bad boy" after tonight. Already—it happened fast when he and Galiana shared a feed—Oxy's blood pressure was dropping, causing the flow of blood to grow weaker and slower. His skin was pallid; his heart raced. Yet Turek could tell, from his sharp panting and jackhammer thrusts, that he was riding that pre-orgasmic wave. So was Galiana, judging from her quivering legs and the way she bucked against Oxy as she gripped the iron bars, her jaw still closed tight around his neck.

Turek fucked and suckled, consuming this human's body as it squeezed and squeezed and squeezed his cock, the pleasure gathering in his veins, in his balls, slamming hard against the ass he was fucking, slamming, slamming...

Over the thundering in his ears—Oxy's heart, not his

own—Turek heard footsteps on the sidewalk as a small group passed the alley. Amid their chatter, he heard a name he hadn't heard in over two and a half centuries: "Ilutu-Lili."

He turned toward the entrance to the alley, his teeth tearing from Oxy's neck in a spray of blood.

"Ilooloo-what? What kind of name is that?" It was a slightly drunk male voice, unrecognizable to Turek. "You sound foreign. Where're you from?"

"I was born in the valley of the Euphrates River."

That voice. That throaty, velveteen, darkly seductive voice...

It's her. It's really her. It's Lili! Turek pulled out of Oxy, ripped off the condom, and tossed it onto the zip-cape.

"Tony?" Galiana had withdrawn her fangs from the ravaged neck of her prey to frown at Turek as he zipped up his jeans. "What's wrong, *marish*? Where are you—?"

"I'll meet you back at the apartment," he said as he turned and sprinted out of the alley and down the street.

They were standing at the corner of West Third, spotlit by a streetlamp as they waved away a cab that had started pulling over. There were four of them, two men and two women.

Turek ducked into a doorway, dragged in a breath, and peered out. One of the women, a delicate blonde with pixie-cut hair who looked to be in her mid-twenties, was rocking the schoolgirl thing: plaid skirt, knee socks, crested blazer over prim white blouse. And saddle shoes; they still sold those? Her only accessory was a pink dog collar attached to a matching pink leash, which was wrapped around the fist of a well-groomed banker type in a chalk-striped suit and tie—nice quality, Armani, or maybe Brioni.

The tall guy with the long blond pony tail was Elic, who lived at the French château where Turek had spent two weeks in bawdy revelry with Sir Francis Dashwood's Hellfire Club in the spring of 1749. Turek had always suspected that Elic was

some type of Follet; how many humans have it in them to pre-
vail over a vampire in a physical confrontation? The fact that
he was still alive and youthful after all these years confirmed
that suspicion. From the looks of him, especially his height, he
was almost certainly a member of one of the Nordic *álfr* subraces, probably two to four thousand years old. Those
Neolithic elves, the ones from Northern Europe, all stood well
over six feet.

Elic was all in black—jeans, boots, T-shirt, and zippered
hoodie.

A hoodie. They'd been out clubbing, from the looks of it—
probably one of the local fetish joints, given the dog collar—
and he'd worn a fucking hoodie. Faded, no less.

He was telling the other couple in slightly accented English
that he and Lili lived in France but kept a pied-à-terre here in
New York. Their friend Inigo used it frequently; they only
stayed there once or twice a year.

"Cities aren't my thing," Lili said.

Lili.

Goddess. Succubus. Witch. Whore. She'd been all of these
things—or rather, been regarded as all of these things—at
some point during her long existence, but tonight…

Ah, tonight she looked every inch the goddess, in ornate
golden earrings that tickled her shoulders and a dress of
aubergine velvet, her sheaf of sleek black hair spilling over one
shoulder all the way to her waist. Her only jewelry aside from
the earrings was something she had been wearing when he
first knew her in 1749: a circlet of hammered gold around her
left ankle, from which dangled a gold-rimmed disc of lapis
lazuli. She had quite possibly been wearing it for thousands of
years.

And her eyes… those drowsy-dark, mesmerizing eyes…
How many hours had Turek spent curled up on his pallet of

rotted straw in that rank little cell in Paris, picturing the profound relief in those eyes as they'd carted him away from
Château de la Grotte Cachée in chains? Elic had been watching
that day, too, his long arms curled around Lili as if to thumb
his nose at Turek for having lost her to him.

Like Turek, Lili had been visiting Grotte Cachée with Sir
Francis and his followers, whose orgies and black masses had
provided an outlet for the incessant lust that held all succubi
and incubi in its grip. But then she'd met Elic, and you would
have to have been deaf, dumb, and blind not to have seen how
besotted they were with each other. Turek had wondered if she
would remain behind with him when the Hellfires bid adieu
to Grotte Cachée and returned to England; it would appear
that she had.

He realized he wasn't breathing. Astounding, that she
should have such an effect on him after all these years.

As the cab disappeared down the street, Chalk-stripe said,
"Maybe we should have taken it."

"Our place is just a few blocks away, off St. Mark's in the
East Village," replied Elic, taking Lili's hand. "And it's such a
pleasant night."

"The pleasure has barely begun." Chalk-stripe stroked Lili's
hair, caressing her breast as he did so.

Lili glanced at Pixie-cut, who was staring fixedly at the
ground, then met Elic's gaze with a look of concern that pro-
voked a smirk from Turek. He would never understand the
sentimental concern that some Follets harbored for human-
folk; they were livestock, not pets.

"Are you cool with this, Nicky?" Elic asked.

"She's fine with it," Chalk-stripe said as he slid an arm
around Lili's waist.

"I asked *her*," Elic said.

"She defers to me in everything."

"But I don't." Lifting Nicky's chin, Elic said, "Do you want to do this? No, don't look at Doug. Do you?"

Lowering her gaze, she said, very softly but with a sincerity that sounded real, "Yes, sir."

"This is the first time I've shared her," Doug said, "but she's known to expect it. And trust me, she loves nothing better than to please her master. Here." He handed the leash to Elic. "See how it feels in your hand. You may find you like it."

They continued on, turning right at West Fourth. Turek followed them, keeping to the shadows as they strolled past Washington Square, then north on Broadway and east on Astor Place toward the East Village.

Forty years.

He'd spent forty long, dismal, famished years in that god-damned prison, forty years that were lost to him, and which he would never get back. And all because of Lili. He'd revered her as the archetype of her race, begged her to let him turn her into what he was so that she could become his queen, his eternal companion. Just as humans fed on the lower beasts, he'd told her, so vampires fed on humans. He'd explained that it was the natural order, the way of the world, yet she couldn't be swayed. Not only had she declined to "spend eternity as a murderous little maggot like you," she had condemned him to a hell on earth deep in the bowels of the Bastille, subsisting on the blood of rats as he grew steadily more desiccated ... and half mad in the bargain.

To this day, every time Turek heard a casual reference to "Bastille Day," or "the storming of the Bastille," it made his stomach clutch. To his fellow prisoners, always few in number, most of them depraved aristocrats locked up at the request of their own families, life in the formidable old fortress wasn't half bad. It was certainly preferable to the alternative of a public jail or asylum. They had spacious accommodations, most

of them, plus personal servants, cooks, barbers, physicians…
Their every need was attended to.

Not so Turek, who was locked up indefinitely on a *lettre de cachet,* which meant that no formal charges need ever be filed. He was meant to simply disappear from the face of the earth. They didn't even enter his name on the prison rolls—not even the assumed name under which they'd incarcerated him: the Comte de Lorges. As far as his guards knew, he was a murderous madman who'd raped, killed, and eaten three of his own children, plus two nieces and a nephew—or was it two nephews and a niece? These monstrous if fictitious crimes had earned him a Hannibal-worthy cell deep in the labyrinthine undercroft of the Bastille.

Turek was permitted to move freely about his little crypt except when it was time to sweep out and replace the straw, at which point half a dozen burly guards armed with torches— for they'd been told of the lunatic count's aversion to fire— would lock him into manacles and leg irons embedded in the walls of weeping rock. There were no windows in his cell, just an iron door with a barred opening and a slot through which his food was pushed by the few guards who knew of his existence, and who were forbidden to speak to him or to speak to others about him.

The food wasn't bad—they fed Turek what they fed the other prisoners—but it wasn't enough to sustain him. Ordinary food is low-grade fuel to an Upír. It will keep his bodily functions slogging along, but without regular infusions of high test—without rich human blood—he will grow steadily more emaciated and dehydrated, as indeed Turek did.

By July 14, 1789, when the Bastille was besieged by a horde of rabid revolutionaries looking for weapons, Turek was gaunt and frail, with a ragged beard down to his waist and a great shock of long, strawlike hair. Even in his little subterranean wormhole, he could hear the muffled drone of a huge, excited crowd surrounding the prison. He heard the pounding of battering rams and bursts of gunfire, sometimes followed by shrieks and groans.

Isolated as he was from the world at large, he had no idea at the time who these attackers were, only that, for some unfathomable reason, they seemed to want *in*. After several hours of this assault, there came a triumphant roar and the thunder of hundreds of feet overhead as the attackers swarmed into the building. He heard people yelling about freeing the prisoners and realized he had an opportunity to escape from that stinking hole if only he could make his presence known. Standing at his door, he screamed through the little barred window until, at long last, a man and a woman appeared in the torchlit gloom of the antechamber beyond his cell.

The woman, thick-boned and with a great froth of red hair, carried a bloody ax and a ring of keys; her cohort, a large knife. He was berating her for having killed one of their fellow *vainqueurs* for those keys just so that she might have the glory of finding the mammoth cache of gunpowder, a dozen tons or more, rumored to be secreted somewhere within those thick stone walls. He called her a murderess who would get her comeuppance when he revealed what she had done. She called him a sniveling, traitorous coward.

The man barred Turek's cell door with his body when she went to unlock it. "This one's name isn't on the list. We don't know who he is or what he's done."

"I made myself the enemy of an important person," Turek said in a voice rusty from disuse and all that screaming. It was the truth, if only a minuscule portion of it. "They don't want anyone to know about me."

"You see?" the woman told her companion. "We'll be heroes if we free him. He's unjustly imprisoned, a martyr."

"Or a very great villain who is also a great liar. You're mad to want to unlock that door. You're mad to have killed Guillaume. I'm going to report you to the Assembly, and then we shall see how heroic you are."

"Pascal," she said softly, reaching out to stroke his cheek. "Put down that knife, *mon chéri*. You wouldn't use that on me, would you? You wouldn't hurt a woman."

He hesitated, then lowered his knife and started to say something.

She stepped back and swung her ax, catching it in his neck. He fell, twitching and kicking, but not a sound issued from him. She kicked him out of the way, unlocked the door, and swung it open.

She said, "You're a free man, comrade. How long have they kept you here?"

"Forty years."

"*Mon dieu!* You haven't seen the sun in forty years?"

"And glad of it. It's not the sun I've been craving."

She gave him a puzzled look.

Turek grabbed her head and slammed it against the wall just hard enough to knock her out without cracking her skull. He managed to get her wrists locked into the manacles hanging from the wall over her head, thus lifting her off her feet. She started screaming as she came to and realized what was happening to her, so he gagged her with a strip of blanket before he began to feed.

She struggled at first, of course, especially when he shoved her skirts up and rammed himself into her, but then the blood-haze overtook her, and she fucked him with wanton gusto. What sheer heaven it was to relieve four decades of pent-up hunger and lust as he drained her dry.

Thus rejuvenated, Turek used Pascal's knife to hack off his hair and beard, stole the murdered man's *sans-culotte* revolutionary garb—pantaloons, short jacket, clogs, and red "cap of liberty"—and disappeared among the howling throng.

The Anton Turek who'd been "liberated" from that hell-hole was not quite the same Anton Turek who'd been locked up there four decades before. The lingering remnants of civilized humanity that he'd retained following his vampiric conversion in 1348 had withered in the face of his consuming fury.

He had thought about Lili ceaselessly during that interminable captivity, her taunts echoing in his skull, stoking his rage. *You're just some vile little bloodsucking insect, a mosquito with delusions of magnificence... a bedbug, scuttling about in the dark, antennae twitching at the scent of blood...*

He'd spent hundreds of hours, thousands, imagining how he would end that bitch's existence if he ever crossed paths with her again. With most Follets, the only sure method of execution was thorough combustion, with the flesh not just charred but roasted past the point of regeneration. Almost all vampires were susceptible not only to fire but to the ultraviolet light emitted by the sun. Some vampire subraces had other weaknesses, as well. There were bloodsuckers, for example, who could be killed by decapitation, by driving a stake through their hearts, or by other, more esoteric means. Turek and Galiana were more fortunate; they could be done in only by fire or lengthy exposure to sunlight.

Lili's only Achilles' heel, as far as Turek knew, was fire. He had envisioned a hundred different scenarios in which she would burn to death slowly, writhing in well-deserved agony.

For some time after his release from the Bastille, he'd tried to locate Château de la Grotte Cachée in order to exact his revenge on her, but it was remarkably secluded for a castle of that size, tucked deep into a valley in the volcanic highlands of Auvergne. Despite his previous visit, he'd found himself utterly at a loss when confronted with the tangle of unmarked roads that crisscrossed the densely forested region—which was particularly irksome, as he'd always prided himself on his sense of direction. The local inhabitants were useless. Time and again, he heard the same refrain, accompanied by a Gallic shrug. *Un château? Non, je suis désolé, monsieur. Je ne sais pas un château.*

After an exhaustive and perplexing search—it was as if Grotte Cachée had been sucked into the very earth—he'd finally come to accept that he would never see Lili again, never make her pay for what she'd done to him.

And now, here she was at last, all these many years later, quite literally leading him right to her doorstep. There were no thick stone walls to hide behind here, no Swiss Guards to do her bidding. There was Elic, who had proven a formidable enemy in the past, preternaturally strong and determined to protect Lili at all costs, but if Turek was clever, he could think of some way to take that bastard out.

And then, at long last, Ilutu-Lili would be his to do with as he pleased. He would torment her as Galiana tormented her pigeons. He would make her suffer. He would revel in her screams of anguish.

And he would smile as the flames reduced her, after thousands of years of existence, into cold, gray bone and ash.

Three

"YOU GOTTA BE KIDDING," Doug said when Elic and Lili paused before a gray-painted, age-scoured wooden door, sans doorknob, which was squeezed ignominiously between a St. Mark's Place brownstone and a brick apartment building with a record store on the ground floor. "*This* is your place?"

As Turek watched from behind a tree across the street, grateful for the nearly full moon and cloudless sky, Elic pressed his thumb to a metal plate on the door jamb. Lili produced a remote control from her clutch purse and pushed a series of buttons, causing a little green light on the top edge of the door to wink.

"Holy shit," Doug said as the door popped open an inch, painting a ribbon of light onto the sidewalk. "What is this, like your secret spy lair or something?"

"It's Penumbra Court, a private residential quarter," Elic said as he swung the door open, gesturing them through. It was a heavy steel door; the gray-painted wood was just a façade.

Turek squinted, trying to see beyond the doorway, but all he could make out was a weathered old brick wall and cobblestone paving. At a casual glance, the door would appear to provide access to the apartment building housing the record store. Looking up to the roofline, however, he saw a tangle of razor wire about five feet wide where the roof above the door should have been.

The door clicked shut. Turek sprinted across the street, scanning the area to make sure he was alone. After hauling himself up by the pipe frame supporting the record store's awning, he clambered swiftly up the building's four-story fire escape and onto the roof.

Galiana probably could have leapt the whole five stories from a standing start. With a backflip and a silent ten-point dismount thrown in for good measure. Turek had seen her bound along rooftops like a Cirque du Soleil acrobat; once, she leapt from one roof to another across the Champs-Élysées. She called that kind of shit her "wireless wire fu," like in those cheesy kung fu movies she couldn't get enough of. Turek called it obnoxious hot-dogging.

Not to her face, of course.

From above, Turek could see that the brownstone next door and the apartment building on which he stood were separated by an alleyway, to which access was gained by the knobless gray door with the state-of-the-art locks. A series of motion sensor lights turned on one by one as Elic guided the others down the narrow passage, leading Nicky by her leash as he dug a key ring out of his jeans pocket.

The alley opened into a courtyard so heavily treed that

Turek could barely make out the three-story town houses huddled around it. Tucked within the embrace of the surrounding buildings—all of them, including that on which Turek stood, rimmed in razor wire with no windows overlooking the court—the little cluster of houses would be indiscernible from either St. Mark's Place to the south or East Ninth Street to the north.

Turek could see little of the houses aside from four gabled, slate-shingled mansard roofs, their flat surfaces carpeted with roof gardens of juniper, boxwoods, and holly. All of the plantings were conifers, like the trees in the courtyard, most of the latter towering over the roofs. Shrouded by evergreens, Penumbra Court would look like any other East Village backyard on one of those satellite maps, even in the dead of winter.

"Dave will go apeshit when I tell him about this place," Doug told Nicky.

"Dave?" Elic said.

"My buddy writes this blog about the little hidden remnants of old New York that people walk right by and don't even notice. You won't mind if I bring him here and let him take some pictures."

"You won't remember where this is," said Lili, exchanging a look with Elic as they paused at the end of the alley.

"Sure I will."

"I don't think so." Elic touched Doug's forehead, then Nicky's.

They both blinked.

Nicky frowned at Doug. "What did you say?"

"What?"

"You said something."

"No, I didn't. And the next time you speak out of turn, or fail to address me as 'Master,' you get five hours gagged and bound in the fucking corner."

Ah, Turek thought. So his failure to locate the château all those years ago wasn't entirely due to having inexplicably lost his sense of direction, nor had it been swallowed up into the valley. It would seem that Elic's bag of tricks included the ability to impose selective amnesia upon those who may have learned just a bit too much for comfort.

The foliage muffled the group's conversation as they disappeared into it. Turek had to strain to hear Elic say "That's our house, the one with the red door. It was the first one put up here in the early eighteen forties. The others were built later, for friends."

"Who lives in them now?" Doug asked.

"Individuals who value their privacy, as we do. *Entrez vous.*"

A door creaked open, and a few seconds later, Turek heard it close. Singling out the closest of the tall spruces, he backed away from the edge of the building, mentally calculating distance, speed, and trajectory. He took a running leap, feeling a snag in his right jeans leg as he *almost* cleared the razor wire.

Gottverdammt. Turek grabbed a branch and held on, grimacing as a barrage of spruce needles scourged his face and hands. His right loafer slipped off and thunk-thunk-thunked to the ground as he scrambled for a foothold. The shoes were no doubt scratched beyond recognition. Ditto the jacket; the black silk scarf he'd worn insouciantly draped over it had flown off in midleap and fluttered to the ground.

Turek paused for a moment, watching and listening, but his blundering foray into this exclusive little enclave had evidently gone unnoticed. Of course, it was late at night. Even if the other residents of Penumbra Court were Follets, as Turek suspected, they were probably fast asleep. To his knowledge, it was only the Vampire race that was primarily nocturnal—and even among their ranks, there were those, like Turek and

Galiana, who could go about during the day with minimal discomfort if they were properly outfitted, especially if it was cloudy or they could keep to the shade.

Vampires had varying tolerances to ultraviolet light on their skin and eyes. With some, it was like what you see in movies, with the poor doomed bloodsucker basically frying to a crisp in short order. Thankfully, the Upír, while still vulnerable to direct sunlight, and therefore repulsed by it, experienced a less dramatic physiological reaction. Most of them had to be exposed to it with no protection for at least five minutes before their skin began to blister. With prolonged exposure—each individual's UV vulnerability varied—came a progressive, systemic sun poisoning known as solar cremation. As with exposure to fire, once the body was damaged past a certain point, recovery was impossible.

For this reason, in the past, the Upír had traditionally slept between sunrise and sundown and done their prowling at night. However, recent technological advances enabled them to mingle with humans during daylight hours with little risk to their health—specifically, high-SPF sunscreen and either good-quality sunglasses or glasses with photochromic lenses, the kind that react to UV rays by turning dark. Turek, who favored the latter, owned upward of fifty pairs of designer frames fitted with nonprescription Transitions lenses; he never left the house, even at night, without a pair tucked away somewhere on his person.

He climbed down, located and replaced his scarf, shoved his foot back in the loafer, dusted off the needles, and fingercombed his hair so that the long, layered front fringe—he hated the word "bangs" in relation to men's hair—was swept off to the side, where it belonged, and not hanging in his eyes.

Dark figures shifted in a pair of ground-floor windows of the house with the red door. By their glow, Turek could see that the courtyard was actually a little deep-shade garden, with vines and flowers growing around the base of each tree and iron benches on the cobblestone paths winding this way and that. The house itself, like the other three, was the type of bourgeois brick town house that had been all the rage in Paris in the mid-nineteenth century, more majestic in design than in size, although it appeared to be the largest of the four.

Turek crept closer to the house, crouching behind a rhodo-dendron bush between the two windows, which were hung with semisheer yellow curtains that afforded a soft-focus view of the room and its occupants. Through the right-hand win-dow he saw a pair of tall bookcases bracketing a fireplace with a painting over it; through the left, more bookcases and a cozy little arrangement of Victorian furniture—couch, coffee table, and a couple of chairs, all upholstered in dark green leather.

Lili and the other couple were in that area of the room, she sorting through bottles at a liquor cabinet as Doug settled into one of the chairs, loosening his tie while he surveyed the room. He'd taken the pink leash back from Elic, and he tugged Nicky down onto the floor at his feet. She sat with her legs curled under her, hands in her lap.

Turek ducked as Elic whipped open the curtains over the window he was looking through, flipped the lock, and tugged it open.

"Good idea," Lili said. "It *is* a little stuffy in here. I hope no one minds, but I'm suffocating in this velvet." She slid down the side zipper of her dress, pulled it over her head, and tossed it over the back of a chair.

"Single malt?" she asked Doug.

He nodded, gaping as she poured a couple of fingers of Cragganmore into a glass.

Turek gaped, too. Lili's undergarments, all black, consisted of a g-string beneath a tube of stretch lace that hugged her like skin from the strapless push-up cups to the hip-length hem, to which sheer black stockings were attached by means of satin garters. With those fuck-me eyes, the ornate gold earrings, and the sex-kitten heels, she looked about fifty times hotter than the hottest Victoria's Secret model Turek had ever seen.

She handed the glass of scotch to Doug, who stroked her hip as he took it, his boner stretching the fly of those elegant trousers.

Elic opened the other window and paused, frowning out into the night. Turek heard him take a breath in through his nose. "Smells like someone spilled about a gallon of Bijan for Men out there somewhere," he said.

A gallon? Turek was wearing Bijan, all right, but just a few splashes applied hours ago, when he was dressing to go out. Its scent had long since faded.

Some Follets had heightened senses. Lili's eyesight, for example, was extraordinary. It would appear that Elic, like Galiana, had the nose of a bloodhound.

"And for you, Nicky?" Lili asked, handing Elic a glass of red wine as he took a seat on the couch.

"She'll have milk, if you've got it," Doug said.

Lili held Nicky's gaze until Nicky met her eyes and nodded.

"I'll get it," Elic said, pushing himself up from the couch.

Waving him back down, she said, "I'm already up."

Turek shifted his gaze to the right-hand window to keep her in his sights as she crossed to a door on the other side of the room. She had a distinctive walk, languid and naturally sensual, about a thousand times more alluring than Mistress G's brassy streetwalker strut.

As she passed the fireplace, Turek's gaze was arrested by the painting hanging over it, a portrait of a raven-haired beauty lounging on a couch—the same one on which Elic now sat, if Turek wasn't mistaken, but upholstered in golden velvet. The styling of her off-the-shoulder maroon gown dated the painting to the 1880s or '90s. It was a very accomplished work, the artfully deft brushstrokes shimmering with light. Turek had no trouble identifying the artist as John Singer Sargent, several of whose works hung in Galiana's private collection.

It was an exquisite painting, but what mesmerized Turek wasn't the quality of its execution but its subject: Lili. Sargent had captured her perfectly—the luster of her skin, the graceful contours of her shoulders and arms, those lush, slightly parted lips curved in a secret smile... But most of all, the eyes, dark, exotic, dreamily seductive. They held Turek's gaze until Lili returned with a tumbler full of milk.

"What do you say?" Doug asked Nicky as she accepted the glass from Lili.

"Thank you, ma'am." Nicky sat looking at the milk until Doug gave her permission to drink.

"I can't recall seeing you two at Tethers before," Doug said as Lili sat next to Elic on the couch.

So that was where Elic and Lili had gone shopping for tonight's playmates. Tethers was a bondage and discipline club on West Houston that attracted a mixed clientele, from posers to longtime devotees of "the lifestyle." Like most alternative sex clubs, Tethers was the site of regular get-togethers, some of them private, anything-goes orgies and others open to the public, at which penetrative sex was verboten.

Some "clubs" were just loose affiliations of fetishists or BDSM types who met at various venues, including each other's homes. Turek and Galiana belonged to a whole slew of them, their members being particularly easy to "harvest," as Galiana referred to it. They were always up for anything: *"Okay, sure, you can bite my neck, but would you mind tying me up with clothesline first and putting clothespins on my nipples?"* And if they woke up in a strange place with bleary memories of having been immobilized and ravaged, well, that was all part and parcel of the lifestyle, was it not? Aficionados of blood fetishism were especially suited to their purposes, for obvious reasons.

"It was our first time," Lili told Doug.

"Our first time at Tethers," Elic said. "We've been to similar events in other clubs. There are some good ones in Paris and Amsterdam, and of course, Bangkok."

"Bangkok?" Doug said. "Cool. But I'm surprised you haven't been to Tethers before, if you're into that scene."

Elic shrugged. "Like I said, we only make it to New York a couple of times a year, at most."

"Tethers's theme nights are the best," said Doug, absently stroking Nicky's hair as she drank her milk. "Masters and Slaves Night is always the first Thursday of the month. We never miss it. And I don't know what you folks are into, but Tethers pretty much covers all the bases. They have Rope Bondage Night, Boot Night, Whip Night, Leather Night, Doctor and Nurse Night . . . That's a good one. I like to dress Nicky up as a nurse and make her give people enemas. She hates it, but she does it with a smile on her face, 'cause all she wants in life is to please me. Isn't that right, Nick?"

"Yes, master."

Elic said, "So, um, how long have you two been, er . . . ?"

"I've owned Nicky for almost six months," Doug said. "She'd solicited online for a commanding, powerful master who could train the willfulness out of her. We met at a coffee shop. She walks up to the booth where I'm sitting and sticks out her hand and says, 'Hi, I'm Barb. You must be Doug.'"

"Barb?" Elic said.

"I changed her name when I took ownership of her," Doug said. "I told her to sit down next to me and put that hand under her skirt and get busy. I told her she had one minute to

186 · Louisa Burton

make herself come, and if she didn't, then I was going to get up and leave, and that would be that. She looked at me like I was crazy. I told her that, as her master, I would demand complete control over her sexual responses. If I ordered her to refrain from orgasm, no matter what the circumstances, she would need to refrain. If I ordered her to come, she'd have to come, and quickly."

"And these were the first words out of your mouth when you met her?" Elic asked as he raised his wineglass to his mouth. "Smooth."

"It wasn't a date," Doug said. "She wasn't looking for a boyfriend, she was looking for a master, and a strong one."

"She didn't balk?" Lili asked.

"No, she did. She said, 'I can't. This place is packed.' I looked at my watch and said, 'You've got fifty-two seconds.' She wasted a couple more seconds chewing that over while she looked around, and then she sat down and slipped that hand up under her skirt and into her panties and started diddling away. Wasn't long before she was quivering and turning red in the face. Took her just forty-one seconds."

"That's pretty quick," Lili said, "especially for a woman."

"How do you know she really came, and didn't just fake it?" Elic asked.

"I shoved a finger up inside her so I'd feel the spasms. It was real, all right, but I did help her along a little. I leaned in close and whispered the things I was going to do to her after we finished our coffee and I took her back to my place. I told her she needed to be disciplined for having been slow to obey me. I said I was going to make her strip and shave her own head with the electric clippers I use on my dog—she had real long hair at the time. Then I was going to lay her facedown on a rubber sheet in the middle of my living room floor, handcuff her wrists to her ankles, and shove an inflatable cock gag in her mouth, and she'd have to stay like that as long as I felt like keeping her that way. Every half hour, I'd rub her cunt and fuck her with a big double dildo till she was squirming and right on the edge, but I wouldn't let her come. Instead, I'd paddle her till her ass was crimson and tears were streaming down her cheeks. And if that got me hot, I might jerk off onto her face, but she wouldn't get any cock, any real cock, till I felt like she'd had enough. Then I'd get behind her and lift her hips and tease her cunt with my cock till she was wet and writhing, and then I'd take the gag out and ask her if she was ready to apologize. If she seemed sincerely sorry, and promised to be a good girl and cooperate with her training, I'd slam it to her, fuck her like a pile driver. I'd make her come so many times, she'd be hoarse from screaming. And then I'd bathe her and leash her and let her sleep at the foot of my bed. And that's just how it went down, and she's been with me ever since. Isn't that right, Nicky?"

"Yes, master."

"She comes on command, too," he added proudly. "In as little as thirty seconds. Show them, Nick."

Nicky turned to look at him, wide-eyed, as he set his glass down and stood.

"On your feet, and lose the skirt and panties," he said, tugging on the leash to force her up off the floor.

Standing with her hands fisted in her plaid skirt, she glanced at Lili and Elic before lowering her gaze.

Elic said, "She doesn't have to—"

"No, I'd like to see it." Lili gave him a knowing little smile as she slid her gaze back to Nicky. The little blonde's eyes glittered just a bit too brightly as she studied the carpet, her lower lip caught between her teeth.

Elic smiled.

So did Turek. It was that hackneyed gesture of reluctance,

the biting of the lip, that was most telling. Their little master-slave melodrama had an author, and although Doug no doubt saw himself in that "commanding and powerful" role, it would appear that Nicky maintained a fair amount of control over the script.

"*Do it*," Doug demanded, slapping her face for emphasis.

She made a show of raising the skirt up just a bit while casting a pleading look in his direction. The pink-stained cheeks were a nice touch, Turek thought.

"Willful little slut." Doug scanned the room. "Do you folks have, like a stool, or an ottoman, or . . . ?" His gaze lit on something outside of Turek's field of vision. "Can I use that?" he asked, pointing.

"Be our guest," replied Elic, fully with the program now.

Dragging Nicky with him by her leash, Doug stalked over to where Turek couldn't see him for a moment, returning with one of those squat, old-fashioned library step stools. Crafted of dark, varnished wood, it was comprised of three well-worn treads connected by two roughly triangular side pieces carved to look like curled-up griffins. Like the rest of the furniture here, it was probably as old as the house itself, if not older.

On Doug's instructions, Nicky knelt on the bottom tread and bent over the top one, gripping the griffins' claw feet for support. Dropping the leash, Doug pressed down on the nape of her neck with his handsomely shod foot, her bottom tilting up as her head dipped almost to the floor.

He took off his jacket and rolled up his sleeves, taking his time about it. "Skirt up, panties down to your knees," he said as he unbuckled his belt.

"Nice belt," Lili said.

It *was* nice, in a vintage-but-not-too-vintage way; looked to be some kind of snakeskin.

Doug thanked her, saying "I picked it up on a business trip

to India a couple of years ago. Can't get anything like it here. The leather is king cobra."

"Isn't that on the endangered list?" Elic asked.

"I think so," Doug said as he folded the belt in half. "Ten strokes, Nicky, and count each one. You know the drill."

Four

ICKY FLIPPED THE LITTLE plaid skirt up, revealing white cotton briefs—of course—which she hesitantly lowered. The slowness with which she pushed them down, revealing her upthrust, deliciously pale little ass inch by inch, only amped up the erotic voltage of the partial striptease. Turek's position afforded him a slightly skewed side view, so that he could just make out the blonde's clean-waxed pussy lips at the juncture of her half-parted thighs.

Elic shifted slightly, as if angling for a better view. Lili smiled and rested her hand on the crotch of his black jeans. Turek felt an absurd little sting of jealousy, like a hot wire burrowing inside him, searing a path from his heart to his stomach. He imagined it was his cock she was stroking, his body she was curled up against . . . her breasts, perfumed with jasmine, pressing heavily against his arm . . . her silken hair brushing his face as she turned to smile into his eyes . . .

Dummkopf. He'd had his chance to possess her, to turn her, and he'd blown it. His desperate longing for her had made him foolish, impatient. How could he have expected her to yield to him so quickly, especially given her loathing for him, her disgust with his hunger for human blood? It was only natural for her to feel that way; nonbloodsuckers almost always did. Had he himself not felt sick to his stomach when Galiana first revealed to him what she was? He'd been so appalled that he didn't even believe her at first.

Turek had been a virgin when she'd first seduced him in January of 1348, initiating a sexual liaison of dark, feral intensity. She was mercurial, brilliant, breathtaking. He was the idealistic nineteen-year-old bastard son of a Bohemian baron who'd chosen medical studies at the University of Bologna over the priesthood, and who used to wonder what a magnificent creature like Galiana Solsa could possibly see in him.

He had been consumed by her, utterly ensnared, until the night he'd found her writhing atop that street cleaner in the alley behind the boardinghouse in which he lived, her face buried in his neck, her mouth dripping blood. He'd fled upstairs to his rented room, and she followed him there, holding his head while he knelt in the rushes, vomiting into his chamber pot.

She told him that she'd been born more than a thousand years before the birth of Christ in Tarchna, now known as Tarquinia, a coastal city northwest of Rome. A priest had converted her into a bloodsucker with the promise that she would live forever as a lasa, which was a type of goddess. Instead, she became feared and loathed as a demoness of death, a role she grew to embrace. Parents would tell their children that if they didn't behave, the dreaded Thanchvil—depicted in a mural in a still-standing Etruscan necropolis with swirling black hair and hawklike wings, the former fairly accurate and the latter somewhat less so—would snatch them at night and suck all the blood from their insubordinate little bodies. She'd been called by many names, she told him. To Italians, she was known as a striga, but in fact, the correct term for her vampiric subrace was Upír.

As an Upír, she told him, she enjoyed all the sensual pleasures in which humans indulged, such as bedsport, food, and wine, but without the "gloomy inevitability" of death hanging over her head. And there was no sensual indulgence available to humans that equaled or even approached the thrill of feasting on blood.

Turek didn't believe her; it was very like her to make up something so outlandish, just to get a rise out of him. He dismissed her claim even after she revealed her fangs.

"They're just rotten teeth," he told her, desperately rationalizing. "They've rotted into pointed stumps."

"A bit long and sharp to be 'stumps,' are they not, Anton?" She showed him how they retracted when not in use, folding back into grooves in the roof of her mouth like the erectile fangs of certain species of vipers, the gaps to be concealed by false teeth crafted from mother-of-pearl secured to gold bridgework.

Yet still he denied the truth of what she claimed to be. The human mind, as he had since come to realize, was pathetically weak and conservative, clinging to its comfortably orthodox notions about what was real and possible long after logic should have swayed it.

Galiana tried to convince him to become what she was by drinking her blood after she had drunk his. It had to be voluntary, she told him; he had to know what he was getting into and to want it for the conversion to take place. He refused as calmly as he could while trying to maneuver her out the door. She knew he thought she was mad; she laughed at his small-mindedness, his all-too-human timidity. Eventually she did leave, telling him she would give him time to think about it.

There was little to think about. She *was* mad. He had fallen in love—for so he'd interpreted her sexual power over him—with a lunatic. He needed to figure out how to break off their affair without enraging her. He'd seen how she abused her servants for even the smallest infractions—whippings, stonings, and even brandings by her own hand, with the subject of her wrath chained hand and foot. When he'd asked her if such punishments were really necessary, she had laughed and called him a little girl. Once he had arrived at her villa outside the city walls to find the bloodied corpse of a young man being dragged away for burial in the woods. She told Turek there had been an accident involving a scythe. Not wanting to know the truth, he had never questioned her about the incident, nor about the whispers on so many lips about a former lover of Galiana's who had simply vanished one day after he was seen boating with another woman.

After ruminating on it for a couple of weeks, he arranged to meet her in the Piazza di Maggiore on market day, reasoning—or hoping—that the presence of so many witnesses would keep her fury in check when he cut her loose.

If only.

"*Bastardo! Cane bastardo!*" she'd screamed, grabbing a clay flagon of wine from a merchant's table and hurling it at his head. He ducked, cringing as it exploded against the horse trough behind him. Two goats tied to the trough bleated and scrabbled about in terror.

"Where in Hades does a spineless mongrel like you get the

stones to cast me off?" she demanded. "I'm Galiana Solsa, not some whore you fuck and then toss into the street for the pigs to finish off."

A matron in a veil and wimple thrust a coin at the greengrocer for the basket of oranges in her hand and herded her three young children swiftly out of earshot. Others stood and stared openly. A butcher said something to his customer in a snickering whisper as he wrapped a coil of sausages in oiled linen.

Oblivious to their audience—or, more likely, reveling in the attention because she saw how embarrassed it was making Turek—Galiana said, "It's that fat little *porca puttana* with the mole isn't it? That Clara. I see how you two look at each other. The coy little smiles, the way she fans those long black eyelashes."

Clara was his landlady, a plumply pretty—*not* fat—little widow with a Cindy Crawford beauty mark above her mouth that Turek wasn't sure how he felt about.

"Are you fucking her yet?" Galiana asked.

"No! Christ, Galiana."

"Not yet, eh? When, then? After you've gotten rid of me? I've been watching you. I've seen how she runs outside to greet you when you come home from your saintly efforts among the walking dead. And the little baskets of food she sends you away with in the morning...One would think she's your wife. It's what she wants, you know. She's found herself a nice young wealthy physician, and now she wants to trap him into marriage. She's no downy little chick, you know. She's at least ten years older than you."

As was Galiana herself, a fact that Turek knew better than to point out.

She was right about Clara, of course. There was a slightly

conniving quality to her attentions—the desperate, incessant flirtatiousness and awkward attempts at seduction. Part of him wondered if she only wanted to bed him in the hope of becoming pregnant, or being able to feign pregnancy, in order to ensnare him into matrimony. Regardless of what her motives may or may not have been, Turek found her genuinely desirable, possibly because she was Galiana's polar opposite, a chirpy, undemanding squab to Galiana's ravenous bird of prey.

"Go settle between the stout little legs of your precious Clara," Galiana told him. "Bind yourself in wedlock and spend the rest of your short, dismal human existence filled with misery and regret. It's what you deserve, what you've chosen over my gift of immortality. You spat on that offer. Now I spit on you."

This she did, before turning and stalking away, her gold-brocaded, sable-lined mantle billowing behind her. Turek wiped his cheek with the back of his hand as the onlookers guffawed.

Partly to avoid a precipitous romance with Clara and partly because of the altruism that had driven him to medicine in the first place, Turek found himself spending more and more time tending to victims of the Great Plague, which overtook Bologna in June of that year after having spent the preceding months crawling northward from the trading port of Messina in Sicily. It was grueling work, not just physically but emotionally. Most victims of that terrible pestilence, no matter what he did for them, succumbed after a mere day or two of fever, vomiting, and diarrhea, with blood oozing from every orifice and their hands, feet, and noses black from gangrene.

During this time, he prayed constantly, not just for his patients but for himself, so that he might be spared the pestilence that had struck them down. In his simple faith and naïveté, he actually believed this would do some good—until the morning he awoke raging with fever, his lungs seizing up, fingers and toes discolored, lymph nodes swollen to the size of eggs.

The disease progressed swiftly. Within an hour, he could barely move, and disorientation was setting in. By that time tomorrow, he would likely be dead. He was all alone in the house, the other boarders having either fled Bologna or died, and Clara having gone to stay with her sister's family in the country, where she felt safer from contamination.

The blood trickling from his mouth reminded him of Galiana as she'd looked after drinking blood from the throat of the street cleaner.

He tossed a silver denaro down to a boy on the street and asked him to fetch Galiana Solsa from her villa. "Tell her I'm dying and that I'm sorry for everything, but that I need her to come to me as soon as possible. She'll know why."

She did come, only to laugh like hell when he begged her to turn him into what she was. "Desperation has made a believer of you, eh, Anton?" she asked as she poured herself a glass of wine.

He didn't know what he believed, except that he didn't want to end his days being hurled into a burial pit with hundreds of other reeking corpses. He knew all too well how impotent the medical profession had proven itself in dealing with this hellish contagion. Galiana was his only hope.

She taunted him as he lay curled up on his sweat-soaked straw mattress, shaking, weeping, pleading... "I'll do anything you ask of me, give you anything you want..."

"What do you have that I could possibly want, you pathetic *pezzo di merda*? I have wealth, beauty, immortality..."

"For Christ's sake," he groaned. "Why did you come, then?"

She chuckled as she sipped her wine. "If you had the opportunity to watch someone you despise bleed to death from the inside, his eyes filled with terror, would you not take it?"

"Christ. No."

"No?" With a nonchalant shrug, she said, "Then perhaps it is just as well you die now. You wouldn't make much of a bloodsucker with that attitude."

She mocked and tormented him through the night as he grew steadily weaker and more insensate. She said she'd been spending much of her leisure time these past few months planning his murder, amusing herself by concocting scenarios that would maximize his suffering. It wasn't just an idle fancy, she told him. She had fully intended to put him to death in as gruesome and painful a manner as possible. "It would appear that fate has taken the burden of dispatching you out of my hands."

At one point, she removed her little jeweled dagger from its sheath on her girdle and told him that when he died, or sooner if she grew tired of waiting, she was going to cut off his *cacchio* and have her cook fry it up for her like a sausage.

A while later, complaining of hunger, she knelt at the side of Turek's bed, opened his linen drawers, and withdrew the organ in question. Laughing at his consternation—"Just a little sip, Anton, something to tease my palate, eh?"—she removed her false teeth, pulled back his foreskin, and pierced the glans very shallowly and delicately. He felt a sharp sting, then the warm pressure of her lips closing around him and the rhythmic caress of her tongue as she encouraged the flow of blood. It rushed into his cock, causing it to fill and rise despite his weakened state.

She sucked and stroked him, then got on top of him and started fucking him hard and fast. Using the dagger, she slit the bodice of her silken gown and chemise to expose her breasts so that she could rub her nipples. The suction of her tight little snatch, especially when it started pulsating with her orgasm, undid him, and he came much harder than he would have thought possible under the circumstances.

As the night wore on, he continued to beg her to turn him; she continued to refuse. Only when he was literally on the verge of death, with his last breath rattling from his throat, did she pierce her right nipple at the very tip with her dagger and slide it into his mouth. He suckled as eagerly as a newborn infant as she stroked his hair, murmuring endearments, calling him *"il mio piccolo cucciolo affamato."* Her hungry little puppy. In the Piazza di Maggiore, he'd been a *cane bastardo*— a bastard dog.

Turek was too far gone at that point to register the reduction in rank. In fact, so delirious was he that he initially mistook the sensations of vampiric conversion—the euphoria, vertigo, and intense sexual arousal—for the process of death. When it was all over and he realized she had turned him, he was pathetically grateful, falling to his knees before her. He kissed her hands and thanked her for her mercy.

"You think this was an act of mercy?" she asked with a smile that looked almost pitying. "You really don't know me at all, do you? I came to realize after you so summarily discarded me that it was really for the best—from *your* point of view— that I hadn't turned you. I realized you aren't the right sort to make a good vampire, that you could never be at peace with it, that you would always, on some level, think of yourself as evil, wrong, unclean. Make no mistake, Anton, my turning you was not an act of mercy, but of retribution."

"Even so," he said, "you saved my life."

"I *replaced* your life with another, very different form of existence. Had I wanted to save it as it was, I could have done so. I could have cured you of the plague and let you live out the rest of your tedious human existence, but that would hardly have satisfied my appetite for vengeance, and as I—"

"You could have *cured* me?" he said. "There is no cure for the plague."

"As a matter of fact, I can cure many conditions subject to humans—and Follets, as well—by the simple expedient of replacing their blood. I have developed the ability to not only extract blood through my fangs but to expel it, enabling me to transfer it from what I call a provider pigeon to a recipient. I simply feed on the provider in the usual fashion, thoroughly draining him, and then—"

"*Thoroughly* draining him?" Turek said. "The provider would have to die, then, for this...transfer to take place."

"Only if he's human. I will choose a human provider in good health if the point of the transfer is to cleanse another human's body of some deadly pestilence, which I will do from time to time in return for a pledge of enslavement. But the provider can also be a Follet with some blood-borne attribute that the recipient, human or non, wishes to adopt, like shape-shifting. Follet providers don't die. They simply generate a new supply of blood, and in less than a day, they're good as new."

"But then how do you replace the recipient's blood?" asked Turek. "If you were to bleed him dry first, he would die."

"Again, only if he's human, but it isn't necessary to empty his veins completely before refilling them. After having thoroughly tapped the provider, I open a major artery in the recipient, and while he's bleeding out, I pierce a second artery with my fangs and begin discharging the new blood. As it flows through his vessels, it helps to flush out the old. When the transfer is complete, I lick the wounds to close them up."

The physician in Turek was astounded and intrigued. "Will I be able to do this, too?"

She gave a scornful little laugh, as if the question were ludicrous. "The ability to transfer blood is exceedingly rare, Anton. Most Upír don't even realize it's possible. It took me almost two millennia to acquire the gift, and a great many years to perfect my technique. I've been able to do it successfully only for the past few centuries. As vampires age, they grow steadily stronger and more powerful. You shall see—if you manage to survive as a vampire, which is by no means certain."

He asked her why he didn't have fangs. She told him they would develop within his gums over the next few days. As they grew, they would push on the two incisors to either side of his front teeth until those teeth loosened and fell out, to be replaced much as a child's adult teeth grow in to replace his milk teeth. She told him that from now on, sexual arousal and hunger would be inextricably linked. In fact, for the foreseeable future, he would be unable to satisfy the first—in other words, to achieve orgasm—without being in the process of satisfying the second. Over time, as his body acclimated itself to its new vampiric physiology, he would develop the ability to climax when he wasn't feeding—although the blood-haze tended to produce orgasms that were incredibly powerful.

She explained which veins and arteries on the human body provided the best access for their purposes, the most efficient and commonly used being the carotid on the side of the neck. Telling him it was best for him to work up a healthy appetite before his first blood-feed, she removed all the food and wine from his room, leaving him only a bucket of water for washing and drinking. He was still too weak and confused to question or resist her, even when she took his keys and locked him in, promising to return when he was good and hungry with "a nice little pigeon for you to break your fast with."

The next three days were interminable as Turek paced the little room waiting for Galiana to return. He felt strong and whole again—better than ever, in fact—and that was something, but there was a crawly sensation in his upper gums that was maddening, and he'd never been so famished in his life.

When his lateral incisors were loose enough to yank out, he did so. Behind their empty sockets he felt two bony ridges in the roof of his mouth. The flesh covering them stretched out thinner and thinner until at last the fangs themselves were exposed, folded back into channels, like scalpels tucked into scalpel-shaped niches in a satin-lined case. He pushed and prodded them, trying to get them to unfold, to no avail.

Eventually he fell asleep and dreamed of pigs being slaughtered, their screams filling the air as the blood sprayed from their throats, drenching him. He awoke with an adamantine erection, his fangs fully extended and throbbing. He stroked them, fascinated with the curved smoothness of them, their length, their hollow, pinpoint tips. The gums from which they emerged were so sensitive that rubbing them felt like rubbing his cock. He was excruciatingly aroused, so much so that he felt certain he could ease his lust by his own hand without being in the process of feeding, regardless of what Galiana had said. However, all he achieved for his efforts in that regard was frustration and eventually pain.

He fell asleep again, only to awaken to the presence of two people in the room with him—Galiana and Clara, whom she'd fetched from her sister's house in the country. Clara threw herself on Turek, babbling about how grateful she was that he was still alive. Galiana had told her how he'd fallen ill with the plague, only to heal himself through prayer, and that he'd been asking for Clara the entire time.

She kissed him, the first time she had ever done so. Turek

returned her kisses carefully, mindful of his fangs. Galiana left, closing the door behind her. He heard the key turning in the lock.

Clara felt incredibly soft and heavy and warm in his arms, her flesh seeming to hum with the blood coursing through it. He couldn't stop rubbing her, squeezing her, yanking at her clothes so as to feel her body against his. She rucked her skirts up, opening her legs for him and saying something about marriage, to which he grunted an affirmation as he licked her throat, tasting salt and savoring the roiling heat beneath the surface.

He sank his cock into her first, and then his fangs, deeply, hungrily, clutching her hard and tight as she struggled, clamping a hand over her mouth to stifle her cries. Driven by newly acquired instinct, he worked his tongue against the flesh of her neck to get the blood flowing. He groaned in bliss when it started drawing up through his fangs in rhythmic surges, creating a sensation similar to that of ejaculation, only in reverse.

The thumping of Clara's heart was like a drum being pounded all around him, echoing, reverberating, driving the fierce, insistent pumping of his hips. Drunk with the novel influx of fresh blood, he was only dimly aware that she had stopped struggling and was ardently meeting his thrusts.

He came with volcanic intensity, ejecting what felt like years of pent-up seed as he bucked and thrashed atop Clara, who was no longer moving. As he lay there sucking in hoarse breaths and shaking, his fangs still embedded in her throat, he felt a cool, soft hand stroking his naked buttocks. Galiana had returned—he had no idea when—and was now sitting on the side of the bed, saying "You can unseat your fangs now, *cucciolo*. There is no more blood to be had in this one. You've drained the little *porca* quite thoroughly."

It was true, he realized. Clara was as white as marble, her filmy eyes rolled up and her mouth agape. She looked for all the world like a statue of a saint depicted in a state of rapture.

"I killed her," he said, both awed and appalled at what he'd done. "*Mein Gott.*"

"Your God is through with you, Anton," Galiana said as she rose and crossed to the door. "You are an abomination in His eyes, a demon."

"*Nein,*" he whispered, shaking his head dazedly. But of course, it was true. A demon. That was exactly what he had become, what she'd turned him into, at his own request—a bloodsucking monster, godless and godforsaken.

Turek's gaze sought out the little crucifix nailed to the wall over the bed, to which he used to offer such fervent prayers. His stomach lurched, and he wretched, but nothing came up.

Standing in the open doorway, Galiana said, "You will leave Bologna and never seek me out again. If you attempt to communicate with me in any way, I will make you extremely sorry. I almost killed you once, in a most unpleasant fashion. I can still do it, *cucciolo.* I can chain you up and burn you to death in increments—first your feet, then your hands, your legs, your arms . . . You'll die in agony with no chance of ever coming back. Do not make the mistake of doubting my sincerity in this."

"I don't," he rasped.

"In future years, you will curse me for turning you. I meant it when I said that you don't have what it takes to live contentedly as an Upír. Just remember that you begged me for this. You were foolish to have done so, and now you will spend eternity paying for that mistake."

"Wait," he said as she turned to leave, yanking his drawers up as he struggled up off the bed, his mouth smeared with blood. "Where are you going? I . . . I don't know what to do. What am I . . . suppose to do with her?" he asked, pointing to Clara's body. "And how do I . . . how do I find more . . ."

"Pigeons? You didn't ask me to teach you how to be a vampire, you simply asked me to turn you into one. You shall have to sort through the details by yourself, I'm afraid. I have no desire to hold your hand while you do so."

"But . . ."

"*Arrivederci,* Anton. We are through with each other until the end of time."

As it happened, they were through with each other only for the next four and a half centuries. After failing to locate Grotte Cachée upon his release from the Bastille in 1789, Turek had returned to Paris, where he spent the next few years venting his bloodlust in a city gone mad with it. Follets of a predatory bent, including vampires of every race and subrace, flocked to Paris in great numbers during those years. Such beings found human turmoil intensely seductive, not only because it made people more susceptible to demonic machinations, but because those machinations were less likely to be noticed in an already brutal and chaotic environment.

Also prowling at night for the blood of unsuspecting Parisians was Galiana Solsa. Turek tried to avoid her, but she tracked him down. Gratified to find him so cold and bitter— evidence, she said, of his "vampiric maturation"—she swept him once again beneath her dark wing. The searing passion of their first few weeks together would never be renewed, but at least he was no longer alone.

She'd been right about him, of course, about the human weaknesses that had kept him—would always keep him— from true fulfillment as an Upír. Most vampires tended to be comfortable with solitude, but Turek could never quite accustom himself to it. For centuries after his conversion, he had

felt his aloneness all too keenly. Had he not, he would hardly
have slid so easily under the thumb of Galiana, with her unre-
lenting, strutting rapaciousness.

Of course, it never would have come to that—his playing
the lapdog in perpetuity to that vicious cunt—had he prevailed in his campaign to win over the only female for whom
he had ever felt true reverence, true devotion: Ilutu-Lili.

In the brief time he'd had alone with her during the
Hellfire's two-week visit to Grotte Cachée in 1749, he'd tried
to reason with her, to make her understand that she was, in her
way, as much of a vampire as he. *You're a creature of dark passions and terrible, ungovernable hungers, as am I,* he'd told her.
*We are really much the same, the succubus and the Upír—both
predators seeking our own particular sustenance, which we de-
rive from humans—willing or unwilling. We both do our prowling at night, for the most part. We are both singleminded in the
pursuit of our prey. And we are both susceptible to the same
means of destruction—immolation—which makes me suspect
that your race and mine are perhaps more closely related than
one would think.*

She'd had none of it, of course. He had used entirely the
wrong strategy with her, a blunder for which he'd paid with
forty years of his life. If he had to do it over again, he would
dispense with pointless logic. He would get her alone somewhere, spirit her away from her home, from Elic and anyone
else who might be inclined to come to her aid. He would keep
her in complete seclusion at his country house in the
Carpathian Mountains with only himself for companionship
for as long as it took to sway her, years if need be. The more
vulnerable she felt, the more quickly she would break down
and let him turn her.

Although of far stronger constitution than humans, both
mentally and physically, even Follets were susceptible to

206 • Louisa Burton

extended isolation, hunger, sleep deprivation, and physical restraint. How long would she be able to maintain her façade of
cool contempt for him, chained naked to a cot? No, not naked.
She was a succubus; she loved being unclothed, because of the
effect her nakedness had on men. It made them want to fuck
her, and she was all about fucking.

Lili reveled in sex; she craved it like humans craved food
and water. Succubi spent every waking hour consumed by
constant, seething sexual hunger that came rushing back almost as soon as it was satisfied—and it could be satisfied only
by absorbing the carnal vibes generated by their sex partners.
Unlike vampires and most other nonhuman races, incubi and
succubi were generally incapable of achieving orgasm through
masturbation, as a result of which they were on the make
pretty much 24/7. The more erotically stimulating the encounter, the greater the boost to their life-force, which was
why they tended to seek out humans with outsize sex drives,
like their own, and a taste for kink.

Lili's unquenchable sexual appetite could be Turek's most
powerful weapon in a campaign to convert her to vampirism,
he realized. It would take a monumental effort of will to keep
from ravishing her once he had her in his complete control,
but if he could manage it, her own escalating arousal would be
her undoing. Forced to go without sex and the vital energy she
derived from it, she would grow weakened, maddened, de-
fenseless. He could even escalate her torment by bringing in
women and fucking them right in front of her, or doing what
Doug had done to Nicky when he first brought her home—
coaxing her right to the edge without letting her come. How
much of that kind of thing could a succubus take without sur-
rendering?

Turek grew hard, imagining her sobbing and straining
against her chains as he fucked some whore doggie style be-

tween Lili's outspread legs, the whore's face right over her snatch, her hair tickling it, her hot breath making it gape and weep . . . *Lick it,* he would order, pushing down on the whore's head. *Just one lick, no more . . .*

Enough of that, and Lili would be begging him to turn her, just as he'd begged Galiana. *Please, Anton. I'll do anything. I'll drink your blood and become what you are. I'll be your queen, I'll be yours forever. Just fuck me. Please, I'm begging you, just fuck me. Fuck me hard . . .*

The crack of leather against flesh made Turek flinch.

"One," Nicky said through clenched teeth as a red-hot stripe materialized on the roundest part of her ass. "Thank you, master."

Doug shifted his aim with the belt; the next blow branded her upper thighs.

Nicky let out a sharp little cry. She also smiled. It was subtle and brief, and seen by Turek only because he had a better view of her face than the others.

"Two," she said a little breathlessly. "Thank you, master."

Each subsequent stroke, which Nicky dutifully counted off and offered thanks for, landed on a slightly different spot, until she was bright, scorching red from her lower thighs almost to her waist.

Turek couldn't help but recall that time in Rome back in '39—or was it '40?—when he seduced one of Mussolini's mistresses because she reminded him so much of Galiana—tall and gorgeous and built like a frigate, with all that thick, gleaming black hair, and of course the stone-bitch, ain't-I-grand attitude. He'd bought Enrica a black satin dinner suit of the type favored by Galiana—low-cut and wasp-waisted, with massive Joan Crawford shoulders—as well as a mannish little hat to go with it, and high-heeled spectator pumps, and of course the much-prized silk stockings. Chocolates and stockings: the

208 • Louisa Burton

universal currency back then. He had her put on these things, and then he bent her over a blanket rack in her bedroom, binding and gagging her with Mussolini's own neckties. He bared her ass and whipped it to ribbons with Il Duce's riding crop, and then he fed on her as he fucked her, nice and slow, reveling in her frantic thrashing and the heat of her abraded skin, timing it so that she breathed her last just as his pleasure erupted.

Turek rubbed his erection as he relived it . . . Her muffled whimpers and pointless, diminishing struggles, the gradual cooling of her flesh as he drained it dry, the drunken bliss as her blood percolated through his tissues and organs, tickling his cock, crackling along his nerves, making him feel as if he were floating, soaring . . . It was rapturous, one of the most memorable death feeds of his vampiric existence.

Having concluded Nicky's punishment, Doug made her kiss the belt. As he threaded it back through the loops, he said, "When I give you the signal, you've got twenty seconds to make yourself come."

Five

"FROM ZERO TO SIXTY in twenty seconds?" Lili asked skeptically.

"She's not starting from zero," Doug said. "To Nicky, getting whipped is like having her cunt licked. She's a total pain freak. Isn't that right, Nick?"

She yelped as he gave her whipmarked ass a sharp slap. "Yes, master."

"Get that head back down." Parting her sex lips, as blood-flushed now as the surrounding flesh, Doug said, "Check it out. She's dripping."

Elic and Lili rose from the couch and came over to take a look. Doug positioned a gooseneck floor lamp so that it shone directly on Nicky's bare ass, then yanked her panties off altogether and pushed her knees as wide apart as they could go on the stool.

Kneeling behind Nicky, Elic and Lili explored her with curious fingers, commenting on how wet and inflamed she was as the little blonde shuddered and gasped.

"On my go," said Doug, standing over Nicky with his gaze fixed on his chunky gold watch. "Twenty seconds, or I'll make you good and sorry. Ready?"

Rather awkwardly, because of the leash restraining her head, she got her right hand between her legs.

"Now," Doug said.

Nicky started fingering herself.

"No, don't close your eyes," Doug said. "Don't go somewhere else. You're right here, with all of us watching you. We can see everything you're doing. We can see your clit getting stiff and red. That's right, work it. Fourteen seconds."

Nicky's breath came in strident pants that evolved into a series of increasingly high-pitched, panicked little bleats of the type some women emit when orgasm is imminent. "Unh... unh... oh... oh... oh, God..."

"Seven seconds," Doug said. "You close?"

She nodded, trembling. "Y-yes, master."

Lili, apparently unwilling to take Nicky's word for it, pushed her middle finger deep inside the other woman's snatch.

"*Oh! Oh! Oh, God!*" Nicky bucked as she came, the step stool creaking so hard, Turek thought it might fall apart.

"Good girl." Doug praised, crouching down to ruffle her hair. "What were you thinking about?"

Gulping for air, Nicky said, "F-fucking, master."

"Getting fucked or watching other people fuck?"

"Getting fucked, master."

"Was I giving it to you in the ass, too? That's her favorite," he told Elic and Lili, "getting a great big vibrator shoved up her ass while I'm banging her."

There came a pause while Nicky ruminated on her response.

Yanking her head up by her leash, Doug said, "Answer me."

"You..." Dropping her gaze, Nicky said, very softly, "It... wasn't you, master."

Doug's incredulity struck Turek as comical. "Well, then, who the hell was it?"

With a wince of apprehension, she glanced over her shoulder at Elic. "H-him, master."

Doug stood, scowling at Elic, who gave him a grinning shrug in return.

Unzipping Elic's fly, Lili asked Doug, "Don't you think, after that impressive display, that Nicky deserves a little reward?" She caressed Elic's erection with loving strokes that incited another little stab of jealousy in Turek. He withdrew his own cock and stroked it in the same leisurely rhythm that Lili was using with Elic, imagining it was her hand pulling and squeezing, her fingers massaging the slippery glans, gliding down the shaft to rub that ultrasensitive flesh under his balls as they grew tight and firm, filling with come...

He really was an idiot.

All the more so because not only was Lili herself evidently devoid of jealousy, but she was actually getting her lover primed to fuck another woman. Petty human covetousness was beneath her. Just more evidence, as if any more were needed, that she was a truly higher life-form, as superior to humans as humans were to the cattle and swine upon which they fed.

"I mean, we did come back here to share our toys, no?" Lili asked Doug as she trailed her fingertips lightly up and down Elic's cock, adding with a sly little smile, "Of course, if you're not into it, I'll just put my clothes back on and we can call it a—"

"No! No, no, no," Doug protested as he ogled Lili in her come-hither lingerie. "Of course I'm into it, are you kidding?"

"Well, then," Elic said. With one hand gripping Nicky's hip, he rubbed the head of his cock against her wet little hole. With a whimper of pleasure, she lifted her hindquarters like a cat in heat, a wordless plea that didn't go unanswered. He penetrated her with one slow, smooth incursion, grabbing her shoulders and pushing hard to force himself in as deep as he could go. She pushed back against him with a ravenous little purr.

Reaching between Elic's legs—Turek thought she must be fondling his balls and the base of the shaft—Lili whispered something in his ear and kissed his throat, his cheek, his mouth...

Turek imagined her bestowing those little intimacies on him while he gave it to some hot, horny little blood-bag, and felt a yearning so acute that it took his breath away even as his arousal escalated, his hips clenching as he knelt there with fingertips trailing lightly up and down his cock...

Lili, Lili...

In the beginning, he'd worshipped her, craved her, *needed* her to banish the terrible loneliness that was the vampire's lot. But then she'd turned on him, and he'd loathed her and plotted his revenge. And now...

Still kissing Elic, Lili reached down the back of his jeans to caress his ass as it rocked back and forth, sliding his glistening cock in and out of the other woman.

Now...

Turek summoned up the mental image that had both nurtured and soothed his wrath during his long incarceration, that of Lili shrieking as the flames licked that beautiful face, bubbling the skin, peeling it away, roasting it to ash...

At one time, that fantasy had felt comforting; now it made his stomach roil, his erection wilt.

Lili . . . Oh, fuck, what are you doing to me?

"I know you said you'd never shared Nicky before," Lili said as she stood and approached Doug, gliding her hands up over her hips and breasts. "Has she ever watched you with another woman?"

He shook his head. "I've been kind of, uh, holding that one in reserve as a . . . sort of as an ultimate punishment."

Nodding toward Nicky, her eyes closed as she moaned in time with Elic's unhurried thrusts, Lili said, "She'll hardly even notice at this point, much less care."

"That won't do. Hey, Nick." He jerked on her leash. "Having a good time?"

"Y-yes, master."

"Yeah, well, I want to have a good time, too. You're going to lick Lili's pussy till she's ready for me, and then you're going to watch me fuck her."

"What a splendid idea," said Lili as she removed her g-string, which tied on the sides.

Turek's cock sprang up again, hard and quivering; it felt like electrified steel in his fist.

"Have you ever done this before, Nicky?" Lili asked. "Gone down on another woman?"

"No, ma'am."

"It's easy. Just pretend you're doing it to yourself."

Doug wanted Lili to kneel, but Lili pointed out that Nicky would have "better access" if *he* were to kneel and hold her from behind with her legs resting on the step stool to either side of Nicky, so that was what they did. Doug struggled to unzip himself while gripping her around the waist as she guided the little blonde's head, murmuring, "That's right, oh, that's

214 • Louisa Burton

good. A little higher, sweetheart, a little softer. Oh, God. Oh, yes. Oh . . . oh . . ."

Turek's quickening thrusts echoed Lili's. *Oh, yes. Oh, here it comes . . .* He gritted his teeth to keep from groaning as the heart-pounding pleasure mounted higher, higher . . .

She came as Doug rammed himself into her, and so did Turek, shooting jet after jet as he watched Lili writhe and buck and moan.

Panting and shaking, he zipped himself back up as Doug pounded away inside Lili, grunting and groaning. She came again, from all appearances just as hard as the first time. Some women, like Nicky, seem pained during orgasm, some reminded Turek of a snorting, rutting she-beast. Lili in the throes of climax was glorious, a vision of sensual passion.

"Perfect," he whispered. The ultimate seductress, the ultimate goddess.

And she could be, if she would only consent to be turned, the ultimate vampire queen.

Lili, Lili, Lili . . . How can you still wield such power over me? How can I still desire you so fervently, not just your body, but you, all of you, heart and soul, until the end of days?

What he wanted of her, what he was determined now, for better or worse, to achieve, was what Galiana wanted— expected, demanded—of him: complete and utter possession, now and forever.

He would have to proceed, of course, with the utmost care and discretion. What, he wondered, would Galiana think if she had any inkling of where he was right now, of the things he was feeling . . .

. . . and planning?

More to the point, what would she do? The last time—the only time—he'd ever presumed to give Galiana her walking papers, back in Bologna, it had detonated a supernova of rage.

I almost killed you once, in a most unpleasant fashion. I can still do it, cucciolo. *I can chain you up and burn you to death in increments—first your feet, then your hands, your legs, your arms... You'll die in agony with no chance of ever coming back. Do not make the mistake of doubting my sincerity in this.*

He didn't.

Six

A FAINT, PREDAWN GLOW was just beginning to bleach the night from the sky when Lili and Elic, in fleece robes, escorted their two fuckmates out of the house and back down the little alleyway. Nicky and Doug looked rumpled, dazed, and exhausted, in contrast to their hosts, who positively glowed, having absorbed a heaping helping of sexual nourishment during the evening's frolics.

Climbing back up the same spruce he'd climbed down, Turek watched and listened from the apartment house roof as the four lingered on the sidewalk, chatting as casually as if they were bringing the curtain down on a dinner party and not a four-hour four-way.

Turek's ears twitched when Lili said to the other couple, "I do hope you two will be able to join us for D and D Week at Grotte Cachée."

"Wouldn't miss it," Doug said. " 'Dungeons and Dominance'—gotta love it. Um, should we plan on bringing our own costumes, or will you have them there?"

"Nicky will be taken care of," Elic said. "We issue specially designed uniforms to the serving wenches and footmen. But the barons and baronesses have to provide their own. Authenticity is encouraged—anything from the thirteen hundreds through the sixteen hundreds will fly. There are those who like to add whimsical little modern touches, which is fine, but we do ask that you make an effort."

"Most of our guests rent from theatrical supply companies," Lili said, "but you can buy something online from one of those outfits that sells costumes for Renaissance fairs—if you think you can get it before next Friday. Just make sure you end up looking like a nobleman, not a peasant. The doms are the lords and ladies, the subs are servants. There is no in between."

Elic asked Nicky if she understood that, by attending this event, she was agreeing to put herself at the sexual disposal of every dom in attendance. "Any or all of those guys can use you however he wants, and you either submit or you go home."

Doug opened his mouth to answer for her, but closed it when Elic shot him a look.

"I understand, sir," Nicky said.

"And you've got no problem with that?" he persisted.

She smiled at the sidewalk. "No, sir."

"So this is, like, an annual thing?" Doug asked.

"Yeah, we've hosted D and D Week every September for the past twenty-four years," Elic said. "It's by invitation only, of course. Our *administrateur,* Emmett Archer—"

"Your what?" Doug said.

"*Administrateur,*" Elic said. "He serves as a sort of right-hand man to the owner of Château de la Grotte Cachée. Archer has connections all over the world, and he finds most of our guests. Our friend Inigo issues quite a few invitations himself. He's always traveling, and he's very gregarious, makes friends easily."

"I'm glad we still have spots for you two," Lili said. "We cut it off at sixty guests, because that's the most we can comfortably accommodate. The barons and baronesses are assigned bedrooms, and the wenches and footmen sleep on pallets in other parts of the castle."

"Are all the guests couples?" Doug asked.

"Oh, no," Lili said. "In fact, most are individuals, subs or doms from all over the world. Some of them come every year, others will be newbies, like you guys. We try to choose people who seem like they'll really get into the spirit of the thing."

"It's not just enthusiasm, though," Elic said. "The subs are chosen in large part on the basis of looks. We like them to be real knockouts, like Nicky here."

Nicky ducked her head bashfully, smiling up at the preternaturally handsome Elic, who had done things to her that night that had her screaming in transports of pleasure, pain, and delicious humiliation. While she was bent over the library steps, he came not once but twice, without pulling out in between, and over the course of the next few hours, he had, by Turek's count, another eight orgasms—but always in Nicky. He brought Lili off by hand a couple of times and with his mouth once—while Turek masturbated again, imagining himself in Elic's place—but Elic never had sex with her, not regular intercourse. Was it possible Elic was that rare type of Follet who could mate only with humans?

"It's not just the serving wenches who have to be beautiful," Lili said. "Back when aristocratic households employed fleets of footmen, they were almost always very tall and very handsome. It was a kind of status symbol."

And why not? thought Turek, who had never met a status symbol he didn't like.

"Just so I know what we're getting into," Doug said, "are we talking a strictly hetero kind of a deal here, or...?"

Elic shook his head. "Anything goes, but the subs get a say in who gets access to them. They let us know when they arrive what kind of livery or uniform they want. Green means they're only available to a dom of the opposite sex, gold means same sex, and a combination of the two colors means it's all good. That's the only choice they're given in what happens to them during the festival. After that, they're at the mercy of their superiors. If they're pleasing and accommodating, they might be rewarded with extra rations of food or some other little gratuity. If they misbehave, however, we've got all kinds of spanking benches and whipping stools and the like. They usually set those up in the courtyard. And we've got a bona fide torture chamber stocked with some very interesting instruments of punishment."

"Seriously?" asked Nicky, wide-eyed.

Oblivious to the fact that his "slave" had spoken out of turn, Doug said, "Holy fuck, a torture chamber. Now, *that's* what I'm talking about."

"Only one dom at a time gets to use it," Elic said, "so it has to be reserved in advance, but it's a very popular feature."

Lili reminded Elic to give the other couple their "cards of entrée," whereupon he produced two thin, flat little metallic devices from the pocket of his robe. "I'll give each of you one in case you end up traveling separately," he said. "These will serve as your proof of invitation, and they're also your only means of finding Château de la Grotte Cachée, so don't lose them. They're custom-designed, dedicated GPS units loaded with one set of directions only, from Aulnat Airport in the

Auvergne region of France to the château. The program is such that you can't even view the directions until the satellites have detected that you're at the airport. Once you're there next Friday, rent a car, turn this puppy on, and let it guide you to our front door—at which point you will be obliged to surrender it to the gentleman guarding the gatehouse. Not that it would do you much good to hang on to it. The directions are programmed to self-destruct after a certain amount of time."

"Why all the double-oh-seven, cloak-and-dagger bullshit?" Doug asked.

Elic smiled evenly. "Like I said, we value our privacy."

When Nicky and Doug finally took their leave, Turek waited until they were half a block away, with Lili and Elic safely ensconced in their house, to climb down the fire escape and tail them. They fiddled with the GPS "cards" as they headed east on St. Mark's, Doug telling Nicky—Turek could just make out their conversation—that she should give him her card to hold on to.

"Nuh-uh," she said, tucking it in a pocket of her blazer. "He gave it to *me*."

"Yeah, but everything that's given to you is automatically mine. And if you back-talk me one more time tonight, or fail to address me as 'master,' I'm gonna—"

"Can we give it a rest, Doug?" She unbuckled the pink collar and thrust it at him. "Just till tomorrow morning? It's been a long night, my contacts are extra crispy, and my pussy feels like it's been Roto-Rootered."

Wrapping the leash around the collar, Doug shoved it inside his suit coat, along with the card. "I didn't notice you complaining when ol' Elic was snaking you out."

"You had to go there," she groaned, scrubbing her hands over her temples. "I fucking knew you'd go there. May I remind you that letting them take us back to their place was *your* idea...*master*?" With an amused little snort, she added, "Probably the best idea you ever had, though."

"How come you never scream like that when I—"

"Trust me, Doug, you don't want me to answer that."

"What the fuck does that mean?"

"Think about it—with the *big* head this time."

They kept on in that tedious vein for a couple more blocks, until Doug paused to peer up and down the street, scowling; Turek crouched behind the front stoop of a brownstone.

"We're never gonna get a cab at this hour," Doug said as they continued on. "I haven't seen a single one pass by."

Pointing, Nicky said, "That's Tompkins Square Park up ahead. We can catch the Fourteen-A, and that'll take us—"

"The *what*?"

"The Fourteen-A. It's a bus that runs along—"

"I know what it is. I'm not taking any fucking bus."

"Oh, for Christ's sake. What—you're worried you'll get cooties all over your precious new Brioni Big Boy suit?

Brioni, Turek thought. *I knew it.*

"You think a bus is gonna come at this hour?" Doug asked.

"Some of them run all night, and most of the others start up at five a.m."

"Yeah, and you know who rides them in the middle of the fucking night? Fucking muggers and rapists, that's who."

Doug continued protesting the idea as they crossed Avenue A and headed north along the sidewalk abutting the park, a heavily treed oasis bordered by a wrought-iron fence. Turek scanned the street in all directions as he darted across it, careful to stay out of their line of sight. There wasn't a soul to be seen, aside from Nicky and Doug, either on the street or in the park, and almost no traffic.

Their bickering escalated as they drew up to an L-shaped, glass-walled bus shelter, with Nicky suggesting they wait for the 14-A and Doug insisting they keep walking uptown in the hope of catching a cab. A streetlamp stood nearby, worse luck, but trees shadowed the shelter itself.

"I'm not getting on any grimy, third-world, fast-food-smelling, diesel-farting public bus, you stupid fucking cunt," Doug growled as Turek, sidling up along the wrought-iron fence, wrapped his scarf around his nose and mouth. For good measure, he put on his glasses, which had big, thick tortoise-shell frames that would help to hide his face. Were he not desperate for a second chance with Lili, he wouldn't dream of pulling a stunt like this. Galiana would go ballistic if she knew what he was up to.

He slid his switchblade out of his pocket and thumbed the button. The blade popped out like a fang.

"Don't call me a cunt, you fucking asshole," snapped Nicky, fists propped on her hips as she faced Doug down beneath the shelter.

"Don't call me an asshole, you fucking cunt."

"Go fuck yourself!" she screeched, drowning out Turek's "Get your hands up, motherfuckers" as he strode toward them, the knife gleaming in his outstretched hand.

"No, *you* fuck yourself, Nicky!" Doug bellowed, prodding her chest with his finger. "Some fucking slave, telling her master to—"

"Some fucking master, whining like a little bitch 'cause he's scared to get on the bus with all the boogiemen and—"

"*Will you both just shut the fuck up and put your fucking hands in the air?*" Turek yelled. "*Do it!*"

They looked him up and down as they slowly raised their arms, taking in the switchblade, the metrosexual finery, the funky glasses and silken bandito scarf. And then there was his to-the-manner-born British accent. Not your basic *Law & Order* breed of mugger.

"Give me the cards," Turek demanded, holding out his hand as he gestured with the knife.

"Cards?" Doug said.

"The cards of entrée, those GPS things. Give them to me. And your belt," he told Doug. "The king cobra belt. I want that, too."

Doug and Nicky exchanged a *What-the-fuck?* look.

"Now!" Turek pointed the knife toward Doug. "Yours first."

"You've got to be shitting me." Doug, seemingly uncowed by the knife, made no move to comply.

"You think I won't cut you?" Turek snarled. "You really don't want to be playing that hand, mate."

Doug said, "I get it. You're some pissant Limey actor who thinks he's Olivier reincarnated, but the casting agents aren't seeing it that way, and now you're two months behind on your big, fat New York City rent, and you'd rather mug honest American citizens than wait tables or tend bar. Sorry, *mate,* but I'm really not buying what you're selling, so why don't you take your little stage knife and—"

"Stage knife?" Turek leapt forward and slashed the knife across Doug's throat, incising a thin red line that flung crimson spatters onto the glass wall of the shelter. "What's that, then? *Stage blood?*"

Nicky shrieked. Doug grabbed his throat and slumped to the ground. From his gurgling wheezes, it would seem that Turek had succeeded in lacerating his larynx and thus silencing the *dummes arschloch* at least temporarily, and quite possibly for good; what became of him was of zero interest to Turek. None of the major arteries appeared to have been severed, though; if they had, the blood would have been pump-pump-pumping from him, not just seeping between his fingers in puny little trickles.

Puny they may have been, but the sight of that blood, and

its warm, sticky-metallic aroma, caused Turek's mouth to water, his gums to throb. Were he not in such a godawful hurry to get those damn cards and split before some early riser glanced out his window and called the cops, he might have wrested the felled man's hands from his throat and lapped at the oozing wound with beastlike relish.

"Oh, my God!" Nicky wailed as Turek knelt to flip open Doug's suit coat. "You killed him! Oh, my God!"

From the inside coat pocket, he pulled a kidskin wallet and the card of entrée. He tossed the former aside and tucked the latter into his own back jeans pocket. He unbuckled the cobra belt and yanked it free, then stood and flashed the bloody switchblade at Nicky, cowering in the corner of the shelter.

"Give me your card," he ordered. *"Now."* Best to take both cards, even though he would only need one; God forbid this little nit should show up at the château while he was there. Even if he dyed his hair darker, she would recognize him sooner or later, if only by his voice. Actually, now that he thought about it, leaving her alive would be a pretty dumb move. He could easily run into her again at Tethers or one of the other clubs. A quick jab to the jugular as he took the card from her, and then he should finish Doug off, as well.

Raising one trembling hand as if to ward him off, Nicky slipped a hand inside her blazer and withdrew a small black canister attached to a key ring.

"Sheisse!" Turek spun around fast enough to avoid a direct blast to the face, but he still found himself enveloped by a scorching haze of pepper spray. Despite the glasses and scarf, his eyes snapped shut and his lungs seized up. He yanked the scarf off his mouth and ran blindly, only to slam into the streetlamp, the switchblade and belt hitting the sidewalk. He fumbled around for them, his eyes tearing, his skin scalded, snot and saliva dripping down his face.

From behind him, he heard Nicky's quavering voice. "Yeah, I'm at a bus shelter on Avenue A between St. Mark's and East Ninth. Me and my boyfriend just got mugged, and he cut my boyfriend's throat, and—"

"*Gottverdammt*," Turek hissed as he shoved the knife into his jeans pocket and started running, hating that he had to leave that kick-ass belt, his eyes slitted open, hacking like a consumptive. She'd called 911. Fucking cell phones. Fucking pepper spray. Used to be, human women were easy pickings. What was *happening* to the world?

Turek may not have had Galiana's physical prowess, but he was still a vampire with six hundred eighty years under his belt. When he needed to, as he did now, he could run as fast as an Olympic sprinter, and then some. He could leap fences, scuttle up brick walls... He could, and did, disappear into the vast, urban night as sirens howled in the increasingly remote distance. Along the way, he stripped off the all-too-identifiable scarf, glasses, and jacket, tossing each into a different Dumpster. He tossed his contacts, as well, which helped a little with the eye irritation.

Thanks to his speedy vampiric healing processes, by the time he made it to the Upper East Side penthouse he shared with Galiana, the skin inflammation had settled down considerably. He was hardly coughing at all, and although his eyes still felt as if someone had rubbed ground glass in them, they were no longer threatening to swell shut.

Turek unlocked the apartment door, thinking they really should get state-of-the-art locks like at Penumbra Court, and opened it as slowly and silently as he could. He took off his shoes, wanting to avoid waking Galiana—thereby bypassing her inevitable interrogation—if she was already asleep, but she wasn't. He had a good view of the living room as he stepped into the foyer. She was lounging at the far end of the sprawling room on her black leather Barcelona chair, one of Mies van der Rohe's 1929 originals, valued at six figures if she were to sell it to a museum, which would happen when they were snowboarding in Hell.

She eyed him as she lifted a cigarette to her mouth. Her hair was loose, and so close in color and gleam to her black satin robe that you couldn't tell where the hair ended and the robe began. Nor could he discern her expression, since she was backlit by the rising sun, which cast a purplish luminescence through the sheer, UV-blocking fiberglass shades cloaking the wall of glass behind her.

She exhaled his name through a curl of smoke. It was "Anton" this time. He didn't know whether that was a good sign or a bad one.

"Hey. Galiana." Turek licked his lips and smiled in a way he hoped looked nonchalant. "You still up?" He set down the shoes and stepped into the cavernous room, lit only by the eerie violet dawn and twelve small halogen picture lights in the ceiling, aimed at the most prized of the scores of paintings that occupied every inch of available wall space.

The most precious of her favored dozen: Jan Vermeer's *The Concert*, valued at five million dollars and stolen from the Isabella Stewart Gardner Museum in Boston on St. Patrick's Day, 1990, by Turek and a professional art thief Galiana had cured of AIDS via vampiric transfusion, both of them disguised as police officers. In addition to the cop getup, Turek had worn a black mullet wig and the fakest fake moustache you ever saw. That haul had also yielded five drawings by Degas, one oil by Manet, a Chinese bronze vessel, and four Rembrandts—although one of the latter turned out to have been the work of some Rembrantish D-list painter nobody ever heard of. This Galiana had fenced, along with the vessel and three of the Degas that she'd found "unmoving."

Also bathed in coronas of halogen radiance: Renoir's *Portrait of Madame Albert Andre* and Bonnard's *Le Petit Café*, which were among nine paintings that disappeared from the Musée de Bagnols-sur-Cèze in France on November 12, 1972, while Turek and Galiana were staying in a nearby hotel. Next to the Bonnard hung Picasso's *Portrait of Dora Maar*, swiped in March of 1999 from a Saudi yacht that was docked in Antibes, where Galiana had owned a villa since 1882.

Galiana gestured with her cigarette toward the Le Corbusier chaise longue. Too wound up to recline, Turek sat awkwardly on the dip in the middle of the leather chaise, which was like perching on a low stool or a child's chair. Perfect. He reached automatically for the pack of Gitanes in his jacket pocket, but of course he wasn't wearing his jacket.

He thought Galiana might ask what happened to it, but instead, she said, "I didn't appreciate having to sink that pigeon all by myself, Anton."

"Did, um, did it go all right, or...?"

"He's under the Whitestone Bridge, with a hundred feet of water over him." Tapping her cigarette into the alabaster ashtray on the seat next to her, she said, "I'm a bit perplexed as to why you would run off that way in the middle of a feed."

"I thought I saw someone I knew walking by on the sidewalk." Lies generally worked best if they were wrapped around a core of truth.

"Who?"

"You don't know them."

"Them? Was it a man or a woman?"

"A man," he said. "A Follet, actually, an elf, someone I met briefly a long time ago. I followed them for—"

"There's that nebulous 'them' again," she said with a wintry little smile.

"Him." Turek wiped his palms on his jeans. "There were

other people with him. And, um, I followed them all over the East Village, but it turned out not to be them after all. Him." *Fuck.*

"So you missed out on a death feed for nothing," she said.

"Yeah. I'm such an ass sometimes."

She offered no polite refutation of that, simply fixed him with that all-too-penetrating Nefertiti gaze. "Your eyes are red and swollen," she said.

"Yeah, I'm toasted. Time to hit the sheets." Feigning a yawn, Turek stood and turned to leave, then turned back as if something had just occurred to him. He almost snapped his fingers, but decided that would just be too hokey. "I keep forgetting to mention this, but, uh, I was thinking about spending some time at Gebirgshaus, kick back a little bit, recharge my batteries." Gebirgshaus was Turek's home in the Carpathians, where he retreated every once in a while when serving as Galiana's compliant little minion got to be just a bit much.

"Ugh." She shuddered as she stubbed out her cigarette. "How can you bear that dank old ruin?"

"You've never even seen it. How do you know it's dank?"

Giving him *that look,* she said, "It's a six-hundred-year-old stone castle."

"It's just a large manor house, actually." Although it *was* enclosed by stone curtain walls fifteen feet thick and festooned with electrified barbed wire.

"It's dank," she said with finality. "And dark and spider-infested, and located a hundred miles from the nearest decent restaurant."

More than a hundred, actually. When Turek had had Gebirgshaus built back in the late 1400s, he'd visualized it as a sort of safe house for when he was being pursued; in fact, it was where he'd convalesced after the Post–Fuck-up Makeover back in '82. To that end, he'd built it not in his Czech home-land but on Romanian soil in the high, craggy southern curve of the Carpathians, which erupted in a thousand-mile-long swath through several eastern European countries. The house and the land it stood on had been bestowed upon him by Vlad III, Prince of Wallachia, in return for helping to mete out pun-ishments to those who were foolish enough to oppose the great prince's rule. The southern Carpathians were vast and desolate. Galiana would have no way of knowing where his refuge was, having refused all of his past invitations to visit it.

"How long do you think you'll be there?" she asked.

As long as it took to coerce Lili into vampirism once she'd had enough of being chained up and tormented in Gebirgshaus's dungeon, where so many of Vlad Tepes's ene-mies had bled their last. "I thought I'd fly out next Friday and stay a week or two, maybe," he lied. "I would ask you to join me, but I know what your answer will be." In fact, if all went as planned, he would never see her again. He would have found a way, at long last, to pry her talons out of his flesh.

"I don't know," she said, choosing another cigarette from the lacquered box on her glass-topped Noguchi coffee table. "Perhaps it's time I finally saw this place for myself. I've always been a bit curious as to why it holds such allure for you."

Oh, fuck me. Leaning over to lift her gold lighter off the table—he'd never once seen her light her own cigarette in the presence of a male—Turek said, "You're more than welcome to come, of course. You should know, though, that it's one of the most remote and inhospitable places on the face of the earth, and very sparsely populated. You'll go stir-crazy, for sure. And when it comes to feeding . . . well, I've had to make do with bears, lynxes, wolves . . ."

230 • Louisa Burton

"I haven't tasted the blood of game in quite some time," she mused, leaning back to savor her cigarette with a contemplative expression.

"It's nowhere near as nourishing as human blood," he said, thinking *Sheisse!* "And it can taste pretty goddamned funky, depending on the animal. And these animals are usually crawling with fleas and ticks, and—"

"I am well aware of the downsides, Anton. I think you forget sometimes how much older I am than you, how much more experienced in, well, everything. More than once I've been forced into hiding in unpopulated areas where I had to feed on wild animals. The novelty wears thin very quickly."

"Then, um, are you sure you want to be stuck at Gebirgshaus for weeks, with little or no access to human pigeons?"

"Weeks? I thought you said a week or two."

"Oh. Yeah, well, um, I'm kind of viewing it as a sort of open-ended—"

"You wouldn't be playing me, would you, Anton?"

"Playing you?"

"Keeping something from me."

"Whoa." He took a step back, raising his hands—which he quickly lowered when he saw how they were shaking. "How—how could you say that? How could you even think it?"

Galiana studied him through a haze of smoke for about ten seconds, during which he didn't draw a breath. She shrugged, tapped her cigarette into the ashtray, and said, "You seem unusually tense tonight. Wired up."

"I'm . . . I'm . . . not wired up, just—"

"If you're stressed out, you probably *should* take a couple of weeks to yourself. Go to your nasty old castle, chill out a bit. I think I'll take a pass, though. Fleas and ticks, for Christ's sake." She shuddered.

"Right. Yeah. Good. That's good," he said, dizzy with relief. "I mean, it's for the best, all things considered. You really wouldn't be happy there. I really think you made the right—"

"Sleep well, *marish*," she said.

Grateful for the dismissal, Turek bid her good night and headed off to his bedroom, a Victorian-style enclave with blackout shades and heavily lined drapes on all the windows. They'd always kept separate rooms; Galiana shared her gray-walled, Bauhaus-furnished royal chamber with no one. When she was horny and wanted him to service her—for such was how he'd come to think of it in recent decades—she came to his room, used him, and left. Sometimes he dreamed that he was smothering; invariably he would awaken with her crouching over his face, rubbing her snatch against his mouth.

After hiding the card of entrée in a secret drawer of his dresser, Turek stripped, showered, and crawled between two layers of cool, sleek Egyptian cotton, only to lie awake, his mind whirring.

Hell yeah, he was wired up. He was getting ready to deceive and betray a three-thousand-year-old vampiress who would toast him to cinders—after dining on deep-fried cock with Chianti and fava beans—if she caught wind of his scheme. That kind of thing tended to focus the senses.

Marish. She'd started calling him that after they hooked up together again in Paris during the Terror. He'd asked her what it meant, and she'd told him it was an endearment in the old Etruscan tongue, and that it meant something like "lover."

About fifty years ago, he'd gotten curious and tried to look up the exact definition. He'd checked a few libraries and well-stocked bookstores, looking for an Etruscan glossary, but it was an obscure dead language, and he came up empty. Maybe if he were to look in one of those big university libraries, he'd have better luck. Or maybe...

He actually smacked his forehead when it came to him. "*Oberarsch.*"

Throwing back the covers, he crossed to his writing desk and opened his laptop. Within seconds, he was scrolling down a web page titled "Etruscan-English Dictionary."

He homed in on the Ms: *Malena, Malstri, Mani...*

"Bingo," Turek whispered when he found the entry for *Marish.*

His grin faded when he read the definition. He stared at it, searing it into his mind lest he falter in his resolve to extricate himself, at long last, from the clutches of Galiana Solsa.

Marish: servant; slave

Seven

Château de la Grotte Cachée
The Following Friday Afternoon

$\mathcal{G}$LUTU-LILI SMILED to herself when she saw Elle accidentally-on-purpose spill a little grog onto "Lord Dragoneye"—a square-jawed, prematurely gray New York trial attorney named Blaine something—while serving pre-prandial drinks to the costumed "barons and baronesses" lounging in the castle courtyard.

Blaine leapt up, wiping at his rented doublet. "What the fuck...Clumsy wench!"

"I'm so sorry, my lord," Elle said with bowed head. "Pray forgive me."

"Forgive you? You ruined my fucking jacket." Some of the attendees liked to throw around the "thees" and "thous," but Blaine wasn't one of them. "It isn't forgiveness you need, it's a goddamned lesson."

Grabbing her by the arm, he strode to the Correction Table

standing next to the central fountain. The hefty antique held a place of honor among the various furnishings set up around the courtyard—spanking benches, fisting slings, even a whipping post—all of which had been used at least once since the official D and D kick-off luncheon at noon.

The stone benches were also popular for disciplinary purposes; a pretty little wench was bent over the back of one at that very moment, being fucked by one baron while another looked on, casually masturbating as he sipped from his tankard. Frequent use was made of the courtyard's hundred-eighty-year-old cherry trees, as well. A baron had chained a strapping, gold-clad footman to one and was tormenting the poor bastard by slapping his cock very lightly but persistently with a cat-o'-nine-tails while he moaned and shuddered.

Inigo, in flamboyant lord's attire and his favorite vintage top hat, had even found a use for the "toy cart." This was a two-wheeled wooden drinks cart, its shelves loaded with playthings that weren't always true to the the Renaissance period: handcuffs, blindfolds, gags, harnesses, butt plugs, dildos, an assortment of crops, whips, and paddles, and about a dozen different brands of lube on a silver tray. The fun-loving satyr had strapped a redheaded wench who called herself Isolde facedown over the top of the cart with her skirts thrown up and the tray of lube on her back. Isolde was a bisexual super-sub with a deep love of pain, degradation, and bondage. With that in mind, Inigo had been wheeling her around the courtyard for the past hour, offering her body as a "test dummy" for comparing the qualities of the different lubes.

Everyone turned to watch as Blaine shoved Elle onto the Correction Table, which somewhat resembled an eight-foot picnic table, the kind with a long attached seat on either side. The main differences were that the seats were actually for kneeling on, and the whole thing was upholstered in scarred, well-worn red leather. Unlike the smaller whipping stools and spanking benches, the Correction Table could accommodate a number of subs at once, if need be.

Blaine positioned Elle not facedown, as was more usual, but on her back with her bottom at the table's edge and her slippered feet on the kneeler. Having chosen by the flip of a coin to play the sub this year, she was dressed, like the other wenches, in a provocative variation on classic Renaissance fair maidservant attire.

The foundation of the D and D wench uniform was an ankle-length, ruffle-sleeved chemise of gauzy linen, its off-the-shoulder neckline gathered loosely with a drawstring. Laced over this was a boned velvet bodice with narrow straps and an under-the-bust neckline meant to frame the breasts beneath their film of sheer gauze. The color of the bodice indicated the wench's sexual availability: green for barons only, gold for baronesses, or striped, like Elle's, if she would submit to either. There was a buff-colored overskirt, but it was tucked so as to drape over the hips while exposing the rest of the lower body, front and back, through the filmy linen chemise; undergarments were, of course, forbidden. The only other items that could be worn were leather slippers and a hair ribbon.

Waving over a pair of footmen, one a hard-cut Asian gymnast whose D and D name was Ailwin and the other a brawny American cop called Fulk, Blaine said, "You two, get over here and make yourselves useful."

He had Ailwin stand across the table from him to pin Elle's wrists over her head, while Fulk, positioned next to him, was charged with lifting her legs straight up by the ankles, exposing her beautiful bare ass and that sweet, pink little pussy. It was the only pussy that had ever turned Lili on, *really* turned her on, in the thousands of years of her existence.

It undoubtedly turned Blaine on, too, but it was hard to tell with his oversized bondage codpiece of quilted black leather accessorized with zippers and buckles.

Fulk's arousal was much more obvious, as the footmen's codpieces were, in true early Renaissance style, triangular panels of the same knitted material as the buff-colored hose they wore with their short boots. At first blush, it looked as if they were wearing seamed cotton hip-hugger tights, but, in fact, they were separate leggings that were tied to each other in back and to the codpiece in front. Naturally, this was worn sans undershorts, the stretchable fabric conforming so snugly to the wearer's male anatomy as to betray the slightest hint of tumescence. On top, the footmen wore color-coded jerkins half buttoned over puffy-sleeved shirts of the same transparent gauze as the wenches' chemises. The shirts were kept as short as the jerkins so as not to interfere with the all-important esthetics of the groin and posterior areas.

Blaine instructed Fulk to move aside while maintaining a grip on Elle's ankles, and then he hauled back and smacked her. He spanked her hard and fast, his expression fierce, his face growing as red as her ass. Elle let out a breathy little cry with each blow, her eyes glittering. It wasn't that she found pain or humiliation sexually exciting in and of itself; she could just as easily have gotten off on being the spanker as the span-kee. Like Lili and Inigo, Elle was aroused by that which aroused her human sex partner. The more stimulating the encounter for the human, the more stimulating—and revitalizing—it would be for an incubus; or, in Elle's case, for an incubus in the form of a succubus.

"I almost hate to do this," Blaine said breathlessly as he unbuckled his codpiece, "'cause it's just what you want, isn't it? It's what all you little sluts want, especially after a good, hard spanking. But I'm not about to end up with blue balls on your account."

Ordering Fulk to keep Elle's legs together and angled toward her head, Blaine knelt on the lower bench, grabbed her hips, and started fucking her with sharp, punishing strokes.

"*Fuck,* your ass is hot from that spanking," he rasped. "Oh, yeah, like a fuckin' oven. And you are *so* fuckin' wet. You liked that, didn't you, whore? Didn't you? Answer me." He gave her hip a stinging slap. "*Answer me.*"

"Aye, m-my lord. Oh...Oh...*Mon dieu.*" She arched her back, pulling her breasts upward and exposing her nipples, erect and flushed, above the gathered neckline of her chemise. Her face darkened, that telltale vein rising on her forehead. She groaned ecstatically as she came; Lili's pussy throbbed in response.

To hold Elle's legs in the required position, Fulk had to lean over the Correction Table, one knee on the lower bench. His erection reared high, pulling at the ties of the codpiece. It was a good-size cock with a nice, thick head; there was a spot of dampness on the tip.

"Can you hold her ankles like that with just one hand?" Lili asked Fulk.

"I believe so, my lady."

"Take that out, then," she said, nodding toward his erection, "and put it to use."

"As you wish, my lady." He untied the codpiece as Lili squeezed between him and the table, kneeling over it next to Elle. She whipped up the skirts of her blue and gold satin gown and spread her legs. With his free hand, the footman pressed his cock into her, gripped her waist, and pushed. She moaned in gratification as he filled her, sliding in easily because she was so slick and ready.

Lili took Elle's face in her hands and kissed her deeply. "You're so beautiful when you come." Looking over her shoulder at Fulk, she said, with as much authority as she could manage, "Make me come first, footman. If you don't, you'll spend the next twenty-four hours in a chastity belt."

"Aye, my lady."

Bracing one foot on the bench, he reached around and fluttered a fingertip right next to her clit as he ground his hips. He really knew what he was doing. It felt like one of those dual-action rabbit vibrators with a rotating shaft attached to a clitoral stimulator. Lili came almost instantly.

Fulk slammed himself into her with a shout, his fingers digging painfully into her hip. She felt him ejaculate, felt his pleasure shooting into her, speeding her heart, pumping her lungs...

"Oh, God, don't stop, don't stop," Lili begged as another climax gathered on the heels of the first. She sucked one of Elle's nipples into her mouth, groaning helplessly. The two women came together, and Blaine, as well, amid a chorus of ecstatic moans.

Lili slumped down with her head on Elle's sweat-dampened breast, listening to the wild hammering of her lover's heart as the stranger's cock inside her slowly softened.

"God, how I wish it was you inside me," Lili murmured. "I love you so much. I wish...I just wish we could—"

"Shh, don't, love," Elle whispered as she brushed her fingers through Lili's hair, not because someone might hear—humans hardly ever put two and two together—but because there was no point in yearning for the impossible.

"That guy's staring at you again," Elle said as she opened the arched door leading from the courtyard to the chapel withdrawing room. The uniforms for the wenches and footmen were stored there, since they had no bedrooms of their own, and she'd asked Lili to keep her company while she changed.

Lili tracked Elle's gaze across the courtyard to a bench under a tree, where a good-looking young blond guy, one of the
doms—a Brit, judging from his accent—sat hunched over
with his elbows on his knees, a cigarette in one hand and a pair
of handcuffs dangling from the other. His elegant fifteenth-
century court attire was gorgeously made and historically accurate right down to the most minor detail—except for the
Ray-Ban Aviators.

"With those shades, how can you tell *who* he's staring at?"
Lili asked. But as soon as he saw her look his way, he dropped
his gaze to fiddle with the handcuffs.

Something that felt almost like a memory tickled the
hairs on Lili's nape and evaporated, leaving a slight chill in its
wake.

"We should give Archer a call and ask who he is," Elle said.
Emmett Archer, *administrateur* to Adrien Morel, Seigneur des
Ombres, coordinated the invitations and guest lists for these
types of events. He had an apartment in the castle, but for the
next few weeks, until Morel and his new bride returned from
their honeymoon, he would be living in the hunting lodge
that was their home, dog-sitting the pair of mastiff pups he'd
given them as a wedding gift.

"He introduced himself to me as Anthony Prazak," Lili
said, "but Blaine called him—"

"Blaine?"

"The guy who had his cock inside you fifteen minutes ago,"
Lili said. "The spanker."

"Blaine, huh?" Elle said with a grin as she held the door
open for Lili. "He fucks like a Blaine." She followed Lili into the
little vestibule and through a second door, locking it carefully
behind them lest one of the wenches or footmen walk in right
in the middle of The Change. Although the subs weren't allowed to go wandering about on their own, they had been

known to break the rules from time to time—usually in the hope of being punished for it.

The chapel withdrawing room had originally been intended for the use of priests celebrating Mass in the adjacent chapel, but since the chapel had never been consecrated, its sizable but homey antechamber had been put to a variety of other uses over the centuries. Currently, it was serving the purpose it did every year during D and D Week, that of a dressing room for the subs. The robing alcove, where vestments should have hung, was occupied instead by rolling garment racks, shoe racks, and plastic stacking bins filled with the components of wenches' and footmen's uniforms, arranged by size. There were also four three-way mirrors set up around the room, and a bank of lockers for the subs' street clothes and other belongings.

Lili wasn't sure which of the castle's many rooms would serve as the subs' dressing room in the future. At Inigo's urging, this one was being converted into a screening room, which was why there was lumber and plywood leaning against one wall and eighteen brand-new home theater recliners, still wrapped in plastic from the factory, pushed against another. Correction: Lili saw that the plastic had been pulled off one of them, and its charcoal gray leather looked as if it had been sat in. There was a wineglass in the cup-holder with a little red wine residue in it, and on the carpeted floor, a half-empty bottle of a local vintage alongside a stack of old-looking books.

Lili homed in on the wine label. "I thought so. That's Darius's poison of choice." The shape-shifting djinn didn't have many places he liked to hang out aside from his cozy little home in the cave, but he'd always been fond of the chapel withdrawing room. In the normal course of events, no one, including the castle servants, had much reason to go there, so it tended to be quiet during the day, an ideal location for relaxing with a book or two . . . or ten. Darius was an obsessive reader, always had been. His library in the cave held uncountable books and scrolls dating back thousands of years.

Elle sniffed the air. "He's still here somewhere. Probably napping."

Crouching down, Lili checked out the volumes du jour. "This is so Darius. While we're playing out our little fetishistic costume drama, he's steeping himself in Renaissance culture. *Paradise Lost, The Sonnets of William Shakespeare, Six Sermons* by John Donne, *The Roaring Girl* by Thomas Middleton and Thomas Dekker, *Selected Poems* by Christopher Marlowe, *The Madrigals of Hannah Vitturi, Una Durata di Piacere* by Domenico Vitturi . . . Wait." She stood up, the latter two books in her hands. "Two Vitturis?"

"Husband and wife," Elle said. "He was the Venetian poet who used to bring young women here to learn how to be courtesans."

"Right, right." When Lili arrived at Grotte Cachée with the Hellfires in 1749, more than a century had passed since Vitturi's visits, but Elle had spoken of him and his wife with great fondness. She used to visit the couple in Venice until it became too noticeable that she wasn't aging in the slightest. It was always sad for Follets, having to relinquish their friendships with their favorite humans at that point.

A cat mewed a groggy hello. Following the sound, Lili and Elle found Darius, in his feline incarnation, squeezed into the narrow space between the first and second rows of recliners. His dusky gray fur blended so perfectly with the recliners that he was virtually invisible except for his eyes and a flash of teeth when he yawned.

"You're actually comfortable, squished in there like that?" Lili asked.

He nodded, laid his head down with a deep, somnolent sigh, and closed his eyes.

"Even when he's not invisible, he's invisible," Elle said as she started unlacing her bodice.

Like the rest of Darius's ancient Semitic race, he was doomed to not only absorb the desires of any human he touched, but to then be compelled to make those desires a reality. In the process, he came to crave what that human craved, to be whatever he or she wanted him to be, to change in ways that he often despised, until such time as the human's longing was satisfied and he was released from his obligation. So maddening was this virtual enslavement that Darius took great pains to avoid accidental contact with human beings. When people were around, he usually either made himself invisible or adopted one of his two favorite personas, that of a cat or a blue rock thrush.

Lili put the books back on the pile and set about detaching Elle's overskirt. "So anyway, Blaine says this Anthony Prazak is a regular in the New York fetish clubs. They call him Tony Prozac."

"Of course they do."

Clipping Elle's overskirt to a hanger in the robing alcove, Lili said, "He's got a gorgeous, six-foot dominatrix girlfriend called Mistress G who scares the hell out of everyone. Blaine told me there's a rumor she's a transsexual, and then right after that, he said she looks kind of like me."

"*What?*" Elle said through an incredulous chuckle.

" 'Cause she has long black hair and 'Cleopatra eyes,' he said. Oh, and 'tits like grapefruit halves, only bigger.' "

"Is she here?"

"We would have noticed someone like that, don't you think?"

"Hey, you know who else didn't come?" Elle asked. "That master-slave duo we hooked up with in New York last week."

"Nicky and Doug, right..." Lili shrugged. "They might show up yet. It's only the first day."

"So, Prazak introduced himself to you?" Elle asked as she hung up her bodice. "By his real name, not Lord whatever?"

"Yeah, he asked if he could take me to dinner in Clermont-Ferrand tonight, just the two of us."

"A *date*? In the middle of a BDSM orgy?"

"I know, right?"

"He should be getting with the subs, not romancing the other doms," Elle said testily.

"Lighten up, love. I turned him down."

"Was he cool with that?"

"He asked me if tomorrow night would be better. I told him I was in a relationship with Elic." If it wasn't for that, she actually might have been tempted. Despite the semicreepy staring thing, Prazak was smart, cultivated, and well spoken. Dinner with him could have been a refreshing break from the D and D experience. As enlivening as it was to have her pick of beautiful, acquiescent sex partners, playing dress-up could get a little old.

"See?" Lili said. "No need to feel threatened. He knows I'm unavailable."

"It's just ... I don't know." Elle scowled as she pulled her chemise over her head. "He's so good-looking, with those dimples..."

"They're just creases."

"And he's blond. You have a thing for blonds."

"I have a thing for *this* blond," Lili said, twirling a lock of

Elle's honey-colored hair around her finger. "Besides, he's just a tad intense, no?"

"Yeah, but intense can be hot. You've said so yourself."

"Now, *that's* hot," Lili said, taking in the spectacularly naked Elle head to toe. She was every man's centerfold fantasy: tall, curvy, and stunning, with skin so creamy, it looked airbrushed. "You are the sexiest female here, hands down."

"I think that honor belongs to you, *mins Ástgurdís,* especially in this." Elle glided a hand down the bodice of Lili's beautiful blue gown, which had a wide, gold-laced opening in front, exposing a swath of bare skin that included the inner and upper slopes of her breasts. The gown was actually on loan from Elle, being part of the vintage clothing collection she had been amassing for the past seven or eight centuries.

"This was Hannah Vitturi's, you know," Elle said as she slid her fingertips through the lacing and under the boned satin to stroke Lili's right nipple. "Or rather, it's a copy of one of the gowns her dressmaker designed for her. I loved it so much, I had to have one just like it."

Elle's teasing caress rekindled Lili's arousal almost instantly. She moaned and pressed her hand to Elle's, encouraging a firmer touch.

"You could lie down right here," Elle suggested in a low, provocative voice as she guided Lili toward the recliner that had been stripped of its plastic. "I'll take your clit in my mouth and suck it the way you like, and I'll take my time, so when you do come, it'll be explosive. And then I'll lick you with my fingers deep inside you—"

"Not with Darius right there," Lili whispered. It was one thing for the reclusive djinn to observe their public sex with humans, another to pleasure each other with him sleeping— or trying to sleep—virtually underneath them.

"I forgot about him," Elle said.

"Later," Lili said, "when you're back to yourself. Maybe tonight, when we're in bed and don't have to deal with all this D and D nonsense. Your fingers will be longer and thicker then, anyway, and rougher. I love the way they feel inside me."

"You've sold me. Meanwhile . . ." Stepping away from Lili, Elle sat on the edge of the uncovered recliner and took a deep breath. "If you don't want to see this, sweetheart, turn around now."

Lili did turn around. It made her queasy to witness The Change, whether it was male to female or "the return ticket," as Elic called it, back to his primary male form. Basically, it was about two minutes of physical metamorphosis, with organs rearranging themselves, bones and muscles and skin changing size, and a profound shift in body chemistry. Although Elle and Elic were the same individual, with the same mind, the same memories, the same long blond hair and aquamarine eyes, the hormones that governed their sexual responses were entirely different.

Lili heard Elle whisper an incantation in the proto-Germanic *dönsk tunga* of ancient Norway. A few seconds later, there came a grunt of pain, followed by deep, rhythmic breathing, like that of a woman in labor. Part of the reason Lili hated to watch The Change was because it was frankly sickening, seeing a body roiling within its skin. But mostly she couldn't bear the sight of her beloved's face contorted in pain and nausea during the transmutation.

Finally, she heard a deep, masculine sigh and turned to find Elic sitting hunched over on the recliner with his hands gripping the arms, his hair a golden curtain over his face. Lili went over and kissed his head, saying, "Welcome back, *Khababu*."

Elic heaved himself to his feet, steadying himself with a hand on the recliner as he reached down to make sure his genitals were intact and unchanged.

Lili smiled to herself. It was always the first thing he did upon reassuming his male form, an unthinking reflex.

He was a little hard, as he always was after having captured human semen, because of the pressure it exerted inside him until he was able to release it into a woman—only a human woman. Racially, Elic was what they'd called in his homeland an *álfr*, but he was also the type of incubus known as a dusios. Any Follet could be born a dusios; it was a random, if rare, genetic mutation among nonhumans.

The biological imperative of a dusios was reproduction—ironic, since dusii were inherently sterile. They "reproduced," in a manner, by transferring sperm from a fit, healthy, intelligent human man—a *gabru* in Lili's native Akkadian tongue—to an equally exceptional woman, or *arkhutu*. This was accomplished by taking a female form to tap the *gabru*'s seed, then reverting to the male to inject it into the chosen *arkhutu*. During The Change from succubus to incubus, the *gabru*'s DNA was subtly altered so as to absorb certain nonhuman characteristics. As a result, if the recipient *arkhutu* became pregnant—a strong possibility, since sex with a dusios triggered ovulation—her offspring would possess what humans referred to as extrasensory gifts.

Mother Nature was a clever bitch. Not only were dusii, like other incubi, unable to masturbate, they were almost always incapable of having sex with other Follets. In order to ensure that they transferred their supercharged human seed to humans, the only way they could relieve their relentless lust was through vaginal intercourse with a human female. They couldn't climax any other way. A dusios couldn't even penetrate a nonhuman. If he attempted to, the blood would drain from his erection, rendering it flaccid. This was how Elic first realized Lili was a Follet, back in 1749.

"So, is Blaine a *gabru* or just a plaything?" Lili asked. Like her, Elic was insatiably horny; it was the lot of any incubus or succubus. He would fuck pretty much any willing human, regardless of their genetic worthiness, and he often adopted a female form simply because the occasion seemed to suit it. However, when he considered the man whose seed he had obtained to be a *gabru*, he took pains to pass that seed on to the right kind of woman. If no *arkhutu* was available, he'd even been known to use condoms rather than gift an undeserving woman with such precious DNA.

Grabbing the longest pair of footman's hose, Elic sat down and started gathering up one of the legs. "Despite the dickish personality, he's a *gabru*, all right. Archer did his homework. The guy's got an IQ of 142, and he's a triathlete to boot."

"Hence your clumsiness with the grog, in the hope that he'd feel the need to 'teach you a little lesson.'"

"You got it." Elic stood to tug the hose up and tighten the waist cord around his narrow hips. His cock, although not erect, was distended enough to look pretty darned impressive under that flimsy codpiece. It would remain that way until he emptied his brimming vesicles through sex with a superior human female. It shouldn't take long for him to find one who was not only willing but raring to go. With that angelic face, long blond hair, and super-tall, shredded bod—not to mention the currently supersized package—Elic looked as if he'd just stepped down off Mount Olympus.

"Who's the lucky *arkhutu*?" Lili asked as he started sorting through the boots for his size-fifteens.

"Alison Southway. Archer pointed her out to me when she arrived this morning."

"Which one is she?"

Sitting down to pull on the boots, he said, "She's one of the Americans. Petite, mid-thirties, shortish brunette hair, big hazel eyes—but you probably haven't seen her. She's been mostly hiding out since she got here. She's not really into the scene, the whole BDSM thing."

"Then what's she doing here? Why did Archer invite her?"

"He wasn't going to," Elic said as he got up and headed over to the rack of shirts. "He told me he'd issued an invitation to someone named Cordelia Meath. She's a Washington, D.C., socialite who dabbles in the scene. Cordelia asked if she could have another card of entrée for her friend Allie, who raises thoroughbred horses and is gorgeous and smart and—"

"Yeah, yeah."

Adjusting the drape of the shirtsleeves, Elic said, "At first Archer refused, but then Cordelia told him Alison was a three-time divorcée who doesn't want to rush into another marriage or even a relationship, but who does want a child, very badly. Cordelia thought it would be a great idea for her to come here, shop around for a guy whose genes look like they'd be worth passing on, and get herself knocked up with no names exchanged and no strings attached."

"And of course, Archer immediately thought of you."

"For which I'm very grateful. It's been too long since I've had an *arhkutu*."

"Now you just have to convince Alison that you've got the DNA she's been searching for all her life."

"It's a done deal," he said as he shrugged on the jerkin and buttoned it halfway. "When I was serving lunch—this was before I changed into Elle—I made it a point to hover around her and Cordelia. I heard her say this whole thing was a mistake, the public sex was freaking her out, and she wished she was back in Virginia on her horse farm. So I told her that I couldn't help overhearing and that I would be happy to escort her to our stable and help her pick out a horse to ride so that she'll have a way to pass the time while she's here."

"Why, what a thoughtful footman you are, *Khababu*."

All the D and D participants knew that this was Elic's home; he might be dressed as a footman and expected to obey the doms, but his duties as a host came first. It was his and Lili's responsibility to greet their guests and officiate over the week's activities. Inigo pitched in when he felt like it, but that wasn't often. Duty was a foreign concept to satyrs, who were biologically programmed to devote themselves to the single-minded pursuit of pleasure, period. By the standards of humans and even a lot of Follets, his self-indulgence and refusal to take anything seriously might be offputting, but by satyric standards, he was an exemplar of his race.

"Alison's meeting me in the stable in about—" Elic glanced at the mantel clock as he rummaged through an accessory bin "—ten minutes." He gave Lili his most seductive smile. "You could come with me."

"You don't think a woman like that might balk at a ménage à trois?" Lili asked.

With little gust of laughter, he said, "Since when do we have a hard time talking people into a ménage?"

Elic filled out that outfit like no other man there. His torso being as lengthy as his limbs, there were no shirts or jerkins quite long enough for him, leaving a narrow band of drum-tight abdomen visible above the low-slung hose. And as roomy as the shirt was, his shoulders still stretched its seams. There wasn't a woman here, Lili knew, who wouldn't jump at the chance to untie that codpiece and have her way with the godlike footman.

Lili considered Elic's invitation for a second, then looked away and shook her head. "I think I'll pass this time."

She'd had enough of watching him fuck other people for one day. It wasn't jealousy; his voracious incubitic sex drive was no different than hers, its appeasement no less vital to his well-being. It was knowing that, as much as she loved him, she couldn't have all of him. That connection between love and lovemaking that humans took for granted didn't exist for Lili and Elic, and it never would.

"Come here," he said quietly, taking her in his arms and pressing her head to his chest. "I know, my love ... *mins Nyidís.* I know. What your heart feels, mine feels, too."

Mins Nyidís. In the *dönsk tunga,* it meant "my Goddess of the New Moon," which was what she had been a very long time ago in ancient Babylonia; it was what the disc of lapis lazuli on her anklet represented. He liked to call her that, to remind her that a goddess was not only what she had been, but what she still was. *You are the same as you always were,* he would say. *The humans just can't see it anymore.*

"I don't begrudge you your pleasure with other women," she said. "I don't think I would even if you and I could make love. You're not like humans, nor am I. We need what we need. But sometimes, when I watch you take a woman, and I see you lose yourself in her arms, I just ..." She shook her head against his chest. "There's always a whisper of despair in the background, knowing that what you're sharing with these strangers, you can never share with me."

"You're not alone in that," he said, rubbing his cheek against her hair. "It's the same for me, sometimes even worse. You know that."

Lili may not have been prone to jealousy, but there had been a handful of times when Elic's resentment of her attraction to certain humans had actually caused rifts between them. And then there was the physical frustration he had to contend with, because although he could make her climax, she couldn't do the same for him. When he became highly aroused with no opportunity for relief, it could be excruciating.

She sometimes wondered how he'd managed to put up with their semiplatonic relationship for as long as he had.

"I know it's hard for you, Elic. And I'm sorry to let it get to me like this. After two and a half centuries, you'd think I would have stopped pining for something we can never have."

Tilting her head up so he could look into her eyes, he said, "We have what's most important, Lili. We may not be able to share our bodies, but we share our souls. Before I met you, I thought that kind of love was something I would never experience, that I would be alone forever."

As had Lili. Using human beings for sexual sustenance was one thing; forming a permanent attachment was quite another. Not only did humans grow old and die with heart-breaking speed, they could never really comprehend and accept the incubitic need for frequent, highly charged sexual encounters. But Elic and Lili understood this and so much more. They understood each other; their bond really was soul-deep.

Two sex-crazed Follets who were madly in love but couldn't have sex . . . The irony didn't strike Lili as remotely amusing.

Elic dipped his head and touched his lips to hers. Taking each other in their arms, they shared a kiss that was deep and dizzying. Lili drew away when she felt his cock rise up hard between them, an ingrained habit to avoid subjecting him to the often agonizing sexual frustration that was the bane of his existence.

"It's all right," he said, pulling her back into his arms. "Don't worry about me. I'll be taken care of soon."

She turned her head as he lowered his mouth to hers. "Go, then. Don't make her wait for you or she might leave, and you'll have to find yourself another *arkhutu.*"

Would he kiss this Alison Southway when he took her in the stable? Probably. He usually kissed them; Elic was not one to restrain a sensual impulse of any kind.

The edge of bitterness in Lili's voice wasn't lost on Elic. He sighed as his erection waned. "Lili—"

A knock came at the door. "You guys in there?" It was Inigo. "We've got a late arrival."

Prying Elic's arms from around her, Lili turned and went to the door. Elic whispered something under his breath and followed her out into the courtyard.

"Bitchin' little roadster just pulled up." Inigo, naked from the waist up but still wearing his top hat, pointed to the gatehouse as he strode toward the fountain. A redheaded wench stood in the water in just her sodden, transparent chemise, scrubbing his already clean shirt in the water sluicing off the statue.

Through the gatehouse's arched passageway, Lili saw the two guards, Mike and Luc, talking to someone in the driver's seat of a streamlined little black convertible. Luc straightened up to inspect something in his hand—a card of entrée, no doubt. Tucking it in his back pocket, he opened the car door and handed out the driver, a woman. Mike hefted a jumbo-size suitcase, a garment bag, and a black leather tote bag out of the trunk, but the woman snatched the latter two out of his hand.

Their visitor was statuesque in the extreme, her height accentuated by the stiletto-heeled boots she wore with tight, glossy black leggings. Her raven hair fell sleekly to her waist except for blunt-cut bangs that echoed the line of her mirrored wraparound sunglasses.

Reaching into the tote bag, she withdrew a small, shiny gold object—perfume, Lili realized when she sprayed it liberally onto her throat and chest. Slinging both the garment bag and tote over her shoulder, she tossed her car keys at Luc and sauntered across the drawbridge with a leggy, hip-rolling stride, her hair flowing out behind her so that Lili could get a look at the upper half of her outfit. It was all black leather: opera-length fingerless gloves and a top comprised of criss-crossing buckled straps securing a pair of breastplates that shoved those puppies up high and round.

"I don't think Tony Prozac will be asking me out on any more dates," Lili said. "Unless I'm mistaken, this would be the scary tranny girlfriend."

Eight

"T HAT'S NO TRANNY," Elic said sotto voce as they walked toward the gatehouse.

Glancing up at him, Lili saw *that look* in his eye. "Oh my God," she whispered, "you think she's hot. She looks like something out of a graphic novel, like if Wonder Woman went over to the Dark Side."

"You must be Mistress G." Elic extended his hand with a welcoming smile as they approached their new guest just inside the courtyard.

"You recognize me," the dominatrix said as she shook Elic's hand. She had a smoky film noir voice. "Been talking about me behind my back, *marish?*"

The question was utterly bewildering to Lili until she realized that Mistress G's eyes, concealed behind the mirrored shades, were aimed at someone else.

Lili and Elic both turned to find Anthony Prazak standing about twenty feet away in front of the bench he'd occupied earlier, his hands at his sides, staring at his girlfriend. The dark glasses hid his eyes, but his fair complexion had gone ashen. The handcuffs he'd been fiddling with earlier were lying on the ground.

"N-no," he said with a wooden shake of his head. "No, I . . . Honest, Galiana, I haven't talked about you at all."

"Another guest mentioned you in passing," Lili said.

"Galiana?" Elic said. "What a beautiful name."

Galiana slid down her sunglasses to get a better look at him, revealing the "Cleopatra eyes" Blaine had spoken of, rendered all the more exotic with generous, expertly tapering strokes of liquid eyeliner. Her lips were stained with the kind of purplish red lipstick that made most women's mouths look clownish, but made hers look as if it was just aching to suck hard on a big, dripping cock.

She cast a fleeting, ho-hum glance at the three-ring circus of deviance taking place in the courtyard, then returned her gaze to Elic, pushed the shades back up and said, "Do you intend to introduce us, Tony?"

Taking a few steps in their direction, Prazak cleared his throat and did the honors, informing her in an oddly strained voice that Lili and Elic lived at the château, as did Inigo, whom he pointed out, and Elic's sister, Elle.

"Is that the new Alfa Romeo Spider you're driving?" Lili asked.

"Lili's crazy about sports cars," Elic said.

Galiana said, "Yeah, the rental company tried to sell me on a Peugeot, but I just had to get my hands on that Spider."

"I don't blame you," Lili said. "I did cartwheels when they reintroduced it, but I haven't had the chance to get behind the wheel of one yet."

"You can give mine a spin any time you want."

"Thanks. I'll take you up on that."

"So, Elic," Galiana said, giving him a lingering appraisal, "you're our host and a footman both?" Her wine-red lips curved up slightly at the edges. "You're not exempt from doing the bidding of your superiors, I hope."

"I am not, my lady," Elic said with a little duck of the head that made Lili's teeth hurt. "I do, however, have other things I must attend to from time to time. In fact, even as we speak, I'm due in the stable to provide my Lady Alison with a mount."

Oh, brother, Lili thought.

"If you'll excuse me," he said.

Galiana watched him walk away through the gatehouse. As she turned back around, she plucked a cigarette from inside her left breastplate. No sooner did she slide it between her lips than Prazak was right there, thumbing a gold lighter.

Galiana scrutinized Lili's blue satin gown over the top of her reflective shades as she drew on the cigarette. She Frenched the smoke, letting it billow luxuriantly from her mouth for a moment before sucking it back in. As she exhaled it in Lili's direction, she said, "That dress. It's the real thing, isn't it?"

Lili nodded. "My friend Elle collects vintage clothing. She's donated the oldest and most historically significant things to the Costume Institute at the Metropolitan Museum in New York. Others she keeps here."

Indicating Lili's gown, Galiana said, "It's held up remarkably well."

"Elle stores everything in special, acid-free wrappings in a windowless room where the air is ionized and kept at a constant sixty degrees. She even has names for some of the garments. This one is *il vestito dallo zaffiro*. It means—"

"The sapphire gown."

"Yes."

"I'm from Italy originally."

"Really? You don't have a trace of an accent."

"I haven't lived there for a very long time. What I don't understand is why your friend, who takes such care with her collection, allows you to actually *wear* a dress that has to be— what, almost four hundred years old?"

"The pieces she keeps here are meant to be worn from time to time. She makes sure they're properly cleaned, and mended if necessary, before they go back into the collection. You're dead on about the age of this gown, by the way. It's late Renaissance, from the first half of the seventeenth century."

"That's obvious from the sleeves. It was made for a Venetian courtesan, I assume."

"You're good."

Galiana smiled coolly. "I've owned quite a few garments from past centuries myself. The 'courtesan' part is a no-brainer, given the peekaboo bodice, which, by the way, screams Venice. You could always tell where a courtesan was from by what she wore. Venice, Rome, Padua, Florence... Each city had its own distinct style of dress."

"Interesting," Lili said, although she'd remembered that from her travels through Italy in those years.

"Whatever possessed this friend of yours to give away her most important pieces to the Met when she could have kept them all to herself?" Galiana asked.

"Why does anyone donate things to a museum?" Lili shrugged. "She wanted others to be able to enjoy them, too."

Galiana's mouth quirked. "The whole philanthropy thing has always struck me as a tad ingenuous."

Not quite sure how she was supposed to respond to that, Lili said, "Are you still into vintage clothes?"

Galiana shook her head as she drew on her cigarette. "I never really was. I've never even been to a costume exhibit at the Met. When I go there, it's strictly for the art. In fact, this—" She twitched the garment bag. "—was inspired by a painting in their collection, *Judith with the Head of Holofernes* by Lucas Cranach the Elder. He painted several versions, but the one at the Met is the best. Are you familiar with the Old Testament story?"

"Holofernes was an enemy of Judith's people, right? And she took him out?"

"He was an Assyrian general who was besieging her city. When he was passed out drunk, she grabbed him by the hair and chopped off his head with his own sword. Took two strokes, so I'm thinking the first one probably roused him from his stupor. What a way to wake up, huh?" Galiana asked laughingly. "With a foxy, spitting-mad, sword-wielding babe standing over you and your blood spraying everywhere?"

Okay...

"In the painting," Galiana continued, "Judith is standing behind a table with his sword in one hand and the other just kind of resting on his severed head. She's incredibly beautiful, of course, and she's wearing the most fabulous sixteenth-century gown you've ever seen, and a big plumed hat and tons of awesome gold jewelry. But the coolest part is his head. It's totally realistic, right down to the bloody neck stump. You just know Cranach painted it from an actual chopped-off head, probably a decapitated criminal. Pretty grisly for a painting of that era. I could stare at it for hours."

"And, um, your costume is based on her gown?" Lili asked.

"It's actually a near-perfect reproduction. I had the best Italian seamstress in New York make it up for me this past week. I didn't bother with the hat—I've never been big on hats—but I did bring a couple of Renaissance-era necklaces that are real close to the ones in the painting."

"You collect antique jewelry?"

"Let's just say I've held on to all the really good stuff that's come my way." Galiana dropped her cigarette butt, crushing it under the knife-point toe of her boot. "Time to suit up so I can assume my proper baronial role and join in the fun. My room isn't ready yet, but that guard, the American one, said I could change in the . . . chapel withdrawing room?"

"Yeah, it's where the subs get into costume." Pointing, Lili said, "Go through that door, and then a second one, and you'll be there. Don't mind the mess. We're turning it into a screening room."

"Tony." The dominatrix said it softly, but Prazak flinched as if she'd snapped a whip at him. Handing him the garment bag and tote, she said, "Be a sweet *marish* and come help me dress."

❧

Galiana's silence was more terrifying to Turek than if she'd pitched one of her thermonuclear fits. Except for ordering him to hang up the garment bag and set the tote on the floor next to it, she didn't say a word as she nonchalantly stripped down in the subs' dressing room.

There were questions he would have wanted to ask her. *How did you know where I went? What are you going to do to me, and how can I get out of it?* But he just stood there in mute dread, afraid to speak for fear it would set her off. He groped around frantically in his mind for some excuse or rationalization for what he'd done, but Galiana Solsa was very smart and very old and very powerful and he was very, very fucked.

The bitch let him wait there like an idiot while she admired herself in front of a trifold mirror. Entirely naked except for the fuck-me makeup, the diamond clit stud, and a pair of nipple rings—yellow-gold barbells with ruby-eyed snakes encircling the nipples themselves—she looked like the star in every guy's darkest, dirtiest sex fantasy. She turned this way and that, plucking at her nipples to make them hard, flicking the diamond to engorge her clit. Her working theory was that male primates, including human men, became stupid and malleable in the presence of an overt display of female arousal. *Let them think you're in heat, and they're yours.* This was little challenge for Galiana, who really was always in heat.

Rubbing her labia to make them flush and swell, she said softly, "Looks like you were playing me after all, Anton."

"What?" It came out as a croak. "No. No, I—"

"My hairbrush."

"Wh-what?"

She pinned his reflection with her hard, black-rimmed eyes. "Bring...me...my...hairbrush. It's in there," she said, nodding toward the tote bag.

It took a while to locate the brush among the tote's jumbled contents: a bulging jewelry roll, a pair of gold satin high-heeled lace-up boots, her favorite gigantic black strap-on dildo, a slender little aluminum cane with a leather belt hook, and the Paramount 900XT Maximum Security Waist Chain. The latter, comprised of over two pounds of steel chain with state-of-the-art locks on the attached handcuffs, was how well-funded police departments secured their high-risk prisoners, and it was Galiana's favorite restraint for subs. Like the strap-on and the cane, she toted it with her almost everywhere she went.

Another item she was never without: the gold-plated perfume atomizer with which she sprayed herself two or three times an hour whenever she found herself among a large number of people. The purpose of this was to mask the mélange of odors that bombarded her on a continual basis, odors most Follets and all humans were unaware of, at least on a conscious level. The perfume she'd been wearing lately was La Fièvre de la Jungle, a chic and pricey new scent that was all citrus top notes, and which did nothing for Turek but make him sneeze.

Galiana took her time brushing her hair while he stood there, soaking his damned costume with flop sweat.

When she was finally done, she held the brush out to him, handle first, and said, "Fuck yourself with this."

He looked at her. This was a new one. Under the circumstances, what did it mean?

She just stood there with her empty black eyes, holding the brush out.

He took it. She told him to strip from the waist up, drop his trunk hose, and stand in front of the three-way mirror "so you can see yourself from every angle."

It was a boar bristle brush with a fat, round lacquered rosewood handle imprinted with "Wick & Carlisle" in gold. Nice brush. Probably cost her three or four hundred bucks.

"What are you waiting for?" she said.

"Um, is there any—"

"Lube? No."

"Can I use a lubricated condom? I've got one in—"

"No."

Under normal circumstances, even as cowed as he was in general by Galiana, he would have pressed her on the lube issue. But he didn't, and he knew that she knew why. He'd fucked up and now he was utterly and completely at her mercy. Apparently, she'd decided to subject him to an S&M

scenario like those she enacted with her pathetic human subs. She didn't normally play these games with him, not overtly, anyway. The question was, how far would she go?

He braced his feet and drew a deep breath. It took him a few long, teeth-gritting minutes to bury the entire handle, as she demanded. Maybe it was the pressure against his prostate, but by the time it was all the way in, his cock was a fucking flagpole.

"None of that," she said when he went to touch it. "Both hands on the brush. All the way in and all the way out, and keep at it till I tell you to stop."

She strolled around him, stroking her pussy while he stood there with his hose around his ankles, ass-fucking himself. Occasionally she would snap at him to stand up straighter or thrust harder, or to direct his gaze to one of the side mirrors so he could watch his own hands shoving the brush handle in and out, in and out. If she was trying to humiliate him, she was succeeding. It was demeaning, for sure, but in spite of that or maybe even because of it, it was also darkly exciting. He trembled with the effort to keep from thrusting his hips, which she forbade.

"Yes," he breathed when she reached for his cock, but she merely pinched the glans to squeeze a viscous stream of pre-come onto her fingertips. This she used for lubrication as she stood right in front of him and brought herself to climax.

Watching her masturbate ratcheted his arousal to a fever pitch, as she had surely known it would do. His lungs were pumping; his cock was on fire. He didn't dare stroke himself, or even ask for permission to do so, but he thought if this went on much longer, he might just come with no contact at all.

When she was done playing with her pussy, she licked her fingers with relish and said, "That's enough. Get dressed."

He stared at her in stupefaction. That's enough? *That's*

enough? Was she fucking kidding him? He's was about a nanosecond from coming, and she knew it, and—

She knew it. Fucking bitch. Sadistic fucking cunt. So that was the idea. Degrade him, torment him, drive him to the aching, throbbing, no-turning-back edge of orgasm, then pull the rug out from under him and see if he'd go along with it like the good little compliant *marish* he was.

But what choice did he have? Defy her and set off a firestorm of rage? No telling what she would do to him then.

You're getting off easy, he told himself as he eased the brush out and raised his trunk hose with quaking hands, taking care as he fastened them not to let the fabric rub too hard against his erection. It wouldn't take much to make him come, and then what would she do?

She watched him in smug silence while he got dressed. As he was buttoning up his doublet, he said, "Interesting punishment, I must say."

She closed her fist around his throat and lifted him off the floor with an outstretched arm.

He clawed at her hands, his lungs convulsing as they strove in vain to suck in air. Strangulation wasn't fatal to vampires— they might pass out, but they wouldn't die—however, lack of air was as panic-inducing for them as it was for humans. And it was anyone's guess what this crazy bitch would do once he was unconscious and helpless. Would he come to soaked in gasoline, with her holding a lit match and smiling that dead-eyed smile of hers?

Keep your fucking legs still! he told himself as he struggled and flailed, bright little pinpoints swarming in front of his eyes. God knew what she would do if he were to kick her.

"You thought that was your punishment?" she asked with an incredulous little smile.

Turek tried to shake his head, but from the neck up, he felt like a lump of meat in a refrigerator. His mouth was agape, his tongue sticking out. He tried to pull down on her arm, but it was like trying to bend the arm on a bronze statue.

A gray fog rolled in, blurring and then obliterating everything...a night fog under a cold moonless sky, growing darker and denser until there was nothing but blackness.

Nine

JUREK OPENED HIS EYES to find himself lying on a plush gray carpet watching three ghostly, white-robed women moving in graceful synchronization.

No, that was wrong, he thought as he blinked the scene into focus. It was three angles of the same tall, black-haired woman reflected in a trifold mirror as she stood behind him, tweaking the drape of a silken chemise.

Galiana.

Sheisse. She wasn't through with him. She was going to do things to him that would have him shrieking and sobbing and begging for death.

He was well and truly fucked.

He lay absolutely still, his eyes slitted, as he watched her adjust the neckline of the chemise to get it as low as possible.

Play dead, he thought, *isn't that what you're supposed to do when a bloodthirsty predator has you cornered?*

Her triple reflection disappeared as she walked off toward the clothing racks. He heard the rustling of fabric, but he didn't dare turn his head to look. A few minutes later, she reappeared wearing a full skirt and carrying something that was made of pieces of gold brocade and the same hunter green velvet as the skirt, with narrow green ribbons trailing off it.

"Figured it out yet?" she said as she ducked her head into the garment—a bodice, he now saw—and started threading her arms through the sleeves. "How I knew you were here?"

Oh, fuck. He sat up, raking his hair off his face. "No idea."

"No, of course not." She didn't look at him as she spoke, just adjusted the bodice, a complicated affair comprised of several disparate elements laced together with the green ribbons. "After I sank that pigeon under the Whitestone Bridge, I decided to find out what had made you bolt like that in the middle of a death feed. I went back to Bleecker and nosed around a little. You'd left a scent trail a human with hay fever could have followed. Bijan and adrenaline. I didn't even have to keep to street level. I tracked you from the rooftops so I wouldn't be seen. At least one of us knows how to be discreet."

Arschloch, Turek thought, scrubbing his hands over his face. *You stupid fucking fuckhead.*

She said, "I ended up at that little secret square off St. Mark's, sitting in a tree right over you, watching you jerk off in the rhododendrons while you played Peeping Tom. I could see through the windows, and I could hear them talking. I couldn't figure out why you'd followed them till I heard the names Lili and Elic. I realized she was the one you'd told me about, the succubus you had such a hard-on for who used to hang with the Hellfires, and he was the guy who kicked your ass and landed you in the Bastille. Looks like you were right about him being a Follet, since he's still around."

"Yeah," Turek said dully.

"He's pretty sexed-up for an elf," she said, positioning a snug band of quilted gold brocade at the top of the bodice to create a cleavage of majestic proportions. "That's got to be what he is, a Nordic elf from back when they supersized 'em."

"I think so."

"He sure knew what to do with that bottomless boner of his. It's been a long time since I've seen a real man have his way with a woman—I mean fucking the hell out of her for hours, taking her however he wants, moving her this way and that, just giving it to her and giving it to her till she's shaking and moaning and can't stand up. Holy fuck, a six-and-a-half-foot Bronze Age Scandinavian elf with incubitic tendencies. He's a goddamned Viking sex god."

Galiana gazed into the mirror with a faraway smile, absently thumbing her nipples through the quilted brocade. Turek had never seen her get this way over a man, human or non. She'd always seemed to view males, Turek included, as being one or two levels beneath her on the evolutionary scale. To see her all dreamy-eyed like this, well, it was a dramatic departure.

And an interesting one.

Rising to his feet, he said, "So, um, I guess you heard them talking about D and D week, and—"

"Get back down," she said calmly as she threaded a ribbon through the eyelets on the front of the bodice. "Sit in seiza. Hands on thighs."

Seiza was the Japanese term for kneeling on one's calves, and it was Galiana's favorite resting position for her subs. Turek hesitated.

268 • Louisa Burton

She glanced at him.

He did it.

"Palms up," she said with an impatient sigh.

When he was positioned to her satisfaction, she said, "I trailed you as you followed those two nitwits to that bus shelter, and I watched you, the third stooge, blunder through that mugging like you were hoping to get arrested all over again. I laughed like hell when she zapped you in the face with that pepper spray. And then when you ran into that lamppost? I thought I was going to choke on my tongue."

Turek's jaw throbbed.

The sleeves of Galiana's bodice were comprised of separate upper and lower arm pieces laced together loosely at the elbows. Plucking puffs of chemise sleeve through the lacings, she said, "After you ran off, I went over to the little blonde— Nicky?—and comforted her till the cops came. She was far too upset to notice me slipping the other card of entrée out of her blazer pocket. Then I just went home and waited for you to show up"—her eyes snapped to his in the mirror—"and tell me you were planning a trip to Gebirgshaus, knowing I'd rather eat steaming dog turds than spend one second in that moldering old relic."

"I... I know I... misled you, but—"

"You *lied* to me so that you could throw me over for that bitch you've been carrying a torch for all these years. At least have the balls to admit it."

Only to have her throw it back in his face and torture him to death? *You think that was your punishment?* The only way to save himself now was to make his deceit seem like a misdemeanor rather than a capital crime.

"I... I did lie to you, Galiana, and I shouldn't have, but it wasn't so I could throw you over. I would never leave you. Why would I want to? You're... you're the most powerful and beautiful creature I've ever known. I'm the envy of every man who sees me with you, human or Follet."

Galiana didn't acknowledge his obsequious flattery as she fussed with her sleeves, but that didn't mean it hadn't made an impression on her. Galiana loved to be told how awesome she was, and it never occurred to her to doubt the sincerity of those who fawned over her. They were just speaking the simple truth, after all.

"You know how I feel about Lili," Turek continued, adding a note of barely repressed fury to his voice to sell the line of bull. It was Galiana herself who'd pointed out to him what excellent actors Follets of all races were. It was a survival mechanism for living in a world of humans who either didn't believe in you or wanted to burn you at the stake; there was rarely a middle ground.

"I would have made her my queen," he said, "and she sent me to rot in the fucking Bastille. Do you honestly think I'd try to win her over again, after what she did to me? I've never loathed anyone in my life as much as I loathe her. For fuck's sake, Galiana, I didn't come here to court the bitch, I came here to fucking incinerate her. How could you possibly think otherwise?"

"And you lied to me because . . . ?"

"I . . ." *Think fast.* "I . . . I knew you'd want to be involved, 'cause you're, like, a take-charge kind of chick, and that's part of what's so great about you, but I thought it would be best to carry this out on my own, keeping as low a profile as possible. I mean, it's not like I can just chain her to a stake in the courtyard and build a pyre around her. I've got to get her alone in some secluded place, without her growing suspicious. And without Elic playing the white knight again. That's just what I need." He made a face and shook his head, then worried he was overselling it.

"You don't think I'm capable of keeping a low profile?" she asked.

Turek risked a little grin, making it look as if he were trying not to. "They, uh, don't come much more high profile than you. I mean, you're . . . Galiana Solsa. You're magnificent. You could cut your hair off and wear a fucking muumuu and glasses and not a stitch of makeup, and you'd still be the most stunning woman anyone had ever seen. You stand out, Galiana. That's all there is to it."

She retrieved the gold boots from the tote bag, sat on one of the recliners, and hiked up her skirts. The boots, with their pointy toes and ultra high heels, were absurdly anachronistic, but Galiana never wore any other style of footwear, period.

She maintained a thoughtful silence until she was almost done lacing up the second boot. "It amuses me that you think you could have pulled this off on your own. I may be conspicuous, but I'm far more cunning than you could ever hope to be. I'm over three thousand years old, *marish*. You're six hundred eighty—and immature for your age, to boot. You lack subtlety. Your schemes are simplistic, your execution sloppy— witness that debacle at the bus shelter, not to mention the great fuck-up of eighty-two. If the cops had nabbed you again, I would have washed my hands of you. You know that, don't you?"

Turek nodded, his gaze on his upturned palms. Was it possible she'd really bought his story about wanting to off Lili? He might survive this experience after all.

"Look at you."

He glanced up to find her standing with her hands propped on her hips, regarding him with disgust. "You really have made a piss-poor vampire, Anton, just as I said you would when I turned you. It was a punishment, remember? For trying to cast me aside? I knew the life of a bloodsucker would just bring you misery, but maybe I should have cured you instead. I could have transfused the plague out of you, kept you mortal, and made you my prisoner. I could have tortured you in very entertaining ways for months, even years, before putting you out of your pathetic human misery. Instead, I sullied the vampire race by making a hopeless loser like you one of us."

She crossed to the tote bag and came back with some rings and an armload of massive necklaces, all yellow gold. "You're lucky I decided to come here," she said as she slid the rings onto her fingers and thumbs. "You would have screwed everything up for sure. I, on the other hand, have three thousand years of scheming under my belt."

She opened a hinged, jeweled choker about two inches wide and snapped it around her neck. "Your job is to cozy up to Lili, make her trust you enough to go off alone with you under cover of dark."

"Tonight?" he asked. "I don't think I can—"

"No, not tonight, you cretin." She added a second choker above the first, encasing her neck in jewel-encrusted gold. "Something like this takes careful planning. It absolutely *must* look like an accident so Elic won't get up in arms and decide to avenge her death. You just work on softening up Lili, and I'll see to the details. Not that I'm going to do the actual dirty work, mind you. You're the one who wants her dead. You get to do the honors."

Of course, it was Galiana who wanted Lili dead, or she wouldn't be making it a project. She didn't do favors; the notion was foreign to her.

"And afterward?" he said.

She gave him a quizzical look as she donned the third and last necklace, a long chain with links as thick as fingers.

Employing his last remaining shred of spinal fortitude, he

said, "Are you going to kill me after Lili's out of the picture and you've got Elic all to yourself?"

Smiling at her own reflection, Galiana arranged the heavy chain so that it hung down in back rather than in front. "I *will* kill you, in an extraordinarily prolonged and creative manner, if you don't follow my plan to the letter and roast that fucking bitch until she's nothing but cinders. Your whole universe will be pain. In the end, when I finally torch you, I'll take my time. I'll make it last and last, an infinity of anguish. You think you know what I'm capable of, but you don't, Anton. You really have no idea."

She stepped back from the mirror to appraise her costume and make a few final adjustments. "If you're smart and do as you're told," she said, "you'll get to live. But not with me. You and I will part ways and never see each other again. For real this time."

"And you'll replace me with Elic."

"Not that it's any of your business, but yes, that's the plan. With Lili gone, he'll be grief-stricken, lonely, vulnerable."

"Are you going to try to turn him?" Turek asked.

"Not at first. I'll assure him I have no such intention. But with the right kind of coaxing, I'll bet I could have him begging for it in no time. I can't tell you how many mourning humans I've lured into vampirism by convincing them it was the only way they would ever find relief from their despair. He'll make a superlative vampire. He's beautiful, strong, passionate... perfect."

It was precisely how Turek felt about Lili. And now, one of the most brilliant and ferocious vampires in existence had given him two options: Kill her or die after suffering "an infinity of anguish."

"My pussy is dripping just from thinking about Elic." She lifted her skirts, planted her gold-booted feet wide apart, and said, "Crawl on over here and lick me, like a good little *cucciolo*."

❧

The first thing Galiana did upon taking her place among the barons and baronesses was to reserve the dungeon torture chamber for an hour that night, beginning at ten o'clock. She asked around for a serving wench who fit her requirements of being both bi and deeply hungry for punishment. One of the doms pointed out a buxom redhead, whom Galiana recognized as the girl who'd been wheeled around the courtyard that afternoon for people to test different lubes on, using fingers, dildos, cocks, and in at least one case, a well-greased fist.

Stepping in front of the wench as she circulated among the doms in the courtyard with a tray of cheese and fruit, Galiana said, "Are you the one they call Isolde?"

"Yes, my lady."

Galiana grasped the girl's nipples through her translucent chemise, pinching and pulling them to make them stiffen up. "They tell me you love pain."

"Yes, my la—" She yelped and dropped her tray when Galiana gave her nipples a good, hard twist.

Galiana slapped Isolde's face, leaving a ruddy handprint on her freckle-spattered cheek. "Pick that up and throw it away," she said, pointing to the grapes and cherries and blocks of cheese scattered on the ground. "That was good food, and it's ruined now. You should be made to pay for it, don't you think?"

"Yes, my lady," Isolde replied as she knelt to clean up the mess.

"Get that slatternly little ass of yours down to the dungeon at ten o'clock tonight. Take off your clothes and finger-fuck yourself until I arrive, but don't you dare let yourself come."

"As you wish, my lady."

Elic needed his instructions, too, but he was nowhere to be seen, so she walked down the gravel drive to the stable, thinking he might still be there with the baroness he'd gone to meet earlier. As she approached the big stone barn, she heard hectic panting from within. With practiced vampiric stealth—Turek should have been there taking notes—she crept along the side of the building to a Dutch door with the top part open. She took off her sunglasses and scanned the dusky interior, lit only by ribbons of late afternoon sunlight.

Diagonally across the central aisle, in a stall enclosed by a grilled wooden partition, stood a big, sturdy chestnut horse with its head down. It appeared to be calmly munching hay while Elic, naked from the waist up, banged a petite brunette in half-undone baroness attire—"Lady Alison," presumably—atop its broad, blanketed back. With one long arm, he gripped the top of the grill for purchase, his other arm wrapped around Alison's back to hold her in place with her legs over his thighs as he fucked her. Each driving stroke forced a breathy little cry from her lungs and whipped his sweat-soaked hair. His body gleamed, every hardworking muscle sharply delineated.

Galiana had come there to give Elic his marching orders, but the sight of that beautiful body heaving in sensual abandon poleaxed her. He really was a Viking sex god, born to do exactly what he was doing right now. She grew wet all over again, thinking about the little threesome she would be presiding over in the dungeon that night. One of the most mind-blowingly sexy men she'd ever known would be completely in her power, obligated to obey her every command. That Elic clearly didn't have a submissive bone in his body, but would be required to do her bidding anyway, made the prospect that much more enticing.

He went still, chest pumping, and looked in Galiana's direction as she ducked behind the wall.

"Don't stop!" Alison gasped. "Don't stop, Elic—please. I'm going to come again."

"Is someone there?" he called out breathlessly.

"Did you hear someone?" the brunette asked anxiously.

"No, but I smell something lemony and kind of . . . murky."

"It's probably just furniture polish."

"No, there's some grapefruit, a hint of bergamot, maybe a little bitter orange. I think it's La Fièvre de la Jungle."

You have got to be fucking kidding me, Galiana thought.

"Galiana, is that you?" he asked.

I don't believe this. Stepping back in front of the Dutch door, she said, "Don't stop on my account. I just—"

"Jesus." Alison cringed and turned her face away. "She was *watching* us?"

"It's all right," he murmured, kissing her head as he gathered her up in a protective gesture that Galiana probably would have found touching if she were susceptible to sentimentality.

He looked toward Galiana, strands of damp hair hanging over his scalding blue eyes, and said, "Sorry, but we're really not into an audience. If you like to watch, try the courtyard."

Galiana turned and walked away, thinking *Holy shit, have I been dismissed? Did he fucking dismiss me?*

He did. And she let him. She couldn't remember the last time anyone had told her what to do, however politely. The ease with which he had done so inspired a little carnal thrill that made her smile, until she remembered . . .

Murky? A thousand bucks an ounce, and she'd been smelling like fucking furniture polish? The first thing she'd do when they showed her to her room would be to wash off every bit of that goddamned overpriced shit and throw the rest in the garbage.

❧

Elic didn't serve dinner or clean up with the rest of the subs, so Galiana didn't encounter him again until around nine, when she was told he'd been seen entering the library. She found him sitting on a leather couch next to another man, both of them leaning forward to look at a book lying open on a table. The book was clearly very old, its parchment pages warped and heavily discolored.

Elic's companion, a darkly handsome guy dressed in jeans and a faded brown henley shirt, was saying "... originated in a cuneiform tablet dating from the Iron Age, which was translated into two or three different Old Italic languages before this Latin translation by a ninth-century Irish monk, but I doubt the content was distorted to any appreciable—"

"Good evening, my lady," Elic said as he rose and bowed to Galiana. So it was back to "my lady" after the familiar way he'd addressed her in the stable. His hair was wet and haphazardly tied back with a strip of leather at his nape. They'd told her there was a bathhouse here; maybe that was where she should have looked for him.

The other man closed the book, which had a cover of ragged tooled leather over wooden boards, and stood, too.

Elic said, "Lady Galiana, may I introduce my friend Darius, who also lives at Grotte Cachée."

"My pleasure." Darius's voice was pleasantly deep, with a subtle accent that didn't sound quite European.

Indicating his mundane attire, she said, "You aren't participating in the festivities?"

"Not really my cup of tea, I'm afraid."

"How may I be of service, my lady?" Elic asked.

Leveling her chilliest gaze at him, she said, "You were impertinent this afternoon in the stable. Meet me at a quarter after ten in the dungeon. I assure you, you'll find your chastisement memorable, and possibly quite painful. I will permit you to bring a tube of lubricant. Other than that, I'm afraid you will find me a rather rigid and unforgiving disciplinarian."

He regarded her in silence for a moment before bending his head and saying, "I am yours to command, my lady."

Ten

BY THE TIME ELIC ARRIVED in the dungeon, Galiana had Isolde just where she wanted her: bent over with her head and hands locked in the antique pillory and her ankles held wide apart by foot stocks, naked but for a leather bondage hood and ball gag. Galiana, wearing nothing but her gold boots, her chunky Renaissance jewelry, and her huge, veiny black strap-on, was giving the super-submissive wench the whip-fucking of her life.

With every few snapping thrusts, she brought her cane singing down onto Isolde's upthrust ass. Aluminum canes hurt like hell, eliciting, in this instance, a muffled cry with every stroke. They also left extremely beautiful crimson stripes, which was one of the reasons Galiana was so fond of hers. Against the redhead's pale flesh, the marks looked as if they'd been drawn on using a red Sharpie and a ruler.

Stunning. The sight made Galiana's mouth water. It made her fangs, tucked away in the roof of her mouth, tickle and throb. The seductive contrast of stinging red against pure, milky white ... the blood so deliciously close to the surface of the skin, she could almost taste it ...

Patience, she told herself. Later, after she had finished with Elic and sent him away, she would sip from the tracery of sweet little blue veins under that marble skin. She wouldn't share her with Anton, either. Fuck him, let him find his own pigeons.

But for now, she had other priorities. There was an investigational aspect to tonight's "punishment" of Elic. How much of it would he accept, she wondered, before he rebelled—*if* he rebelled? It took iron-cast balls to resist Galiana's innate authority. Look at Anton. If one discounted how he acted with her, he came off pretty goddamned menacing. His lifelong body count was probably higher than hers, considering his perverse love of death feeds, yet he'd been her toady since the French Revolution. True, he'd deceived her about this little visit to Grotte Cachée—for which he would pay with his life after he helped her to land Elic, regardless of what the gullible little nit believed—but to her knowledge, he'd never pulled a stunt like this before.

Would Elic bend over for her, as Anton had, or would he push back a little bit? The answer to that question would determine what kind of strategy she should employ in winning him over.

Galiana made a show of ignoring Elic as he walked toward them through the torchlit stone undercroft. Grotte Cachée's medieval-era torture chamber made your average BDSM dungeon look like a Sunday School classroom. Each of its six vaulted bays housed several instruments of punishment, some clearly as old as the castle itself, such as the rack, the iron chair, the whipping stool, the hanging cage, and the pillory Galiana was making such excellent use of. There were a few furnishings that clearly dated from the last few centuries: a Berkley horse, a triangular flogging ladder, a bondage bed with a pillory headboard, and a steel St. Andrew's cross. Shelves held myriad smaller implements of malevolent design, and racks of whips, paddles, ropes, leather straps, straitjackets and the like adorned nearly every wall. Two massive stone columns were embedded with rings and hooks festooned with archaic manacles, modern handcuffs, leg irons, and chains.

From the corner of her eye, Galiana saw Elic watching her intently as she rammed the big black phallus into the captive sub. Every thrust caused the strategically placed nubs on the inside of the harness to rub against her clit, stoking her pleasure.

He eyed her hungrily, his cock rising thick and hard.

"I like to have a nice, full pussy when I come," she told him. "Do a decent job of it, and I might show you a little mercy when it's time for your punishment." As if the word "mercy" meant anything at all to her.

"At your service, my lady."

As Elic untied his codpiece, she bent over Isolde with her legs spread to present her wet, gaping cunt to him. The dildo itself was made of a flexible gel, and the vinyl strap-on was styled with thigh bands like a jockstrap, so that she could fuck and be fucked at the same time, which she loved.

Her hips jerked reflexively when Elic slid his fingertips between her pussy lips and spread them wide. He held them open as he stood there, lightly stroking his erection, making Galiana feel exposed and vulnerable—not a sensation she was accustomed to; the very novelty of it was strangely arousing.

Just when she was about to tell him to go ahead and fuck her already, he shoved himself into her—or tried to. The moment his flesh touched hers, he went limp.

"What the hell . . . ?" he muttered.

"You're kidding," she said. An incubus with erectile dysfunction? Of course, as far as he knew, she regarded him as an ordinary mortal—which was, of course, what he took her to be. She'd given him no reason to suspect otherwise.

He pumped his cock to full tumescence and tried to penetrate her again, with the same result.

"Are you drunk?" she asked.

"No."

"Um . . . do you have this problem with other women?"

There came a pause. Very quietly, no doubt so Isolde wouldn't hear, he said, "Not human women. Ever."

Galiana turned to look at him over her shoulder. He was regarding her with an expression of revelation and curiosity, as if wondering what kind of Follet he had on his hands.

Meanwhile, it was suddenly all too fucking clear what he was.

God*damn.* The most incandescently hot male she'd come across in centuries, and he couldn't fuck her?

Straightening up, she pulled the dildo out of Isolde, who mewed petulantly at its removal. "Fuck *her,* then. I'm bored with her."

"Very well, my lady." He eyed Galiana longingly as he worked on renewing his erection. "It won't be the same, though."

"I'm sure you'll manage." Galiana said. "Just don't make her come. That's her punishment for *her* transgression, denial of orgasm."

"Not the caning?"

"No, she loves the caning. And while you're punishing her, I'll punish you. Did you bring the lube?"

"No."

"No?" Sliding her fist up and down the fat dildo, she said,

"This may be gel, but it's a hell of a lot for a guy to take without a little help. But if that's the way you want it, that's the way you'll get it."

Chuckling, Elic said, "I don't think so."

There it was, his statement of defiance, his line in the sand. She held his gaze for an electric moment, and then she brandished the cane, saying "Bend over and drop your—"

Elic seized her wrists, the cane falling to the floor. He grabbed a pair of manacles off the column and locked her hands in front of her, then yanked off the strap-on and tossed it onto the Berkley horse. The entire maneuver had taken him all of about five seconds.

She said, "What the hell—*Oh!*"

Banding an arm around her waist, he bent her over, lifted the cane off the floor, and whipped her fast and hard on her bare ass. She screamed with every blow, not so much because they hurt, although they did, but because of the sheer mortification of being treated like a . . . like a . . .

Like a miserable little fucking sub.

When he was done, he let go of her. She collapsed to the floor of beaten earth, thinking *Did that really happen? Did I really just take a caning?*

He planted a booted foot on her back as she started to rise, shoving her facedown with her bound hands under her. "That alpha bitch routine of yours is pretty hot," he said. "Up to a point."

"Fuck you."

Leaning down, he pushed a couple of fingers up into her and moved them around, her drenched cunt clutching at them greedily. In a deeper, softer voice, he said, "So it does get you off, being whipped. I thought it might."

Only if it's you doing the whipping, she thought. But she

said, with a petulance that surprised and embarrassed her, "Let me up, you bastard."

He lifted her easily to her feet. Her hair was snarled, her hands were manacled, she was grimy from lying on packed dirt, and she knew all too well what her ass must look like after that caning.

Brushing her hair off her face, he said in a quiet, earnest voice, "God, you are hot. I'd give anything to fuck you."

"Yeah, right," she muttered as she yanked at the manacles. They were cast iron shackles connected by about six inches of chain, probably nineteenth century. They weren't very thick, and cast iron was weaker than steel. A quality set of modern handcuffs would hold her, but with these, one good surge of vampiric strength would suffice to bend them and free herself. Hell, given ten seconds, she could just wriggle out of them, as could many humans for that matter.

Instead, she just stood there, heart pounding in anticipation, waiting to see what he would do with her.

"You should see yourself as I see you," he said, touching the tip of the cane to a barbell-pierced nipple, which grew instantly erect—as did he. "You look amazing right now. Furious, aroused, mortified, confused..."

"I'm not used to being treated this way."

"No, you're the one who dishes it out." He trailed the cane down over her hips and thighs, raising goose bumps. "Have you ever been forced to take it?"

"Why are you even dressed like that if you won't act like a footman? You're supposed to give me what I want."

"That's what I'm doing. It's just that you don't know what it is you really want, deep inside."

"And you do?"

He answered her with a smile that said he didn't have a

doubt in the world. Standing there with that gleaming cane in his hand, fully dressed but for his marble-hard erection, he was the very picture of the primal male, ready to fuck or fight at a moment's notice.

Isolde made a little grunt of impatience and shifted her hips in a silent plea.

"Shh, I know, I know," Elic soothed, gently stroking her pussy. "Soon."

"Don't make her come," Galiana said.

"Still trying to issue orders? Tsk-tsk." Lifting her bound arms over her head, he lightly tapped the diamond in the hood of her clit, inciting spasms that reverberated throughout her, making her moan like a little bitch. He slid the aluminum rod back and forth along her wet slit, her hips trembling as she tried not to thrust. She couldn't remember ever having felt so empty, so desperate for penetration.

He knew, goddamn him. He said, "Since I can't give you the full pussy you need, you're going to have to fill it up with that." He nodded toward the strap-on. "Put it on inside out. Turn it from a strap-on to a strap-in."

Galiana hesitated. It was one thing to be bullied, another to actually hop to when you were given an order. If she obeyed him in this, he would know she could be mastered. If she didn't, if she fought him for dominance, she would have little chance of making him her consort. Elic was no trembling syncophant like Anton Turek. If Anton was a puppy, Elic was a wolf. And wasn't that, after all, what had drawn her to him?

He raised the cane and cocked his head, as if to say, *Well?*

Galiana took the device and attached the thigh straps, no easy feat with her bound hands. Widening her stance, she pushed the oversized phallus into herself, wondering how he'd managed to get her in his thrall in a matter of minutes. She felt impossibly stuffed when it was only halfway in, but she kept pushing until it was fully inserted, and then she buckled on the waist strap to hold it there.

Elic said, "Isolde's punishment has lasted long enough. Get down under there." He pointed between the girl's legs with the cane. "You're going to use your mouth on her while I use this." Taking his cock in his hand, he stood behind Isolde and penetrated her gradually while she moaned through her gag. Rather than have to crouch, because of his height, he lifted the girl by her thighs and stepped over the leg stocks so that her widespread legs extended behind him.

Galiana dutifully crawled beneath them. For a moment, she just knelt there, relishing the sight of Elic's cock plunging in and out of Isolde with slow, deep, churning strokes. He was holding her fairly still, making Galiana's job a little easier than it otherwise would have been. She rarely performed cunnilingus, except occasionally to underscore her power over a female by forcing her to come against her will. She didn't mind it, though, and in fact, she was pretty damn good at it, as Isolde proved by coming not once, but twice, in short order.

From Elic's ragged breathing and strained thrusts, she knew he was close. She raised her hands to cradle his scrotum, feeling it draw up hard and tight in her palm as she caressed it. He rammed his hips forward, shaking. With each low groan, she felt a pulsing in his balls.

A trickle of semen, creamier than that of humans, slid down Isolde's inner thigh. Galiana indulged the urge to lick it, growling deep in her throat because it made her think of feeding. Her fangs didn't just tickle now, they quivered, straining to unfold.

Elic didn't uncouple from Isolde after coming, or even set her back down. Instead, he paused for a few seconds to catch his breath, then resumed his unhurried thrusting, again holding the redhead conveniently still.

Galiana slid off her denture. Her fangs popped down, sharp and ready. She glided her tongue along the crease of Isolde's groin, feeling a racing pulse under the skin—a lovely femoral artery just waiting to be tapped. The proximity of all that hot, rushing blood made Galiana's nipples stiffen and tingle. Her pussy swelled around the thick, unyielding phallus.

She licked her lips, touched the tips of her fangs to the sweet spot where the pulse was strongest, and snapped them down, piercing the flesh and puncturing the artery. It was a little deeper than she'd anticipated—femorals were unpredictable that way—but her three-thousand-year-old fangs were long enough to do the job.

Isolde's gag-muted cries took on a frantic quality. She squirmed and bucked, or tried to, but Elic held her tight, no doubt assuming she was merely reacting to Galiana's ministrations. Galiana was glad of that; she didn't want to have to open her jaw and bite down on this pristine white flesh. She stroked the artery with her tongue until the blood started pumping up her fangs, every nerve in her body vibrating with the rapture of the feed. The position of the dildo tugged the waist strap down, exposing her upper vulva. No sooner did she touch her clit than she came hard, so hard she almost unseated her fangs. She rocked her hips and stroked her aching flesh and came again and again as she fed, groaning in feral bliss.

Elic shouted hoarsely, snapping Galiana out of her blood-haze. Evidently his semen wasn't just thicker than a human's, but more copious, as well; it dripped from Isolde's body like heavy cream as his climax ebbed.

With much reluctance, Galiana extracted her fangs, licking the pair of puncture wounds to speed healing and muddy Isolde's memory of what had transpired here. Elic withdrew from the girl, cleaned them both off with a handkerchief, and retied his codpiece as Galiana surreptitiously replaced her denture.

After helping her off the floor, he took a key from a hook in the column and freed her from the manacles. He removed Isolde's mask and gag and released her from the pillory and foot stocks, grabbing her as her legs started to crumple beneath her.

"Whoa, are you all right?" Frowning in concern, he took a step back to look her over while supporting her by her upper arms. His gaze lit on the two little half-healed puncture wounds in her groin.

He stared at them. Galiana could almost hear what he was thinking: *So this is what I'm dealing with, a fucking bloodsucker.*

He turned to look at Galiana. She held his gaze with a look that said, *You got it. That's what I am.*

"How much did you take?" he asked.

"She'll be fine. The marks will be gone by tomorrow, and she won't even remember it."

"Remember what?" Isolde asked.

Galiana smiled at Elic. *You see?* "Have you learned your lesson?" she asked the girl.

Ducking her head, Isolde said, "I'm not sure, my lady."

"You mean you might need another punishment session before your behavior improves?"

Isolde nodded.

"Very well. Tomorrow, I'm going to lock you in that—" She pointed to the hanging cage. "—with the two biggest, strongest footmen I can find, all three of you naked. The first footman to penetrate you anywhere but your mouth will get extra rations and the loser will spend the rest of the day in a chastity belt. I want them motivated. When the first match is done, I'll lock two more footmen in there, and then two more, until I grow bored with it—or until every footman here has taken a stab at you. I'll invite the other barons and baronesses down here to watch and place bets. I anticipate it will be quite the show."

A flush of arousal swept up Isolde's chest and face as she studied the iron cage hanging about four feet off the ground. It was dome shaped and about as tall as a man, but not even wide enough to lie down in. What a sight it would be, three bodies grappling and fucking in that narrow cage while it shook and swayed on its chain. Galiana could hardly wait.

"You are dismissed," Galiana told the girl. "Thank me for your punishment and be on your way."

"Thank you, my lady!" the girl exclaimed as she fell to her knees and kissed Galiana's boots, that beautiful, whip-striped ass raised high. "Thank you so much. I'm humbly grateful for the time you've taken to improve me."

"Don't forget your clothes."

"Yes, my lady."

Elic helped Isolde into her chemise, kissed her cheek, and whispered in her ear, "You're so sexy. That was great."

A gallant incubus. Galiana wanted to sneer at that, but she couldn't help but find it appealing—a schmaltzy response one might expect of a human.

"So, you're a dusios, right?" she said after Isolde left. "That's why you can't fuck other Follets. A factor in your blood makes it drain from the penis the moment you attempt to enter a nonhuman." She should have suspected this, despite the rarity of dusii, after watching him during that foursome back in New York. He banged that little blond schoolgirl slave at least half a dozen times, but not once did he stick it in Lili.

"That's right," he said.

"And you know what I am."

He nodded. "What kind, though?"

"Upír."

He nodded again. To his credit, he betrayed no hint of distaste, although most Follets, like humans, had little use for vampires.

"It doesn't repulse you," she asked, "knowing I suck the blood of humans?"

"Do you kill them?"

"Not as a matter of course," she said, although she didn't hesitate to thin the flock when it was called for, as with that pigeon she dropped from the Whitestone Bridge last week; but why bring that up now? There would be plenty of time for him to get used to her ways.

He expelled a weighty sigh as he rubbed the back of his neck. "We're all children of Frøya. We all have a reason for being here."

"I call her Hecate. But yes, we all serve a purpose in the greater scheme. Humans may regard my kind as evil, but it's a simplistic and artificial construct, good and evil. Without darkness, light would have no meaning. Light wouldn't even exist, not as we know it."

The warmth of Elic's smile was a relief; it meant she had a chance with him, despite what she was. "Vampiric philosophy?" he said.

"Galiana's philosophy."

"Galiana is a woman of many dimensions." He regarded her in silence for a moment, as if sizing her up now that he knew what she really was. "You can take that out now," he said, indicating the dildo strapped into her.

"Maybe I don't want to," she said. "Maybe I want to imagine it's you inside me, impaling me with that beautiful hard cock of yours, making me wet, making me come."

The rapacious glint in his eye as he came toward her was such a shock that she actually stumbled back. He hooked a hand around the harness, yanked her toward him, and closed his mouth over hers. Holding the base of the dildo, he shoved it in and out of her while deftly fingering her clit and the slick, ultrasensitive folds of her inner labia. She gripped his hard-muscled shoulders, groaning into his mouth as the pleasure detonated into a heart-stopping orgasm.

He didn't let up, just kept kissing her—and damn, what a kiss—as he brought her off a second time with those nimble fingers and that big, pussy-stretching dildo. He thrust it faster now, faster, faster, rolling the diamond between his fingers as he fucked her mouth with his tongue. Convulsing with plea-sure, she heard stifled screams and realized it was her. He di-aled it back as the spasms subsided, grinding the dildo hard but slow, caressing her with a whisper-light touch as his mouth flirted with hers and—*oh yeah, oh yeah, here it comes, here it comes*—she climaxed again, just as hard as the other three times, a low, strangled moan grinding out of her throat.

He held her until her heart stopped slamming and the shaking ceased, his arms tight around her to keep her from slumping to the ground.

"Holy *fuck*," she said through a wheezy chuckle. Oh, yeah, she had to have him. This one wasn't going anywhere. He was hers.

His erection prodded her stomach. She reached between them to stroke it, but he clamped a hand around her wrist. "It already aches like hell just from watching you come apart like that. You're so responsive, so wild."

"It almost felt like you were fucking me for real," she said.

"I wish I could. God, how I wish I could. I can't imagine what it would be like to be inside someone like you when you lose yourself like that." His chest shook with a little laugh. "I'd probably come so many times in such quick succession, I'd pass right out."

" 'Someone like me' . . . You mean vampires, or Follets in general?"

"Follets in general, I guess, though I've got to say, I don't think I've ever met one as hot as you. Your sexuality, it's ferocious. Human women . . . I mean, I love them. They're great. They can be incredibly sexy, but not like you."

"Even Lili?" she asked.

His chest stopped moving.

Galiana said, "I gather she's a special favorite of yours. What kind of a lover is she? I mean, she *is* human, right?" *Might as well get all our cards on the table right now,* she thought.

The air left his lungs. "No."

"No?" Galiana tilted her head to look at him. "So you can't . . ."

He shook his head without looking at her.

She said, "How long have you two been . . . ?"

"Since the mid-seventeen hundreds."

"Holy shit. If that isn't a recipe for frustration, I don't know what is."

" 'Frustration' is an understatement. It's been . . ." He released her and stepped back, his jaw tight. "Not easy."

"Not easy?" she said. "And *I'm* guilty of understatement? It sounds like hell. I'd lose my fucking mind if I could only do it with humans. My God, how banal. Don't you ever get fed up?"

With a sigh of resignation, he said, "I've learned to cope. Look, there's no way to change the situation, so what's the point of talking about it?"

Stepping closer to him, she said, "What if I told you there *was* a way to change the situation?"

He gave a dubious little snort. "I'd say prove it."

She smiled.

Eleven

"DRINKING ALONE?" Turek asked Lili as he came up behind her the next afternoon. She was standing just inside the main entry door to the great hall, peering out at the courtyard, an open bottle of red wine in her hand. No glass, just the bottle. She'd changed out of her baroness costume into a saronglike garment made of gold-shot gray silk.

She started at his voice, but smiled when she turned and saw who it was. "Not anymore," she said, handing him the bottle as he came up beside her. "Hi, Anthony."

Anthony. Lili was the only person here who called him that. In fact, she'd asked him when he sat next to her at lunch that day whether he preferred Anthony or Tony. It would be nice if everyone was that thoughtful.

He took a swallow and returned the bottle to her, saying, "Great cab." He loved the intimacy of drinking from the same bottle, loved even more that she'd been the one to initiate it.

"Where've you been all afternoon?" she asked.

In Clermont-Ferrand, buying the cordless reciprocating saw, utility knife, and five-gallon can of gasoline Galiana had sent him for. She told him to buy matches, too, but it seemed pretty lame to actually pay for something people gave away all over the place, so he just figured he'd keep his eyes open and snag the next book he saw lying around.

But of course he couldn't tell Lili what he'd really been up to, so he grinned and said, "Why? Were you looking for me?"

"You seem to be the only person here who can carry on a conversation that doesn't involve fucking, sucking, whipping, or spanking."

He said, "D and D Week has barely begun, but you sound like you're more than ready for it to be over."

She sighed and returned her gaze to the courtyard, lifting the bottle to her mouth.

He followed her line of sight to a cherry tree near the gate-house, beneath which Elic and Galiana stood kissing, seemingly oblivious to the orgiastic frolics taking place all around them.

"Do you ever get jealous when Galiana goes all gaga over another guy right in front of you?" Lili asked him. "I mean, obviously, you have an open relationship, but still . . ."

"You and Elic aren't exclusive, either," he said, "yet here you are, spying on him and sucking down—"

"I'm not *spying* on him, I'm just . . ."

"Lurking and watching him from a distance while he makes out with another woman?"

"Yeah, what's that about?" Lili asked. "I mean, *making out*?

What are they, fourteen? This is a freakin' BDSM orgy. What are they going to do next, organize a game of spin the bottle?"

Turek knew that Lili wouldn't be nearly this put off if Elic and Galiana had been fucking under that tree instead of kissing. Fucking was mere entertainment at an event like this—a shared bodily function, no big deal. Kissing, on the other hand, was the sensual expression of emotion. Lili couldn't help but feel threatened by this evidence that what was happening between Elic and Galiana might involve more than mere hormones and genitals.

Just as Galiana had planned. *The more alienated she feels toward Elic,* she'd told him when she gave him his instructions this morning, *the more likely she'll be to go off alone with you when the time comes.*

A mental image ambushed him: Lili enveloped by flames, shrieking as that exquisite olive skin blistered and charred.

In the end, when I finally torch you, I'll take my time, Galiana had promised, should he fail to carry out Lili's execution. *You think you know what I'm capable of, but you don't, Anton. You really have no idea.*

Bile surged in his throat. He fumbled for the pack of Gitanes in his trunk hose and shook one out. "Do you mind?"

Still staring across the courtyard, Lili absently shook her head. "How long have you and Galiana been together?"

About two hundred twenty years, he thought, lighting the cigarette, but he could hardly tell her that, since she assumed he was mortal, so he just said, "A long fucking time."

"You mind if I ask what you see in a cold-blooded piece of work like that?"

There was nothing in the question to suggest that Elic had disclosed Galiana's vampirism to Lili. *Let me know if he told her,* Galiana had said, *'cause then we'll have to switch tacks.*

"I didn't see that side of her in the beginning," he said, which was true.

"You never do, with her kind. They reel you in, and then one day you suddenly realize you're in a relationship with a sadistic control freak who's got you on a tight leash, and there's no way out. It's a classic situation, happens to people all the time."

Not just people, Turek thought grimly.

"Mostly women." Lili added.

And not just women.

"Aren't you worried she'll double-cross you someday?" Lili asked.

Turek paused with the cigarette halfway to his mouth. "Double-cross?"

"You know, replace you with someone else and get rid of you?"

"Get rid of?"

Laughing, Lili said, "Do you always repeat what people say?"

That's right, start irritating her just when she's warming up to you. "Sorry. I, uh … It just seems like such a dramatic way to put it—'get rid of.' Like you're talking about offing someone."

"That's not what I meant, but it happens. You find yourself in a relationship you can't get out of, 'cause no matter how hard you try, the other person always has to be the one to call the shots. They'll never let you break up with them. They'll kill you first. Or if you do manage to leave them, they get into this stalkerish head where they spend all their free time plotting your demise."

Just as Galiana had done after Turek broke it off with her in the Piazza di Maggiore in June of 1348—not as an idle exercise, she'd assured him later. She had fully intended to torture him to death. It was the same fate she'd threatened him with the day before, a fate he could avoid only by burning Lili to ashes.

Assuming she kept her word and really did let him live in exchange for taking care of Lili.

Aren't you worried she'll double-cross you someday?

Across the courtyard, Elic and Galiana looked up from their necking session to greet Inigo. They spoke for a few seconds, and then the three of them headed out through the gatehouse together.

"*Et tu,* Inigo?" Lili murmured.

"Hm?"

"Looks like they've got a three-way in the works."

Not quite. According to Galiana, Elic had been balky but intrigued when she'd revealed that she was one of only three or four vampires in the entire world with the ability to replace all the blood in the body of a human or Follet. If he allowed her to transfuse him, she explained, he would be able to have sex with her or any other nonhuman, assuming the donor could do so. The catch: When she left Grotte Cachée, he would go with her. He was tempted, but troubled by the prospect of losing Lili, so she said he could sleep on it, but that it was a one-time only offer; if he turned her down, he would never get another chance.

That morning, he told her he'd decided it would be best for Lili and him both if they stopped torturing themselves and went their separate ways. *It's about time he figured that one out,* Galiana told Turek. *An incubus and a succubus in a platonic relationship? It's a sitcom that should have been canceled after the first episode.*

Inigo had agreed with typical satyric good humor to act as donor. Given that Elic's replacement blood would be that of another Follet, he would still be virtually immortal afterward.

There was also a strong likelihood that he would retain his ability to change genders, since genetically, he would still be a dusios. The dusiian blood factor only controlled penile hydraulics, not the rest of it.

Galiana told Turek that the transfusion was to take place that afternoon at a shallow stream in the woods. This was so the water could carry away the blood draining from Elic's femoral artery as she discharged Inigo's blood into his carotid. *Then, while Elic and Inigo are recovering, you and I can set the stage for Lili's little accident.*

The fatal "accident" would be Galiana's insurance should Elic be tempted then or in the future to reneg on his deal with the Devil and remain at Grotte Cachée. And, too, Elic's grief would make it that much easier for Galiana to manipulate him into accepting vampiric conversion.

"Anthony?" Lili said.

"Hm?"

"I said I'm sorry I blew you off like that when you asked me out to dinner yesterday. You're obviously a nice guy. I hope I didn't come off as a bitch."

"*You?*" Turek laughed. "Look who my girlfriend is."

Lili laughed, too, but her smile soon faded. "Yeah, she really knows what she's doing. Elic . . . It's like he's a teenager with his first crush." She looked down, swallowing hard.

"Are you all right?"

She nodded and gave him a watery smile. "Here." Taking his hand, she closed it around the wine bottle. "You finish it before I start blubbering."

His hand was warm where she'd touched it. He took a long pull on the bottle. And then he took another.

"Is something wrong?" she asked.

"Hm?"

"You're scowling."

"Oh. Just lost in thought for a minute. I was wondering, um…"

"Yes?"

"I was, um, reading online about a mountain near Clermont-Ferrand that has a Roman temple on it."

Nodding, she said, "The Temple of Mercury. The mountain is the Puy-de-Dôme. It's about eight or ten miles from here. Amazing view."

"Yeah, the article I read said the sunrises and sunsets are spectacular. I was thinking, if you felt like taking a drive, it might be a nice break from all this."

Her gaze shifted from Turek to the spot in the courtyard where Elic and Galiana had been kissing. She nodded. "Yeah. Why not? I think I'd like that. And God knows I could use a break from…all this. What time is sunset tonight?"

"Tonight?" he said. "I was thinking about setting out before dawn tomorrow and catching the sun*rise.* There's something about sunrises. They feel like…beginnings."

"I know what you mean," she said. "Shall we say six o'clock tomorrow morning?"

"Why not make it five? I like to see the pitch-black sky start to lighten little by little. Oh, and maybe we should keep this little outing under our hats. If Galiana finds out about it, she'll go postal on me, and I really don't need that."

"Sounds like a plan."

Sure as hell does, Turek thought.

Elic gazed up at the sun-spangled leaves overhead, his thoughts as dreamy and insubstantial as the breeze waltzing through the woods. From time to time he would realize he was lying naked on his back in six inches of burbling water and forget why. And then he would feel the tickle of her hair on his face and chest, feel the fresh blood, Inigo's blood, surging into him through the fangs buried in his throat, feel the warmth of his own blood pumping into the water from the incision in his femoral artery and swirling downstream...

He couldn't turn his head because the vampiress was holding it in a steely grip, but he could slide his eyes to the side and see his old friend lying nearby in his garish Renaissance garb, his face a death mask leeched of color, of life.

No, not quite. Already Inigo's waxen pallor was just a bit less white, and there may have been a hint of pink on the pointed tips of his ears. He was regenerating the lifeblood that he had granted Elic with such careless generosity. *Bro! We'll be the ultimate blood brothers! This totally rocks!*

Mesmerized by the sun glittering through the branches of the sacred oaks far above him, Elic closed his eyes and saw her face, her beautiful, beloved face, and smiled to himself, and thought, *Not much longer now,* mins Ástgurdís...

Twelve

"SHAME ABOUT THE CAR," Galiana said as she smoked a cigarette in the driver's seat of the Alfa Spider, parked on an overlook of the Puy-de-Dôme access road with its top down under a star-strewn night sky. She was in normal clothes tonight—vinyl leggings and a leather bustier.

"What?" Anton shimmied out from under the jacked-up chassis and stood, dusting off his ridiculous designer jeans as he aimed his flashlight in her face. "I'll have to throw these out now."

"Will you get that fucking thing out of my eyes?"

"Sorry." He opened the passenger door and wedged the flashlight between the gear shift and the dashboard with its beam aimed downward to illuminate a square foot of neatly cut, peeled-back carpeting. In the middle of that square was

the small hole he'd cut in the floor pan with the cordless reciprocating saw lying on the pushed-back passenger seat.
Threaded through that hole was Galiana's Paramount 900XT
Maximum Security Waist Chain, five feet of heat-treated,
nickel-finished carbon steel, one end of which he'd just finished padlocking around the front crossbar of the car's steel
frame. Attached about a foot and a half apart at the chain's
other end, which lay on the passenger seat next to the saw, was
a pair of heavy-duty handcuffs fitted out with Medeco locks in
polycarbonate housings.

"I said it's a shame about the Spider," Galiana said as Anton
smoothed down the square of carpeting with unsteady hands.
He'd been a nervous wreck all night, seeing to these prepara-
tions for Lili's final drive. "I hate having to destroy a beautiful
machine like this just to take out that tiresome little bitch."

"It's your plan," he reminded her as he gathered the business end of the waist chain and tucked it under the passenger
seat. Then, as if worried that he'd overstepped himself, the little weasel added, "And it's a great plan. You're right, this road is
perfect."

It *was* perfect, a treacherously winding mountain road
with rock face on one side and a drop-off on the other. The
spot she'd chosen for Lili's predawn "accident" was an especially sharp curve over a plunging drop about a hundred yards
back.

Checking out her lipstick in the visor mirror, Galiana said,
"I told the guard when he gave me the keys that I'd be giving
them to Lili when I brought the car back tonight, because
she'd asked if she could take it out for an early morning drive
tomorrow—or rather today," she said, checking her watch.
"Elic will think what everyone else thinks, that she was driving
a little too fast in the dark in a car she wasn't used to, went off
the road, and roasted to death in the ensuing fire. *Alone.* You

302 • Louisa Burton

did tell her to keep her mouth shut about your romantic little sunrise date, didn't you?"

"I told her."

"And you won't let anyone see—"

"I won't let anyone see us leaving together." Anton lifted the floor mat from where he'd tossed it onto the pavement and replaced it over the carpet, covering the incised square and most of the chain snaking under the seat.

Galiana said, "Pull the seat forward to hide the rest of the—"

"Way ahead of you," he said as he adjusted the seat. "But thanks. The devil's in the details."

Rolling her eyes at the pedestrian cliché, Galiana leaned back against the headrest and blew a plume of smoke at the winking stars. "Make sure one handcuff is where you can reach it easily from either the passenger seat or the driver's seat. In the unlikely event she doesn't want to do the driving, you're still going to have to immobilize her."

"We've been over all this." He didn't apologize for his insolence this time.

Galiana closed her eyes and shook her head. You'd think, after having tried to hoodwink her with that Gebirgshaus shit, that he'd be walking on eggs, but no. She'd promised to let him live if he helped her get rid of Lili, and like the trusting moron he was, he believed her—all the more reason to thin him from the ranks of the Upír. As soon as Lili was dead and she'd gotten Elic away from here and under her control, Anton Turek was going to get the slow roasting he'd been begging for all these years.

Tapping the cigarette onto the pavement, she said, "Go over it again, *marish*. One bungled detail could ruin the entire thing."

Anton grimaced as he stowed the saw in the trunk along-side the five gallons of gasoline he'd picked up that afternoon. "I tell her she's about to hit a deer, and when she stops, I hand-cuff her."

"Both hands." Even if Lili possessed extraordinary strength, there was no way she could work free of such a secure restraint.

"Right. Of course. I drain her completely, leaving her too weak to move, and then I douse her with—"

"*No!*" Galiana bolted upright. God, the *imbecile*. "After you drain her, remove the handcuffs and unlock the chain from the car's frame. You're going to take it with you, remember? So it looks like an acci—"

"Right, right. I knew that, I'm just . . . a little keyed up."

"Speaking of which, you've got both keys, right? For the handcuffs and the padlock?"

"Right here." He patted his front jeans pocket.

"And remember," Galiana said, "if she's in the passenger seat, you're going to have to move her to the driver's seat and strap her in. Then comes the gasoline."

"I soak her down and take the can."

"Don't forget to bring a backpack or something to put the chain in. The can you can carry. You'll just look like you ran out of gas. Don't run, it'll attract too much attention. You can hoof it back to Grotte Cachée in about two hours. Don't let anyone give you a ride. Stay off the local radar."

"Gotcha. So then I figure I should put the car in neutral so it's easier to push off the—"

"Did I tell you to put it in neutral?"

"Um, no."

"The cops might be able to tell from the wreckage that it was in neutral, and then it won't look like an accident. You want the engine running and in drive—with something to brace the front wheels, like a rock or a log. Aim them toward the drop-off, release the parking break, toss a match in—remember to bring the matches, not your lighter, so you can throw it and don't have to try to—"

"*Sheisse*. The fucking matches." Anton slammed the balls of his hands against his forehead. "*Fuck!*"

Leaning back, she said, "God, chill, Anton. You still have time. You can scrounge some up before five o'clock. There are, like, a hundred fireplaces around the castle. Check them."

"Fucking matches," he muttered, shaking his head.

"Toss the match in. She'll go up like a torch. Then just roll away whatever was bracing the wheels and push the car off the mountain. The engine will probably explode immediately. Cars burn at super-high temperatures. She'll be toast within minutes. Dead and gone. Kaput."

Galiana hurled her burned-down cigarette out the window, plucked another one from her bustier, and looked toward Anton for a light.

"Um, yeah, okay. Hold on." He slid into the passenger seat, reaching into his back jeans pocket.

"You didn't forget your lighter, too, did you?"

"What? No," he said, fumbling in the pocket. "I don't *think* so."

"Oh, for God's sake," she muttered, leaning her head back and closing her eyes. "You are the most worthless fucking—"

Something cold and hard snapped around her right wrist. She opened her eyes to find him reaching toward her with the other handcuff.

She swatted him away with a snarl, teeth bared. He landed on the pavement with a grunt of pain.

She jerked at the handcuff, rattling the chain, as he scrambled to his feet. In a voice deepened by rage, she said, "Very funny, *marish*. Unlock this now."

Digging in his front pocket, he produced the two keys, held them up in a quavering hand . . .

And threw them over the side of the mountain.

A growl of fury thundered from her lungs as she strained toward him.

"I know what that means," he said in a voice that was at once tremulous and irate. "*Marish.* I know what it means. It means slave. That's what I am to you. That's what I've always been. Your personal fucking slave."

"What are you doing?" she demanded as he hauled the five-gallon can of gasoline out of the trunk and unscrewed the cap.

"You're so smart, such a brilliant schemer. *You* figure it out." His old Germanic intonations were creeping in on the British accent he'd been affecting for the past century or so.

She tried to wriggle her hand free of the cuff, but it was no use; he'd snapped it on good and tight, and it was probably the best handcuff in the world, which was why it was her favorite. Willing her voice back to its normal timbre, she tried to reason with him. "Why are you doing this, Anton? Our plan is that close to completion. After today, you can go your way and I'll go—"

She shrieked as he splattered her with gasoline, standing just far enough from the passenger side of the car so she couldn't reach him. He stumbled back anyway, when she lunged for him.

"Lili said something really interesting to me today," he said. "She asked me if I wasn't worried that you'd double-cross me someday. Like, try to get rid of me. And I realized what a fucking *asshole* I've been, thinking you would ever let me live after—"

"She's manipulating you, you fucking—" Galiana bit off the rest of that. "Don't you see? I get it now. Think about it.

Somehow, they figured out who we are and what we're up to. And . . . and that I can transfuse blood from one Follet to another. We were talking about it in the subs' dressing room yesterday, remember? Someone must have overheard us and told Elic and Lili."

"There was no one there."

"There could have been," she said, cringing at the desperation in her voice. "Hiding behind the racks of clothes, or those chairs, those recliners—"

"You would have smelled him."

"Not over all that perfume. Anton, think about it . . ."

"*Nein!*" he screamed, shaking another stream of gasoline onto her. "*Erzaehle mir nicht so einen mist!*" Another splash. "*Blöde Fotze!*" And another.

Choking and sputtering, Galiana said, "Elic played me. Lili played you. All Follets are fucking awesome actors, you know that. She has no intention of going anywhere with you, Anton. She poisoned your mind against me so you'd do this—or something like it. Neutralize me, take me out of the equation."

"This was *my* idea!" he yelled as he hurled the half-empty can onto the front seat. "*Mine!*" He kicked the passenger door shut. "You don't think I can think for myself? You don't think I can scheme like you?"

Anton reached into his back pocket, produced his gold lighter, flipped it open, and thumbed the flame to life. He crept toward her, arm outstretched. Galiana's deeply ingrained instinct was to cower from the flame, but that was suicide. The only way she could keep him back long enough to talk some sense into him was to go on the offense.

She made a grab at him. He dropped the lighter, cursing, but picked it right up again and lit it, glowering at her.

"Anton," Galiana said in a tight, quivering voice, her hands raised placatingly. "Please just stop and think. You're setting yourself up for another long imprisonment. This"—she gestured to the handcuff, the car, the gasoline can—"isn't going to look like any accident. It'll be a murder scene, plain and simple."

"I'll be gone—with Lili—by the time the sun comes up tomorrow. I'm going to keep her at Gebirgshaus till she lets me turn her. No one knows where that is. You're the only one who even knows it exists, and you'll be dead."

"No, Anton. No. Just stop and think—"

"Stop telling me to think!"

"Elic and Lili set this up so I'd transfuse him, then disappear from the picture. When you get back to the castle, they're going to be waiting for you—guards or cops, or whatever. They're going take you into custody and—"

"Liar! Bitch! *Halst maul!*"

"Anton, just think—"

He struck in a blur, flames blossoming with a *whump* all around her.

Howling in pain and rage, she seized his arm as he started to retreat.

"*Nein!*" he cried as she grabbed the second handcuff and locked it around his wrist, tethering them both to the car. He looked toward the gas can, opened his mouth.

A white-hot concussion roared through her world.

Darius, perched on the wall of rock above the black sports car, having followed it to the Puy-de-Dôme from Grotte Cachée, shot into the air on a bloom of heat when the gas can exploded. Flames boiled high into the night sky, along with billows of soot-black smoke.

Gaining his bearings, he flew in a circle over the burning automobile, his gaze on the two charred, twisted, roughly human-shaped figures chained to it. Neither one moved—which didn't mean they were dead. Follets clung tenaciously to life, and vampires especially.

Within seconds, there came a second, larger explosion as the fumes in the car's gas tank ignited. The fireball came close to singeing him because his lousy avian depth perception had him flying closer than he thought. He flew as hard as he could to the safety of a nearby walnut tree.

Darius found himself captivated by the liquid-gold flames dancing in and around the distorted exoskeleton of something that had been, until moments before, a machine of great beauty and elegance. It was a cleansing fire, steadily devouring the blackened figures as sirens began to whine somewhere out there in the darkness.

It's done, Darius thought as he flew back to Grotte Cachée, *or it will be soon.* The fire would be extinguished, the scene photographed, investigated, and pondered over. The vampires' remains, carbonized fragments by the time they were cool enough to extract from their chains, would end up in a morgue drawer pending identification, which would likely never occur. The mystery of their presumed murder would go unsolved, and eventually what was left of them would be disposed of and forgotten. They were gone from this world, and more important, from Lili and Elic's world, these beasts of the night.

Darius had suspected what they were the moment he awoke in the chapel withdrawing room yesterday, ears flattened and lips drawn back, tasting a whiff of raw meat beneath the lemony perfume filling the room. He remembered Anton Turek from the first time he'd set his sights on Lili two and a half centuries ago, loathed him and feared him for her sake. Then there was the older, stronger female, and her tantalizing reference to transfusion. It tickled his memory; he'd read of this, but where? It had taken hours of research among his ancient demonological texts, but he had found it, a reference to vampiric blood exchange dating back to ancient Etruria, translated by a monk laboring in a Dark Ages scriptorium.

As Darius flew over the castle courtyard, he saw eight of their guards, good men and worthy successors to the Swiss Guards who had served the seigneurs of Grotte Cachée for centuries, awaiting the return of one or both vampires. They were armed not just with handguns and rifles, which would only slow a vampire down a little, but with flamethrowers, as well as piles of chains. As soon as Darius reverted to human form, he would call them on his cell phone—one of the few modern conveniences he embraced, since it helped him to avoid personal contact with humans—and let them know there would be no bloodsuckers to capture tonight.

Darius flew past the castle toward the bathhouse at the entrance to the cave in which he lived, slowing down when he saw a faint glow from within the white marble structure. He lit upon the edge of the big skylight over the pool and dipped his head, taking in everything at once with his panoramic vision. A handful of candles burned at the lip of the pool, their flames twitching on its glassy surface. There was no one in the water, but between the pool and the mouth of the cave, among a heap of silken pillows, two naked bodies lay with arms and legs and hair all entwined: Lili and Elic.

Darius was about to give them his "hello" chirp when he noticed the slow, sinuous movements of their hips and grasped the magnitude of this long-awaited moment. He could hear Elic speaking softly into her ear, his voice hoarse and damp, but he couldn't make out the words. Lili nodded, a droplet glimmering on her cheek.

Darius pumped his wings and spun away, soaring off into the starry night.

AUTHOR'S NOTE

The Bastille, the fortress-turned-prison that had become, by the time of the French Revolution, a detested symbol of the corrupt French monarchy, never housed more than a handful of men. Often these were aristocrats incarcerated there rather than in some public jail or madhouse, their relations paying well to have their every need attended to by scores of attentive servants and guards.

On July 4, 1789, the Marquis de Sade was transferred to the substantially less swank Charenton Asylum, leaving only seven names on the Bastille's prison roles: the forgers Jean de la Correge, Jean Bechade, Bernard Laroche, and Jean-Antoine Pujade, arrested two years before; an elderly Irish lunatic named Major Whyte, who imagined himself at various times to be God, St. Louis, and Julius Caesar; the Comte de Solanges, committed there by his family on suspicion of murder and incest; and the sole political prisoner, a fellow named Tavernier who'd been locked up there since 1759 for participating in the Damiens conspiracy against King Louis XV.

As every student of history knows, on July 14, 1789, the Bastille was besieged by revolutionaries, many of whom died at the hands of their own while plundering arms and ammunition. All seven inmates were liberated from their cells and paraded around Paris (with poor Major Whyte convinced he was Caesar being cheered by the Roman citizenry), only to be swiftly reincarcerated.

History does, however, record a mysterious eighth whose name never made it onto the official list, but who was freed along with his fellow prisoners. The "Comte de Lorges," as he was known, had been held since 1749 on a *lettre de cachet,* which was how the French aristocracy at that time made people disappear without benefit of trial, appeal, or even official charges. Presumed to be an unjustly accused victim of tyranny, he came to represent the quintessential Noble Prisoner liberated during the storming of the Bastille.

A journalist subsequently raised doubts as to the existence of this martyred count after failing to find his name in the prison register, and it's now thought that he was a fictional *héro de roman* meant to fire up the sympathies of the French populace.

The truth will likely never be known.

ABOUT THE AUTHOR

LOUISA BURTON, a lifelong devotee of Victorian erotica, mythology, and history, lives in upstate New York. Visit her website at www.louisaburton.com.